Gardens of Hope

A Novel

Michael Holloway Perronne

CHANCES PRESS

Gardens of Hope: A Novel

ISBN: 9780977050642

www.chancespress.com

For my mother.

"A fallen blossom
returning to the bough, I thought --
But no, a butterfly."
— **Arakida Moritake,**

Acknowledgments

Special thanks to the park rangers at the Manzanar site who patiently answered the questions I had during my visit to the site and my many emails that followed. Also, much gratitude goes to Karen Gibbs for her editing assistance.

A wounded deer leaps the highest. - Emily Dickinson

Prologue- April 2004

I couldn't tell you what I had for lunch the day before, but with complete and total clarity I can remember the smile on Hiro's face the first time we met back in 1941. I had startled at the sight of him sitting on the bench across from me with the moonlight providing the only illumination. Something shifted inside me when we made eye contact. What seemed impossible before, more than a quick, hushed encounter with another man, suddenly became attainable. That chance meeting was so different than the ones I had had before which consisted of fumblings and quick moments of physical intimacy. With Hiro, mutual tender touches and words of affection opened a whole new world to me even though we both realized the strict limitations of what society would allow us to have at the time.

Don't get me wrong. I loved Howard, the love of my life I met many years later. We spent twenty-eight good years together. Sure, we had our challenges like any couple, including watching so many of our friends pass away in the 1980s that funerals frighteningly became as common as a trip to the grocery store.

I met Howard in 1972 at the Twin Peaks bar in the Castro area of San Francisco right after it became the first gay bar to have actual windows where the patrons could see outside and vice versa. He stood out to me with his fit build and thick silver hair. Just a few weeks earlier, I had turned fifty-three. I had long given up on love at that point, but in this case love seemed to find me and not the other way around. We bonded that night over our dislike for the loud music the bars were so fond of blasting. At the time, there weren't many other options for meeting men like us, so hanging out at a bar was the default for socializing. We both made our way outside to smoke cigarettes and continue our conversation. Six weeks later he moved in with me and our lives gradually merged, and four years ago a stroke, quickly and without any warning, took him away from me.

Still, I kept his reading glasses on the end table next to the sofa as if he might walk into the room at any moment and ask, "Did you see where the hell I put my glasses this time?"

Many, many years before, I had told Howard about Hiro not long after we met one night over dinner at a coffee shop close to Nob Hill.

"Who was your first love?" Howard asked, over a corned beef sandwich.

"You," I said, giving him my best mischievous grin.

"Don't bullshit me," he said smiling and cocking an eyebrow.

Howard always got right to the point.

I told him about Hiro, Pershing Square Park, the Japanese evacuation from Little Tokyo in Los Angeles, and my surprise reunion with Hiro in a place that would change me and shake my worldview for the rest of my life.

After I told him the whole story, he looked like he was on the verge of tears. Howard, the man whose emotions were made of proverbial steel, began to choke up a little.

"You don't know what happened..." he started to say.

"No, I don't," I said, cutting him off. "I try not to think about some of the possible outcomes, either."

Howard had just nodded, and then he reached across and took my hand into his. He didn't care who saw or what they might think, and at that moment, I knew he would be the one.

Lately, most of my time was spent staring out the window at the nameless people who went about with their days, listening to classical music, reading the classics, and watching life go by. At eighty-five this was usually enough to keep me content, and my only company tended to be the home health nurse Rita, a gentle soul from the Philippines who visited three times a week and my eighteen-year-old cat, Tabby, that was as slow and tired as I was, visits from my sister, Jane, who lived near San Jose, and my grand-nephew, Tate.

Just a little past seven in the morning, I heard a knock on the door of my Victorian walk-up in the Castro, a neighborhood I could never afford to live in if I hadn't bought my house forty years ago.

"Uncle Jack!" I heard Tate yell through the door.

"Just a minute!" I called back.

I sat my book of Shakespearian sonnets on the side table and pulled myself up from my favorite chair next to the bay window in my apartment. Slowly but surely, I began to shuffle toward the door with my leg aching from a decades-old injury. The aches were a constant reminder of a long ago event in my early teens, one in which I learned a split-second decision could change everything. But most times when my mind started to recollect the accident that caused the injury, I would still, even to this day, and shift my focus to something else.

Tate, my younger sister Jane's grandson, lived in San Francisco, too, in a tiny one-room apartment in the somewhat dicey, somewhat affordable Tenderloin area and worked for a marketing company in the Financial District. He was thirty, quite handsome in a boyish blond-haired, blue-eyed way, gay and very much enjoying playing the field. Or at least that's what he said. I, on the other hand, could sense that he longed for his ex-boyfriend, Connor, a ginger-haired social worker who had relocated to Los Angeles for work, and regretted not telling him that he still loved him. Youth stubbornly continued to give young folk the sense that they had an endless amount of time to tell those who meant the most to them how they felt. I knew Tate would learn the lesson, as usual for most people his age, a tad too late to right some of the wrongs of the past.

Tate visited me every couple of weeks to check on me. I was sure my sister, who lived an hour away, urged him to do so, but I always enjoyed his visits. I lived vicariously through his stories of the latest clubs he and his friends went to, the gorgeous boys he would date and eventually drop, and the latest international trips he took. He'd humor me for a good couple of hours while he usually drank one of those coffees served in an impossibly big container by one of those cafés that appeared to have popped up everywhere, and he always brought me one, too. Black. Two sugars. During our conversations he'd constantly check that cell phone he brought with him everywhere and read things called text messages. I didn't understand them. Didn't we invent the phone so we wouldn't have to write messages to each other?

When I had called him a few weeks ago to ask him to drive me to the opening of the Manzanar Interpretive Center, he asked, "You want me to drive you to an apple place?"

At first I was confused, but then I remembered that the word *manzanar* meant apple orchard in Spanish. Ironically there were no apple orchards there by the time Hiro and I arrived in 1942.

"No," I said. "The internment camp."

There was silence on the other end of the phone.

"What's that?" he asked.

I no longer felt any surprise that so many people had never heard of Manzanar or any of the other nine camps to which Japanese-Americans had been forced to relocate to and leave their entire lives behind. The few times I spoke about it with anyone, especially those younger than me, they appeared shocked as if it couldn't possibly have happened. Otherwise, they surely would have learned about it in school. But just like any other culture, Americans were hesitant to include information in school curricula that might not fit with the overall narrative we had chosen for ourselves.

A younger ex-colleague of mine who was still teaching social studies, as I had for thirty-five years, told me once that the textbooks had only in the past few years begun discussing the camps. So I hadn't been surprised when Tate had no knowledge of what I was speaking about.

"Do that Google thing and look it up. I think you'll be surprised by what you read," I told him. "I worked there for a very short period of time, but what I saw changed me in my soul in ways I can't entirely describe. It's also where I started my teaching career, and they're opening a new museum. I'd really like to go if you'll take me."

I'm sure there were many other things he'd much rather done on his day off that drive his old great-uncle to a museum he'd never heard of before. So I added, "You know. While I still have time."

I wasn't above twisting the knife of guilt to get my way if needed.

"Okay," he'd reluctantly said with a sigh. "But then you need to read my graduate school admissions essay for an edit."

"Deal," I agreed.

Tate had reached a kind of crossroads in his life, and he'd decided to return to school to get a Masters in Marriage and Family Therapy.

"Uncle Jack!" Tate called, knocking on the door again, this time a little more frantic.

My sometimes drifting mind jolted back to the present.

I swear, at my age, if you didn't answer the door on the first knock or pick up the telephone almost immediately, people went into a panic mode. I wished they'd give me at least enough time to walk across the room.

I opened the door, smiled, and said matter-of-factly, "You're late."

"I know," he said, walking in and slinging his messenger bag on my sofa. "Sorry. I was held up getting the rental car."

Like many in San Francisco, he used the extensive public transit system versus driving. I couldn't even remember the last time I was behind the wheel.

"Look, I gotta go pee before we leave," he started. "But first, I googled that place we're going to, and that is some messed-up shit! How the hell did that happen here in the US?"

"Fear is not always rational. In fact, it's usually the opposite." I'd witnessed this more times over the past eight decades than I cared to remember. Somehow people never learned, but they just kept repeating the same patterns in a desperate bid to create an "us-versus-them" society.

"Well, I still can't believe it," he said, shaking his head. "And we're so going to have to stop and get more coffee on the road. This is way earlier than I usually roll out of bed."

"I made a thermos of it for the road," I said.

He wore his standard sweatshirt with a hood, jeans, and sneakers.

I, of course, had on one of my usual knit sweaters I even wore in the summer and polyester pants that expanded or contracted depending on my diet at the time.

"And you used to work there?" Tate asked. "Why haven't you ever mentioned this story to me before?"

"It's a long tale. I don't like to talk about it much because of the memories, but I'll fill you in," I said.

"Well, hold that for the road. I'll be right back," he said, heading for my bathroom.

I grabbed my cane that sometimes helped relieve the pain in my leg and the thermos of coffee I had prepared for the seven-hour car ride. I didn't especially relish the idea of being stuck in a car for that long, but I knew Tate would stop when I needed to stretch the old bones in my legs.

The plan was to arrive at Manazar midafternoon, explore the museum, and then stay the night in nearby Lone Pine before heading back the next morning.

When Tate returned, looking much relieved, he said, "Okay! Ready to hit the road?"

"As ready as I'll ever be," I said.

Tate helped me get down the stairs to the sidewalk in front of my home. I noticed that he had taken two spaces to park the car, which made me question his driving skills, but I realized that beggars can't always be choosers.

Once in the car, we snaked our way through traffic on Market Street while Tate sang along to some new dance song on his CD player.

"It's Britney Spears," he told me.

I smiled like I knew who this was, this girl who kept begging someone to hit her.

I took a sip of my coffee. All the kids might have been into buying their Morning Joe at one of those fancy places, but I was quite satisfied with my Maxwell House, thank you very much. So I carried a thermos of it most places I went—not that I got out too often these days.

Once we were on the freeway and out of some of the traffic, Tate said, "So, are you going to tell me how you ended up at this place teaching? What's the deal? I feel like there's a story here. Give me the scoop, Uncle Jack."

I sucked in a deep breath and stared out the window.

"You really want to know?" I asked, turning to him.

"Well, sure. We've got seven hours to kill," Tate pointed out with a slight eye roll.

"Okay, then," I said, clearing my throat. "I should probably start before I went to Manzanar and what life was like for men like us in the early nineteen forties. It was often a life of fear and shame, you know."

I felt myself unexpectedly start to tear up, and I quickly turned my gaze back toward the window.

"And it was also the time that, despite the odds, I managed to find a window of light in my often otherwise dark life, the beginnings of a strong crush or love or whatever you want to call it. It may have been short-lived, but that relationship…"

My voice trailed off, and I took a deep breath.

"…gave me the strength to carry on at a time I desperately needed it," I finished.

"But how did you end up at this internment camp?" Tate asked, merging into a new lane of traffic.

"I suspect many people wondered the same thing about how their own fate delivered them to Manzanar," I answered, as San Francisco grew more distant in the background.

Chapter One- December 1941, Los Angeles

Gay.

Back in 1941 Los Angeles, this word still meant happy and carefree.

As a result, I didn't really know a word that described the feelings I had. Of course, I had heard the word *homosexual* used to describe someone you did not want to be associated with. That couldn't refer to me I tried to rationalize to myself. After all, I was a young man who had recently become engaged to Sally Jenkins, the all-American girl next door with a peaches and cream complexion, auburn hair, and a ready smile. Sally would, as my mother would say, make a great mother, wife, and homemaker. She had a laid-back friendliness about her that suggested she could get along with most anyone.

We met while going to a local teacher's college when she joined one of my study groups. She was planning to teach elementary school while I planned to teach high school social studies with the hope of being a principal one day. When she asked to borrow my notes from a psychology class, we struck up our first conversation, which ended up spanning four hours. Besides both of us planning to teach, we enjoyed reading British literature and loved Charlie Chaplin films.

From the outside, people probably thought Sally and I had a great "normal" life ahead of us filled with children, an automobile, a white picket fence, and a nice radio for the living room. Yet I already knew that this scenario didn't exactly fit me and seemed somehow "off" to what I truly desired. But I, for the most part, did what was expected of me especially after my spunky youngest brother, John, died at the age of twelve, when I was fourteen, in an auto accident that left me with a bum leg and slight limp. I felt as if I owed it to my parents to somehow live up to not just my potential, but that of John's as well, of what his life could have been. But I always thought that my other brother, Edward, who had been thirteen at the time of the accident, was doing a much better job at being the perfect son with his macho bravado that I sorely lacked. To say my self-esteem wasn't the highest back then is probably a vast understatement, and Sally, through her own confidence and zest for life, made me feel uplifted.

Beyond my secret life in the evening shadows I'll tell you more about later, I thought of myself as less than other men my age due to my damaged leg. My injury kept me out of the draft and, ironically, may have saved my life because of that, but to me it was just one more way I didn't think I measured up to what a man should be.

But first, I will start the story right before all of the country was up-ended by the ugliness of war. You need to know just how different my feelings were for...Hiro.

Hiro.

It's been so long since I've said that name out loud. I always feared if I said his name that my emotions would start to get the better of me. People come and go throughout one's life with just a precious few who always keep a grip on your heartstrings no matter how many years go by without you seeing them.

I'll start at a day with events that eventually helped lead Hiro and me to not just cross paths in the first place, but to actually *see* each other as we hadn't seen previous men we'd met in the darkness of the evenings.

"Why don't you go home? Call Sally. Maybe you two could go to the picture show," my mother said, placing her hand on my shoulder and giving it a gentle squeeze.

I turned away from the storefront window of the family jewelry store on Broadway in downtown Los Angeles and faced her.

Mother more often than not had a kind smile on her face despite what sadness seemed to trail her in this lifetime. She always dressed simply in a neutral-colored dress, sensible shoes, and with her salt-and-pepper hair pulled back in a simple bun. She often said having a neat, professional appearance was essential to good customer service. The shopping experience should be all about the customer and nothing to distract them from the beauty of our merchandise.

"I'll close up," she said, straightening up a display of costume earrings.

"No, I'll do it," I said with just the smallest hint of panic in my voice. "Go on home. You know Father will be expecting dinner soon once he gets back from the wholesaler."

She looked at me, and I noticed just the slightest look of suspicion in her eyes. Recently, I had been offering to close up the store, where I worked part-time while in school and mostly kept up with the accounting, a lot whereas before I had always tried to get out of there as soon as possible. I found the tiny storefront claustrophobic, and I'd spend my time mostly staring out the window and watching people rush by heading off to their next destinations without noticing much around them as people in the city often do. Selfishly I wished that could be me going someplace, maybe someplace new. I wished I could buy a bus ticket to anywhere, take off, and go to a place I'd never been before, and I don't know, maybe breathe and not feel trapped. But I had no idea where or if such a place existed for a person like me, someone hiding secret desires.

I needed my time this evening to go off on my own.

Even though it seemed more and more of my life was spent living in the shadows at dusk, those few precious hours I could sneak away had become more important to me than Sally, school, my family, or working at the store my parents had owned for twenty years. During these secretive hours spent with others in the same predicament, I somehow found myself feeling like I was getting closer to the real me despite the shame that often went hand-in-hand with each encounter I had.

"You've been very agreeable lately," Mother said. "You usually can't wait to run out of here fast enough."

Mother had been right. I had little to zero enthusiasm when it came to selling our jewelry. I had to force myself to smile and go through the motions. If I had to help one more young man pick out an engagement ring, I thought I might have to scream. I found myself angry at their excitement and eyes full of promise for the years to come.

I'm ashamed to admit it, but when it came to Sally's engagement ring, I just reached into one of the cases and pulled out the first one my hand found despite my parents telling me I could choose any. Proposing to Sally just seemed like the logical next step after we'd gone steady for a year. She'd always been so kind to me when I felt guilt about surviving the accident that killed my younger brother, John. She'd coax me to open up and talk about it when I couldn't with anyone else. I couldn't have asked for a better friend. She'd hold my hand, embrace me, and wipe my tears away as we'd sit privately on my parents' porch, and my thoughts kept going back to how all of this was my fault and what a bad brother I had been.

I did love her, but I knew I hadn't fallen *in love* with her. Sometimes I felt pangs of guilt that I wouldn't or couldn't give her what she really wanted and deserved. Yet I still went along with what society expected of me at the time. Remember, this was 1941 and decades before Stonewall or Harvey Milk in 1970s San Francisco when *parts* of society just barely started to open up to the idea that people who were gay weren't mentally ill. I felt trapped like one of my mother's parakeets in its tiny cage and knowing, somewhere on some level, that there was more to the world out there. But all I could do was look through the bars of the cage and resign myself to my fate.

"I just want to help out while I can," I told my mother, shrugging. "When I start teaching in the fall I won't be able to be here as much."

Mother sighed loudly. I knew she dreaded my leaving her, forcing her to once again balance the books, a business chore she hated. But then she had been enormously proud of the fact that I would be the first one in my family to graduate from college.

"I know, sweetie. You'll be moving on," she said, reaching up and brushing back a few stray hairs from my forehead like she used to do when I was a child. "You and Sally will be starting whole new lives. I'm so excited for you. Everything's going to be great. You'll see," she said, giving me a little awkward hug. My family never did affection well. "Will I see you at home for dinner?"

"Nah. I have a study group later. A big exam is coming up," I said.

She nodded, and glanced at the clock.

5:15.

"Okay. I'll leave something in the icebox for you if you come home hungry. Go ahead and close up at six. It's been dead all day," Mother said.

She put on white gloves and a green hat. She may have dressed simply compared to some women, but she always dressed for what she considered proper including a hat and gloves. Mother would catch the streetcar and then have a twenty-minute walk home since Father had the car, but she was never one to complain.

"Bye," I said, as she walked out the door.

I glanced at the clock hanging on the wall. Forty-five minutes was sure to feel like an eternity. Rarely did customers come in this late, and all I'd be able to think about was where I would head next and whom I might find there.

The minutes ticked by in mind-numbing slowness. After finally closing up the store at six, I locked up and began to walk toward the park at Pershing Square in downtown Los Angeles. The December evening air was especially chilly, and I could feel my heartrate quicken with each block I walked. Part of me wanted to turn back around and head home to my family, Sally, and the comforts of the norm at the time. Yet my innermost desires proved to be much stronger, and as if they had a mind of their own, my feet continued to move forward to my place of both excitement and shame.

I had found out quite by accident exactly some of the goings-on at Pershing Square when I went there one night after work and not wanting to go home yet. It had been a particularly bad day I remember. I couldn't concentrate in my classes. Sally and I argued about something so insignificant I don't even remember what it was. And to top it off, I had to deal with a very pushy customer in the store who kept insisting that the gold ring we sold him was not 18k.

To try to clear my head before heading home, I had taken off on a walk. When I felt anxious, scared, or uncertain, the therapeutic nature of a walk tended to be something that helped me refocus. Before I knew it I had walked into Pershing Square. A few teenage boys were horsing around and chasing each other. They were still young enough for the idea of a possible draft and being sent to World War II to feel as if it were a long way away. My brother Edward, who started working at the Port of Los Angeles after high school, knew he could be called at any moment. President Roosevelt had called for the first time ever peace-time draft, many assumed to ready the country if we had to enter the war going on in Europe. Because of my injured leg, the fear of the draft didn't hang over my head like my brother. However, at the same time, I felt guilt for not joining up to serve my country. But I knew how important it was for my parents that I finish school, and they depended on me at the store.

Other than the young teens, the park was pretty much deserted. I headed to the fountain in the middle and took a seat. The sounds of the gushing water calmed my unquiet mind for a minute, and that's when I noticed him.

Sitting on a bench across the way was a guy about my age. He had light brown hair that was just a tad bit longer than was the norm for guys at the time. He was tall, and I could tell he had a muscular torso in his fitted, collared blue dress shirt. He wore suspenders and cotton trousers, and I suspected he might work in one of the office buildings nearby. In one hand he had a cigarette and in the other a cup of coffee. His eyes were fixated on me in a way that made me both extremely uncomfortable and, oddly at the time, excited.

Why was he so fascinated with me?

Uneased by his intense gaze, I shifted uncomfortably on the bench and tried to remain casual, but every time I sneaked a look at the guy I found him still staring at me.

My palms began to sweat, and I glanced over at him yet again.

He stared me down…hard. Then he got up and headed toward a patch of dense brush. In the middle of walking, he turned, looked at me, and I knew then he wanted me to follow.

I swallowed hard, and my mouth turned dry.

Clenching my hands, I knew I should just head home to where my mother would have a warm meal ready, and I could study for an exam I had coming up.

But as if under a trance, I got up and followed the man to a point in the bushes and trees where we were more or less hidden, especially as nightfall began.

When I stood face to face with him, I could see, despite the dark, he had a pretty much expressionless face. But then he reached out and grabbed my crotch. I hardened and wanted to touch his so bad my body practically ached for it. When I felt him, erect and thick in his pants, he stepped even closer to me and shocked me by placing his mouth on mine and giving me the most intense kiss I'd experienced, nothing like what I had felt with Sally. His hand began to grab my penis harder and started stroking it through the fabric of my trousers.

The whole encounter only lasted a few minutes, but despite the secrecy and the dark, I somehow felt more alive. My nerves practically tingled throughout my body as if they were all coming alive for the first time. Stunned, my head spun as I tried to understand what just happened as I stood there with my underwear wet and watched him walk away.

I immediately rushed home where I found my parents, Edward, and my little sister, Jane, with her pigtails and only nine years old at the time, eating slices of apple pie and listening to big band music on the radio.

"There's some meatloaf and potatoes sitting warm in the oven for you," Mother said.

"Where you been? You look...flushed," Father said.

Father was a man's man, if you will. After serving bravely in World War I, he returned to Los Angeles and took over his uncle's ailing jewelry store and turned it around, even thriving during the Depression. He always prided himself on noticing the little things others wouldn't. He said that's what made him a good salesperson. He could sense what others wanted to hear, whether it was true or not, and he could sniff out a weakness that resulted in a cash transaction.

"I was just rushing to get home," I said. "Stomach problems. I've got to go to the bathroom"

I bolted up the stairs so fast you would have thought each previous step was on fire, but all I could think about was taking a bath and washing this sin off my body.

That night I lay restless in my twin bed while Edward snored in the bed next to me. I couldn't get the guy from the park out of my head or how natural touching another man had felt. Sally and I had, of course, heavy petted on our dates, but it never gave me the feeling of an intense shot of adrenaline that touching and being touched by another man gave me. Being physical with her, more or less, had the feeling of a duty I should fulfill being a man my age.

Now, months later, I walked into the park knowing the game after numerous encounters. The stares from other men held just slightly too long to mean indifference. The circling of each other and playing chicken, who would make the first real move. If there was a match, we would head into the bushes of a nearby dark alley. Even though I had heard from some of the other men I briefly encountered that the police had taken to patrolling the park at times since word had gotten out that perversion was taking place there, I couldn't seem to stop myself from returning there time and time again.

I knew that, if I were arrested, my life would be destroyed, but at the same time I couldn't stop going to the park, stop having hurried sexual relations with men that had gone beyond just touching at this point.

As I walked toward the middle of the park where the fountain was located, I noticed a young man with dark wavy hair and olive skin. I'd caught glimpses of him before and found myself attracted to him, but the timing had never been right. This time he leaned against a tree, smiled, and I knew the inevitable would soon take place once again.

That Sunday sitting around the breakfast table with my family, my parents suggested that I invite Sally over to join us for our family dinner. So I called her, and she said she'd be happy to do so.

"She's going to be family, after all," Mother said. "We should include her more often."

I dutifully nodded.

"The more time we get to spend with her before the wedding, the more our bond will grow," Mother said, with a small smile. "When are you two going to set a date?"

I groaned.

"We will, Mother. Soon. We're just both busy trying to graduate this year. Once that's done, and we start teaching, we can set a date."

"What about babies?" Mother pushed, raising her eyebrows.

"Leave the kid alone," Father said, before taking a big gulp of my mother's extra strong coffee that could wake the dead.

"Yeah, what about babies?" Edward said, laughing and kicking me under the table.

I shot him an annoyed look, and he just gave back that crooked smile of his that somehow made him endearing even if you wanted to be mad at him. Edward was one to talk about marriage. While I had been going steady and was now engaged to Sally, he left behind a string of broken hearts of women who fell for his rugged masculine charm. He showed no hint at slowing down.

"I'll be an aunt then!" Jane exclaimed, jumping up and down. "I want to be an aunt."

I always had a soft spot for my little sister. She, like Sally, had an overwhelmingly pleasing personality mixed with her natural curiosity about things. She loved for me to take her to the local museums on the weekend, and as if she were twenty years older, she would carefully examine all the exhibits and soak any and all information that she could.

With the differences in our ages, I had always suspected that Jane had been an unplanned surprise for my parents. After all, my mother had been in her late thirties when she had her, when she was just about to help usher Edward and me into our teenage years.

"I like Sally," Jane said matter-of-factly, before devouring her scrambled eggs.

Sally had taken the time to get to know Jane and asking her about school and what she liked to do with her friends. I knew my parents loved Sally from the first time they met her, too. With Sally's bubbly personality, smattering of cute freckles, and easygoing demeanor, she won my parents over from the start. Even Edward mockingly told me how surprised he was that I'd managed to snag such a great girl.

I knew Sally would be an amazing catch for any man, and part of me still couldn't believe she'd chosen me. She came from a well-to-do family with a doctor for a father. And she and her brother lived with her parents in a Victorian designed house in Angelino Heights.

"I knew the moment I saw you on campus," she had told me one night while we sat on my parents' front lawn and looked up at the stars.

"How did you know?" I asked.

She grinned and said, "When you helped the professor bring her books into class since she had a broken leg and was on crutches. Remember? You were the first one to jump up and assist her. I knew that's the kind of man I wanted, someone who just naturally helps others."

I had smiled, and she squeezed my hand. I noticed she didn't ask me how I "knew" about her which I was grateful for. It's not that I didn't think Sally was amazing or a terrific gal, but I couldn't deny that we weren't equals in this relationship concerning emotions. She'd been the first girl I'd ever really dated. In high school, I played off my seeming lack of interest in girls as being very focused on school. It's not that I didn't try. God knows I did my best by taking a few girls out and actually getting on my knees and praying to God that I would start to have the kind of feelings other boys my age had about girls. So when Sally came along, and she had so many great attributes, I just decided she'd be the one I would go after. I had given up on feeling that "spark" other couples had.

That evening after dinner, Sally insisted on helping my mother clean up the dishes and thanked her for the delicious roasted chicken and potatoes. Sally and I, hand in hand, took a walk down the sidewalks in the streetcar suburb, Larchmont, where my family resided. The evening air was just a tiny bit crisp for December and a nice breeze slightly swayed the trees. It was a Los Angeles fall, cool not cold, and the kind of weather people in most of the rest of the country would envy. We passed other couples strolling by with baby carriages and dogs. They all looked like perfect families cut out from pictures of the Sears and Roebuck catalog.

"Your parents are so sweet," Sally said, as she leaned into me, and we started to walk by the local shops in the neighborhood, with their Christmas window displays.

"And they think you're quite swell," I said. "But you already know that."

From the time I spent with Sally's parents, they seemed to like me well enough and were always unfailingly polite. However, I couldn't shake the feeling that they weren't 100 percent sure I was a match for their daughter. I worried that they could somehow see there was a struggle inside me, and I was nothing but an imposter posing as a "normal" all-American guy. There was a look in their eyes, particularly her father's, that made me just a tiny bit uneasy and made my stomach clench.

"So..." Sally said, stopping to look in the store window at some dresses. I knew from the sound of her voice and the "So..." that she had something important she wanted to talk about.

"What's going on?" I asked.

She looked down at the engagement ring on her finger with the small but respectable diamond.

"Are we ever going to set a date?" she asked. She shifted her weight from one foot to another and smoothed down the front of her polka dot cotton dress. "I mean it's been six months since you popped the question."

I chose my words carefully as Sally still feigned interest in the window display.

"I thought we agreed we would pick one after graduating and finding teaching jobs," I pointed out.

"I know, but…" She trailed off.

"But what?" I asked.

She turned her gaze back to me and said, "Why should we wait that long? We love each other, and getting married is an inevitability. Wouldn't it be wonderful to already be married when we graduated? It'd be you and me, together, and ready to take on the world."

I swallowed hard. Somehow I had managed to dodge the date setting by coming up with a series of excuses that were believable enough, but now I looked into her eyes. I could see the hope and desire in them. I could see the *love*. How could I keep denying her no matter what other feelings I had? Those feelings, those experiences with the men in the park didn't matter. Building a life with Sally *did*.

"What about…." I said, trying to come up with a good answer. "We talk about it after Valentine's Day in a couple of months. We'll set a date then. Promise."

Her face lit up, and she threw her arms around me.

I had made her so happy, so easily. Would anyone else ever love me like this? Probably not. So she was right. Why should we drag it out any longer?

As she squeezed me harder she said, "I love you, Jack."

"I love you, too," I said, and I meant it…just not in the same way.

But I couldn't stop thinking about the electrical shock of emotions I felt with every man I met and touched at the park. Maybe that would just be a secret I carried through life. God knows I wouldn't be the only one judging from the wedding rings I noticed on many of the men. And besides, if I wasn't with any other women, wasn't that being faithful? I tried to rationalize it.

"Jack! Sally!" we heard someone yell out our names.

We turned to find our friend, Ethel, from college rushing toward us. She looked like she'd been crying.

"Ethel, what's wrong?" Sally said in a calming voice, taking Ethel's shaking hands.

Ethel had always been a bit on the dramatic side, such as when she wept for days after getting a C on a midterm, but the look in her eyes suggested something very different this time, something serious.

"You haven't heard, have you?" she asked, and continued before she could answer. "It's on all the radio stations."

"What?" I asked.

"My mother sent me here to go to the drugstore to get something for her heartburn, but I'm so upset," Ethel rambled.

"Focus," Sally told her. "What's happening?"

"The Japanese. They bombed Pearl Harbor! It's bad. We're going to war now for sure. Petey…" she said, referring to her fiancé, "said he's signing up for the Army tomorrow. He's going to go fight the Japs and help protect his country!"

Ethel really began to sob now, and Sally hugged her tightly.

"It's going to be okay," Sally said, but her voice betrayed her. I could hear the fear in it.

Ethel's words rang over and over in my head.

We're going to war.

Of course, I knew this was a possibility with the war in Europe and all the tensions building. But now there could be no denying that war was imminent.

I knew immediately life for all of us would soon drastically change, and things such as wedding dates would suddenly not seem so urgent.

When I arrived home and walked into the kitchen, palpable tension hung in the air like a wet blanket. My parents sat at our pine breakfast table with the radio sitting in the center and listened with grim faces. The announcer read off what was known so far about the bombings, the damage, and the Americans killed. Edward paced the kitchen with a look of intense anger on his face as if he were ready to fight someone at any moment.

"You heard?" Edward asked and leaned against the counter.

He took a pack of cigarettes out of his pocket, took one out, and lit it even though he knew our mother hated being around smoke.

"Yeah, I heard about it from Ethel Mitchell when Sally and I ran into her," I said.

"I'm going," Edward said, taking a long puff on his cigarette.

"What?" Mother asked in surprise, her voice tense.

She held a ragged dish towel tight in her hand as if it were a life preserver.

"I'm joining the military. *Tomorrow.*"

"But what about the mechanic job you just got?" Mother protested, but we all knew her concern was about more than just a job.

"You heard them…how many people died, and that number will probably go higher," Edward said, turning his gaze to me and obviously waiting for me to chime in. His stare practically drilled holes into me. I knew he expected me to say how I would find a way to contribute despite my injured leg.

When I said nothing, he looked down at the floor barely disguising his look of disgust.

Our whole lives I knew he was disappointed in me, as if I had never been the role model older brother he could look up to growing up.

"I'm taking a walk," I announced.

"You just got here," Father said surprised, motioning to a chair. "Have a seat. This is a sad day for our country. Families need to be together."

"I gotta go," I said, quickly turning around and heading back out the same door I had entered through barely a minute ago.

I couldn't wrap my head around all this. It was one of the few rare moments in life when you realize the whole world has changed, everything has been shifted, the axis tilted.

The December evening air had already gotten chillier as the last tiny bit of the sun disappeared. I pulled my light sweater closer as I quickly walked to the streetcar stop. I practically ignored our neighbor, old Mr. Thompson, as he waved from his front porch while smoking a cigar. I gave a weak wave and picked up my pace.

There was only one place I knew I wanted to go now. Pershing Square. I needed that rush that came with desiring another man and feeling desired. It would be the only thing that would cancel out my fears of what would happen next, even if only for a few minutes, and the fact I felt so inadequate in so many ways. Edward was so sure of himself and going off to fight the good fight. I feared having to really get serious about Sally and the wedding date. I feared that these connections, if you will, I made at the park were just making me feel lonelier than I felt before, yet I couldn't seem to stop going there. I feared my brother going off to war and not coming back. Even though Edward and I had never been particularly close, I still loved him.

Deep down though, I knew those few moments of a high I'd get from being with another man would turn into a deep crash of sadness and a scalding hot shower afterward as if I could wash off the shame. But like someone with a drinking problem, I couldn't resist the allure of being able to forget for just a few minutes even knowing the pounding hangover that would follow.

At the streetcar stop, I tried to be patient as a young, exhausted-looking mother tried to herd her three children, all of whom had to be under five, on the bus. I could feel my irritation starting to reach a boiling point though, as the mother knelt down to rebutton the jacket on the youngest girl and blocked the door to the bus.

"It's cold, honey," she said to her daughter in a weary voice. "You have to keep your coat buttoned."

I wished the driver would tell her to hurry up and that people had places they've got to be, but instead he just smiled kindly at her.

Lately, when I made the decision to go to the park, I just wanted to get there as fast as I could before I thought about it too much. I found myself not wanting to think too hard or a lot about my life in general these days, but now the thought of possibly being sent to war put a need of rush inside.

Finally, the mother managed to get her children on the bus. I paid my fare and found a seat in the back, leaving rows between me and anyone else.

I leaned my head against the cool window and watched the city pass by as the streetcar made its way toward Downtown. I watched the couples walking hand-in-hand as they strolled down the sidewalks, and all of them looked so much in love and as if they *fit*. My stomach twisted as I thought of the fact that I'd begun to realize that I'd never feel that way with a woman, yet I could never have a similar type of life with a man. That was something I couldn't foresee society ever accepting back in 1941.

My emotions had overwhelmed my thoughts to the point that I almost missed my stop and just barely had enough time to hop off the bus before the driver shut the door.

I stuffed my hands in the pockets of my pea coat and continued to walk faster and faster toward the park, fast enough that I began to sweat even though it had turned downright cold at this point. I walked by the May Co. Christmas window displays with their Santas and snowmen and wondered how anyone could have a jolly holiday now knowing the danger that threatened us all after the attack on Pearl Harbor. Sure, we had been listening daily to the news on the radio describing bombings in Europe, but I knew that having a mass attack on American soil woke many people up to the fact that we were not immune to the violence or the war.

When I eventually reached the park, it was dim and looked deserted. Usually there were a few men milling about and trying not to look obvious about why they were there and a few other people who had come there simply to go to the park. Maybe everyone was as shaken up by the bombing that they were staying home with their families—which is probably exactly where I should have been if I hadn't been so weak, I admonished myself.

Finding the park so deserted felt like another kick to my stomach. There was no way to run from or ignore my feelings at the moment, and defeated, I slumped down on a park bench by myself. I could hear the distant voices of people walking outside the park and even a few laughs. I wondered if the laughing people had heard about the bombing yet. News traveled much slower back then with no TV or Internet. It was possible to be "out of the loop" for a period of time when it came to bad news. Now it just hits you like a high-speed train throughout the day with one breaking news story after the next.

I looked up at the clear sky, and even with the city lights, some stars shone brightly.

Increasingly, I felt lonelier.

I knew I should probably be with Sally, my family, or friends instead of by myself in this deserted park in Downtown, but none of them would understand all the confused feelings I had swirling in and dominating my brain. I didn't even understand it all.

Suddenly, I heard a loud chirping sound and felt a small but sharp peck on the top of my head.

"What the…." I started to say.

The bird loudly squawked again before diving down and pecking at my head again. I threw up my arms and waved them around to scare off my tiny attacker.

That's when I heard a chuckle coming from across me. In the dim light I could make out another man. Back then, he would have been referred to as Oriental. He was a few inches shorter than me and about my age with short-cropped black hair, and I could see his wide smile even in this light.

"You must be near her nest. That's why she's attacking you. They do that sometimes. I'd move if I were you," he said.

Quickly, I got off the bench and walked toward him, and the bird stopped attacking.

"Thanks," I said.

As I got closer, I got a much better look at him.

He had broad shoulders that hinted at a somewhat muscular body. He wore a black knit sweater with fitted gray slacks. His cheeks had dimples when he smiled, and just his gaze on me quickened my heart. The more he came into focus, the more I saw how incredibly handsome this man looked, even bordering on the term pretty.

"Sorry, but I couldn't help laughing," he said, his smile growing bigger as I got closer.

I paused and continued to look at him to see if I could recognize that tell-tale look in his eyes and the possibility that he had ventured out here by himself for the same reason I did.

"That's okay," I said, conjuring up a small laugh on my end to appear relaxed. "I hadn't expected to be harassed by a bird."

He nodded and said, "Yeah, by the police maybe but not a bird."

The police?

Even though anything resembling a real conversation had been short, I had heard from a couple of the guys I met up with at Pershing Square to keep an eye out for the police who showed up on occasion to make sure nothing happened in the bushes and grass that shouldn't. Some men's arrest reports ended up in the newspapers and their lives were basically ruined. One man described the arrest and beating in the park of a guy with premature salt-and-pepper hair and bright blue eyes. I immediately recognized his description. The two of us had gone off together just a couple of nights prior.

My heart fluttered. His comment did strongly hint at something. Maybe he was here for the same reason as me.

This young man with his warm smile could help me forget....at least for a few moments. In his arms, I would be able to block out the rest of the world just long enough not to feel so low about myself. I wanted to take him to the back of my parents' shop. I wanted to run my fingers through his black crew cut, let my hands run up and down his arms to feel his masculine torso, and pull him close to me enjoying the buildup of warmth between our bodies.

"What's your name?" he asked, his eyes darting around every now and then to stay aware of who was around.

"Jack," I managed to say.

All I could think about at that moment was how badly I wanted to kiss him and taste his lips. I could now see a bit of stubble on his check that I wanted to stroke with my fingers.

"I'm Hiro," he said. "Sounds like h-e-r-o but spelt with an 'I' instead of an 'e.' It's Japanese."

"Hiro," I repeated. "Nice to meet you."

"I...uh...have seen you here before," he said, his eyes searching mine, too.

He is here for the same reason, I realized for sure now.

"Really?" I said. "I'm surprised I haven't seen you then."

"I stay off on the sides most of the time. I don't really like..." He trailed off.

"Jack Henry?" a voice called out.

I turned and saw Thomas Keats, a guy a couple of years older than me, who lived a few houses down from me. He carried some large bags that I assumed contained Christmas shopping.

"Oh...uh...hi, Thomas," I said as he got closer.

Damn.

Damn.

Why now of all times?

Hiro looked frozen, not knowing what to say or do next.

Thomas stopped next to me. His eyes darted over to Hiro and back to me again.

"What are you doing out here tonight?" he asked, a little suspicion coming through in his voice.

"Just getting some air. Needed to leave the house for a bit," I answered.

Thomas looked back at Hiro, and I knew I needed to quickly come up with a cover.

"This is Hiro. We just met. This small bird was attacking me, and I didn't know why. Hiro said she must have a nest close by," I said, knowing that this all sounded rather odd and flimsy.

Thomas nodded, but he looked unconvinced that that was the whole story. He eyed Hiro with a disgusted and hateful look.

"Well, I'm headed back home and going to catch the streetcar. Want to come with me?" he asked, no longer acknowledging Hiro's presence besides the quick glances he'd take at him every few seconds.

"Uh..." I stammered.

Going with Thomas and leaving behind this especially good-looking man who actually appeared interested in *me* was the last thing I wanted to do. I wouldn't have described myself as handsome, but in retrospect I suppose I was better looking than I realized at the time. I was close to six feet, with dirty-blond hair, and baby-blue eyes that my mother said reminded her of the waters off Catalina Island. My nose was a bit crooked, and my ears were a bit big. I also remained self-conscious about my small limp. Overall I was decent enough, but not close to the level of handsome that described Hiro.

Thomas stared at me and waited for a reply. What excuse would I have for staying? I couldn't think fast enough to come up with anything plausible.

"Sure," I answered. "Thanks."

Thomas shot Hiro another quizzical look.

"Well, uh, thanks for saving me from the crazy bird," I told Hiro.

He nodded and said, "Sure. You two have a good evening."

I gave him a small unenthusiastic smile that I hoped told him I hated having to leave. Sure, he said he'd seen me before, but maybe this moment would be the last one. I wished I had the ability to think quicker on my feet and dodge Thomas and his invitation to go back home, the last possible place I wanted to be at that moment.

When Thomas and I were out of earshot and on our way to the streetcar, I broke the silence.

"Nice night for shopping. Did you get any good stuff for the family?" I asked, trying to sound interested.

I so badly wanted to turn around to see if Hiro still stood there, and if I could somehow let him know with my look that I hoped to see him there again.

"Just stuff for my nieces and nephews mostly," Thomas said, before lowering his voice as if someone may be listening to us. "You have to watch out for those Japs."

"What?" I said.

"The Japs, the guy you were talking to. They bombed Pearl Harbor in Hawaii today, you know? Lots of people killed," Thomas said, shaking his head. "You have to be careful with them. Who knows what they're up to. He should stay in *his* part of town. That's a lot of nerve sitting in a park over here."

I thought about saying something along the lines that Hiro was probably an *American* and not just a *Jap*, but I decided against it. As we crossed to Olive Street, I quickly turned around and caught a glimpse of Hiro crossing Fourth Street, and as if he could feel my stare, he turned toward me. For the briefest second our eyes met, and my gut told me he also hoped we would run into each other again.

Chapter Two

That next day was a Monday, and the entire campus of our university would normally be swept up into the stress of finals this time of year. Instead, all anyone could talk about was Pearl Harbor and what would happen next. The US would surely retaliate big, and then the military draft would pick up steam.

At lunch, Sally and I sat at a picnic table under an evergreen tree on campus, picking at the egg salad sandwiches we'd purchased. Neither of us had much to say. I knew Sally worried about her brothers, especially Steve, who had only recently turned eighteen.

"What if the war is still going on then?" she asked, setting her sandwich back down on its wrapping paper.

I knew it was the draft that concerned her.

"I don't think this will last all that long," I tried to assure her, even though I didn't believe a word of it myself.

She looked on the verge of tears, and she avoided eye contact with me by staring down in her lap. I placed an arm around her and gave her a small squeeze.

Sally looked up at me, and I thought she was about to say something. But then she just smoothed down her wool green A-line skirt.

"What is it?" I asked. "You can tell me."

She shook her head, and said, "It's just…"

"Just what?" I asked when her voice trailed off.

"This may be horrible of me to say in some ways, but I'm sort of glad about your injury. If I knew you had to leave too, I'm not sure I could handle it," she said, placing her hand over mine.

I nodded and said, "That's nothing to feel horrible about."

I couldn't bear to tell her that part of me felt *guilty* to know I'd be a military reject, and that it made me feel less of a man somehow. When combined with my secret time at the park and going off with other shadow men there, I felt not only guilt but shame for two things I felt I couldn't control.

Sally leaned into me, wiped a couple of small tears from her eyes, and placed her head on my shoulder, and the two of us didn't move even though we were already late for our next class. Neither of us could imagine sitting in a classroom and taking notes when it seemed as if everyone's future had just been given a hard and brutal shake.

Later that day, I sat at the desk in the back office of the jewelry store balancing November's books while my father cleaned some new ruby necklaces before putting them on display. I could hear my mother in the front of the store helping a man pick out an anniversary present for his wife.

Father carefully cleaned each of the intricate parts of the necklaces with a thin cloth.

"Presentation is everything," he always told us growing up. "Both in business and how people perceive you on a personal level."

Presentation is everything.

I wondered what would happen if my secret trips to Pershing Square came out. Something so scandalous could hurt the family business. This I knew. Los Angeles might have been a sizable city back in 1941, but word still traveled fast within the business community especially if it was something salacious.

"Wasn't Edward going to come by after work this evening to help with inventory?" I asked.

"Not today. He was going to go sign up for the Army right after work today," Father said, each word practically dripping with patriotic pride.

"Already?" I asked.

"There's no time like now especially after what happened. These Japs aren't going to see what's coming for them once we hit them full force. You just wait and see," he said.

In classes that day, I had heard other students making similar vows of what would happen to *those Japs*. No one else seemed to notice, but I realized that Henry Nakamura, a guy who had been in many of my classes, was absent that day despite final exams quickly approaching. He had mentioned once while we were working on a group study project that he had never been to Japan, but he hoped to go one day to visit his grandparents while they were still alive.

On the desk, I noticed a folded copy of that day's Los Angeles Times on a shelf next to the desk. I wondered what it must have been like for other people of Japanese descent. Did they feel caught between two worlds? Did those who were born here, who had never visited Japan, have any loyalty to that country? After all, they were American citizens. My grandparents on my father's side had immigrated from Ireland, but I certainly didn't feel Irish.

I thought of the heart-stopping handsome Japanese man from the park.

Hiro.

I wondered if he lived in Little Tokyo and what the people in that neighborhood must be wondering and feeling now that America had declared war on Japan. As a child, we would sometimes go to Little Tokyo for food and trinkets, as if it were a tourist destination and a mini-visit to a foreign land. No one I knew had so much as visited a restaurant in Little Tokyo for quite a while at that point.

How did the newspaper headlines make the Japanese-Americans feel? I could hear the downright hatred in people's voices when referring to the Japanese, and I could tell it didn't matter where any of them were born. They were all seen to be the same and all put into the same category.

Potential.

Enemy.

I thought of Hiro's smile. Would he find it possible to keeping smiling now?

My father cleared his throat, and I turned my gaze back to him and watched him continue to meticulously clean another piece of jewelry. For the first time in who knew how long, I really noticed him. His hair had more salt than pepper at this point, and crow's feet had begun to spread from the corners of his eyes.

He had spoken of his time fighting in World War I with great pride, and I knew he regarded it as one of the most important times in his life. His level of patriotism knew no bounds, and Father often told us how lucky we were to be born in the "land of opportunity." Edward would undoubtedly make him very proud with his eagerness to join the fight and help protect his country.

Maybe it had been only in my mind, but at that moment, my injured leg began to give me the dull ache it had been prone to do since the accident. The throb served as yet another reminder that I couldn't and wasn't the son my father had truly wanted when John might have been. I never played sports. I certainly hadn't been good with the girls growing up. It was only by lucky accident that Sally landed in my life. If he knew what had happened between me and some nameless men in the park, he would feel such a deep shame. Yet, I knew deep down that I would continue to bring these men here as the touch of another man had grown increasingly into an itch I had to scratch, and I so wished that I had been able to bring Hiro to this room.

This surprised me in a way. The men I had "met" previously, the men whose bodies I had explored, had remained anonymous for the most part. Rarely was any personal information, including names, exchanged. But with Hiro, even though I didn't get the chance to so much as kiss him, I found my thoughts continuously going back to him and found myself wanting to know more about him…to actually talk to him. These feelings excited and scared me at the same time.

"Thank you," I heard Mother say from the front of the store, and then there was the familiar sound of the click that came from locking the front door.

I glanced up at the clock and saw that it was a few minutes past six o'clock.

"It looks like it's that time," Father said, putting the necklaces back in their individual boxes.

I stayed silent and kept working.

A few minutes later, Mother walked into the back, and I could tell the level of her exhaustion from the bags under her eyes. At the breakfast table that morning, she had looked just as tired, and I knew she hadn't slept well. As much as Father felt pride at Edward joining the war effort, I knew that Mother worried about what could happen to him. She would probably never voice her true concerns to Father as she often went along with what would make him happy. But I knew her well enough to see beyond the nods of agreement she gave my father as he gave his opinions on any situation.

"You boys ready?" she said, trying to put some chipper in her voice.

"Ready here," Father said, putting some of the more expensive pieces he had been working with into a safe. "Edward should have some news for us."

Mother didn't respond to the last comment. Instead, she reached into the small closet in the backroom to retrieve her coat.

"Mrs. Sheffield is probably more than ready for us to pick up Jane," she said referring to the neighbor who took care of Jane for a few hours after school each day.

"I'm going to stay here and try and finish up the November books," I said, staring down at the ledger with great intensity to suggest I was in the middle of some very important work.

"Can't you finish tomorrow?" Father said, putting on his gabardine overcoat. "We should all be there to hear what Edward has to say."

"It's not like I won't see him tonight. We share a bedroom," I said a little too sharply.

Mother shot me a pleading look that I knew meant to urge me not to pick a fight.

When I finally arrived at the entrance to Pershing Square, I found myself short of breath from the rushed pace I used to get here and my bum leg had begun to throb. I entered the park and immediately caught the eye of a man I had taken back to the jewelry store a couple of months ago. He was older than me by maybe a good twenty years and looked slightly like Cary Grant but with a little more white in his hair. He had a tall and brawny build. Just like the last time he wore a well-tailored brown suit. We barely spoke when we met before, but I could easily picture him as an insurance agent or maybe an accountant.

He sat on a bench under a tree and smoked a cigarette. His hat and a newspaper sat next to him on the bench. The man immediately locked eyes on me, and he gave me just the barest of smiles. Then he leaned back and placed his arm along the back of the bench in a gesture of openness.

I knew he might have been old enough to be my father, but since he was undeniably handsome, the age factor hadn't meant anything to me, especially since our time together mostly consisted of desperate, yearning grabs and pulls of each other's bodies in the back alleys of down-town. I remembered that he pulled me in tight and gave me the deepest, longest kiss of my life. His mouth had tasted of cigarettes and whiskey. Once the hardness of his body was factored in, I had turned to jelly in his arms. But just as fast as it happened, it had ended. And this was the first time I had seen him since.

Admittedly, I thought about turning around and heading back to the store to see if he would follow, and by the intense gaze, I had no doubt he would. But instead of doing so, I just gave him a slight nod and kept walking through the park. I didn't want to linger in the least to give him any ideas, so I picked up the pace even further.

I had only one thing, one person, on my mind.

Hiro.

I hoped he would be here, and I would get the chance to get close to him. He'd been the only man I'd thought of since I saw him which I found odd. I had never felt the same about another man. I just assumed that the person didn't matter as long as I was attracted to them because the only outcome would be a few minutes of fumbling and grabbing.

But with him, it seemed different despite our not so much as touch-ing each other, and I couldn't exactly say why.

I was far too pragmatic to believe in such things as love at first sight, but here I was searching throughout the park with my gaze darting all around as I made my way along the walkway looking for him.

Every man I had met at the park before I assumed would just be a one-time encounter, but here was a man I hadn't even touched yet. All I could think about was finding Hiro and getting the chance to speak with him again.

There had been a kindness in his eyes and a warmth I hadn't found in other men, who tended to avoid eye contact once the connection for the evening was made.

Finally, I had made my way down all the paths of the park, and besides quickly passing a few other men probably there for the same thing, I had not found Hiro. I finally stopped searching and walked over to a tall palm tree and leaned against it. My leg, my reminder of the accident, ached with a deep throbbing worse than I had experienced in quite a while.

The lights from The Biltmore Hotel shone through the trees, and I considered going there for a drink before heading home. I needed something, a liquid courage, to face another evening with my family. I knew the conversation would be dominated by Edward's upcoming future with the military which would result in hand-wringing from my mother and back slaps and "Atta boys" for Edward from my father.

My thoughts turned to John, the brother who had died in the accident that left me with my injured leg. He, too, I'm sure, would have wanted to sign up and protect his country first thing. Knowing John, he might have already been in the military for a good amount of time.

I tried not to think about John, the accident, or what led up to it. Doing so just reminded me of how I was less than my brothers and how the whole family and hell, even Sally, would have been better off if I had just never been born.

"Hey there again," I heard a voice on my right side say in a half whisper.

I turned and saw Hiro now leaning on the other side of the same tree and eyeing me with a smile.

"Oh!" I said startled but very pleased. "You snuck up on me."

"You sure looked deep in thought," he said, cocking an eyebrow.

"Just a lot going on right now with…well, everything," I said.

He nodded and gave me a knowing look.

I thought about all the anti-Japanese sentiment I'd heard since I'd first seen him. I wondered how it must feel to be lumped together in people's minds with the enemy.

He motioned over to a black wrought iron bench.

"Want to sit for a few minutes?" he asked.

I realized that in our two brief encounters we had probably already had more conversation than I had had with the other guys I met in this park. How odd to think about the level of physical intimacy I had had with men in the park. It had basically consisted of nothing but carnal urges. Silence and secrecy were considered necessary to protect oneself.

"Okay," I said, excited but still a little lost on how this should go.

We made our way over to the bench, sat down, and made sure to leave a good bit of distance between us. I knew we were both aware of the dangers that came from meeting up like this. If the police happened to come by and keep an eye on us, we could act as if we were just casual friends. Just the slightest touch of the knees or the feet could raise eyebrows and bring about all sorts of unwanted scrutiny by passersby who might even call the police if they suspected something. I knew that people sometimes still *did* things out of desperation of nowhere else to go in darker areas of the brush. Luckily, I had the backroom of the store. Thankfully, neither of my parents had decided to come back in the evening if they forgot something for example. I couldn't even begin to imagine how horrible that would be.

Hiro wore a blue collared dress shirt with a checked tie and high-waisted trousers that gave him a clean, professional look. I wondered what he did for work, and I also suddenly felt oddly underdressed in my plain cotton twill trousers and hunter-green wool V-neck sweater. It was as if I was on an important first date. But what would you call this that was happening? I didn't even know if there was such a word for two men meeting up like this.

A couple of moments of awkward silence went by when the only sounds came from the cars on Olive Street. I could see Hiro taking quick glances over at me. I wondered what he was thinking. Did he feel regret meeting with me this way after seeing me for a second time?

There was more light this evening from the streetlamps where we sat. Was he disappointed seeing me now? He was so handsome with his strong jawline and shock of black hair. I felt lowly in comparison.

The butterflies in my stomach went into overdrive. I suddenly felt clammy despite the cool, crisp December air. Being so close…yet far away…from him was just about more than I could stand. I so wanted to reach out, touch him, run my hand along his smooth cheek, and look into his dark eyes. But I knew not here.

Hiro finally broke the silence and said, "I was hoping to run into you here."

"Really?" I asked. Could it be true? Had he been thinking of me also?

"Yep. I'm glad you were here. I wanted to talk to you some more, but I know you needed to leave with your friend."

"I would have rather stayed here," I admitted.

That comment brought another smile to his face, and I once again got to see the dimples I was sure he must get complimented for having.

"I just decided to take a chance and to see if you might be here," Hiro said. "Things in Little Tokyo are very…tense right now."

Hiro looked down at the ground and kicked a small rock with his shoe.

"Some people say it's not safe for us to leave Little Tokyo and go to other parts of the city especially at night. But I wanted to take the chance to see you again."

"People are worked up about Pearl Harbor," I said.

"That's an understatement," he nodded and said. "And I understand. All of those innocent people died. And I've got a Japanese face. I just walk down the street and some people see the enemy. One of my cousins got punched in the face by some guys close to Union Station. They jumped him and screamed at him to go *home* like he hadn't been born right here in Los Angeles."

"I'm sorry," I said.

Hiro shrugged and although I barely knew him at this point, I could see the concern in his eyes.

"It's just the world we live in," he replied solemnly. "Things aren't always fair."

"Is he okay? Your cousin?"

"Yeah, he'll be fine. He's just uncomfortable leaving Little Tokyo now. All of us are."

"But you came here to see me?" I said, perplexed in a way that'd he'd be so interested.

"Well, yeah. I had to see how well you were doing after your bird attack," he said, a smile returning to his face.

I wanted so badly to reach out and put an arm around him, pull him close, and make him feel safe, but I knew I couldn't here.

I worked up some additional courage and asked, "Would you like to go somewhere?"

"Where to?" he asked.

"We could go…uh….to The Biltmore and have a drink. My treat," I said, with a hopeful smile.

"I'd like that, but…"

"But what?"

"I'm not sure I'd be welcomed there, especially now," Hiro said, stuffing his hands into his pockets. "What to do then, huh?"

"Well, we could…"

Where could we go and actually spend time together that went beyond my usual quick encounters? I thought of the guy I had met who'd been arrested. We needed somewhere where we could be safe. Finally, an idea occurred to me, but it had its own special dangers. However, compared to the alternatives it was all I could come up with at the time.

I thought of the backroom of my parents' store.

"Could what?" he asked.

It was the only place I could think of going though where we would be safe this time of night.

"My parents have a business not far from here and just down Broadway. No one's in the office this time of night," I said, before quickly adding, "We can talk."

"Just talk?" Hiro said, with a wink.

I could feel my face flush but I tried to play it off by shaking my shoulders and saying, "Yeah, sure. Why not?"

"Lead the way then," Hiro said.

I got up and took a quick glimpse around. All I needed was to be seen by someone I knew. Only this time I wouldn't be alone, and I'd be with a Japanese guy. I can imagine the questions my father would have about that one. But the idea of spending some time alone with Hiro and finding out more about him proved to be tempting enough to override my fears.

"This way," I said, motioning to one of the paths in the park. "This is the quickest route there."

"Why don't you walk a few feet ahead?" he said. "Just in case someone sees us. My luck one of my friends from Little Tokyo ventured out this way tonight, too."

I nodded and started heading in the direction of the store. Every now and then, I couldn't help but look back just to make sure he was still there and hadn't decided to drop me. I always felt so embarrassed about my limp that I often assumed it was the only thing people noticed about me.

After walking a few blocks down Broadway, I paused at the alley that led to the backroom of the jewelry store. I turned around, made eye contact with Hiro, and turned down the alley.

Part of me wondered if at this point he'd decide this wasn't for him and would disappear. But within a few moments, there he was turning down the alley to meet me.

"You into dark, questionable places?" he asked, sounding half-serious, half-joking as he walked around a fallen trashcan and a feral cat hissed at us from a windowsill.

"It's right here," I said, walking to the door that led to the backroom and digging into my pocket for the keys.

I fumbled a bit out of nervousness since I wanted to get us inside and away from prying eyes as soon as possible. To add to my anxiety, the door felt jammed and I had to push against it with the weight of my body.

Finally, the door popped open, and I flipped on the light switch.

"In here," I said, suddenly feeling a little foolish. After all, where else would I be going?

I stepped aside, and he walked into the room. My accounting books were sitting on the table where I left them, and there were two wooden office chairs next to the desk and a small coffeepot that kept my parents caffeinated throughout the workday.

He seemed uneasy and unsure of what to do with himself once he walked inside. He took off his hat and held it and looked to me for what to do next.

I hadn't been used to making pleasantries with men I met at the park, so it took me a couple of seconds to remember to be in hospitality mode.

"Have a seat," I said, motioning to one of the chairs.

He sat his coat and hat on the table and took a seat.

"Would you like some coffee? Just to warn you my parents only buy the really strong stuff," I said, trying feebly to make some sort of a joke.

"Sounds good," he answered.

I noticed him eyeing the imposing metal safe in the corner.

"My parents have a jewelry store," I said. "This is the backroom."

"My parents own a restaurant in Little Tokyo," he said.

"Really? For how long?" I said, carefully and slowly measuring out the coffee.

It felt like I didn't want to rush any part of this moment.

"It's been in the family for many years, but business is slow. Few visitors make it to Little Tokyo with the war and all. Just the local Japanese now, and no one is spending money. Everyone's scared that…things…may get worse. So, I help them in the restaurant in the evening and attend UCLA during the day. I'm studying linguistics," he said, before adding quickly, "and minoring in art."

I could tell from the tone of his voice that his heart was much more with art than linguistics.

I sat in the chair next to him. We were closer than ever now, just a few inches.

"It must be difficult," I said. "With everything going on right now."

"Let's just say it's not easy being Japanese-American right now. I'm *Nisei* which means second generation. I've never been to Japan. The other day this woman on the street yelled at me to go back to my home," he said with a chuckle that sounded humorless to me. "The only home I've known is Los Angeles though."

The expression on his face turned dark now, and I could tell he was deep in thought.

"I can't imagine anyone saying that to you," I replied.

And naively it was true. Ashamed to say, but if I hadn't met Hiro, I would have probably never even thought about what it must be like to be Japanese-American when Japan was now the enemy that must be conquered before another Pearl Harbor happened. I was part of the white, Caucasian, all-American part of the population. Before Hiro, I had barely known any Japanese persons nor did I really know anyone who wasn't part of my ethnic group on any sort of a personal level. In just the very short time I'd known Hiro, I was beginning to start to see the world in a different focus and viewpoint in the way you only can once you truly take the time to get to know someone who has been lumped into the category "different" from you.

"The tension in Little Tokyo hangs in the air now like a wet blanket. My grandmother, who lives in Seattle, called and said that she can feel in her bones that something awful is going to happen to all of us in the United States because of what Japan did. People are scared there, too."

Without thinking, I reached out and placed a hand on his knee. He looked back at me and our gazes locked. I knew both of us were wondering what the next move would be, what *this* would be.

"I have to believe that things will turn out right somehow," I said, knowing how unworldly that must have sounded.

He gave me a small indulgent smile and his eyes drifted down and looked at where my hand lay on his knee.

That simple touch between us felt electric and more intense than any other time I had been with a man, and I couldn't explain it. When I had heard people mentioning love at first sight, I thought they were full of crock. I simply couldn't imagine feeling so strongly about someone you barely knew. Yet, here I sat feeling an immediate connection to someone who remained a virtual stranger.

"I hope you're right about things getting better. I wish I had your optimism," Hiro said, sighing. He then turned to the coffeepot. "Smells like it's ready."

"Oh, yeah," I said, getting back up and grabbing two clean mugs that sat on the desk. "How do you take yours?"

"Black is fine," he said.

Before pouring the coffee, I turned on my father's wood table top radio from Montgomery Ward he would play while cleaning and fixing jewelry pieces. The "Chattanooga Choo Choo" played sending such a cheery tone in the air you could almost forget a war raged across Europe and now at home.

I could feel his eyes on me as I poured the coffee, and it made me more than a little self-conscious to the point that I almost spilled the coffee while pouring. I wondered if he had noticed my limp on the way over. I had concentrated and tried my best to straighten my stride as much as possible. I still had trouble believing that this guy with the angular features and perfect skin might be interested in me. While many people considered Sally beautiful I knew that women were thought to sometimes overlook certain physical imperfections if they thought the man was kind or would be a good provider. Men, however, weren't usually so forgiving.

"How did you find out about the park?" he asked suddenly, when I sat the mug of coffee in front of him.

I felt embarrassed by the question despite the fact that that had been exactly how we met. If anyone should understand my predicament when it came to meeting like-minded men, it had to be Hiro.

With my coffee in hand, I sat back down in the chair next to him. "I sort of stumbled on it you could say. I just went to the park to clear my head and then I noticed this man staring at me."

I looked down into my mug of coffee and continued. "It was unexpected. I just found myself following him...you know...into..."

"The bushes?" Hiro asked.

I nodded.

"I never got his name. I mean it all lasted just a few minutes. But he did tell me to be careful of the cops, and that they sometimes monitored the park."

"Yeah, I've heard that, too. I knew of one guy. They put all the details in the newspaper. He lost his job over it. I can't imagine what his family thought."

I shuddered. I couldn't imagine looking my parents or Sally in the eye if they were to find out about this other side of me. They'd never understand. Hell, I'm not sure I understood.

"What about you?" I asked. "How did you end up going to Pershing Square?"

"I found out about it from a customer at our restaurant who had been eying me all night. A Japanese guy. He had actually been at the restaurant with his fiancée believe it or not. He slipped me his phone number on a crumpled paper napkin. At first, I hid the piece of paper at the bottom of a drawer in my room. Then I worked up the nerve and called a few days later, and we met up at a bar he told me about a bar where men *like us* go," he said.

"What do you mean?" I asked perplexed. "What kind of places?"

"Bars," he answered. "For men who…well…like other men. They're pretty secret with the locations. You have to know someone to tell you."

I couldn't believe such a thing even existed and just the thought flabbergasted me.

"I didn't know about those," I said, shaking my head in amazement.

The idea of a room full of men…of men who had these feelings for other men…meeting together at a local watering hole proved hard to wrap my head around. At that point, I had only begun to realize that there were others like me. As far back as I could remember, something told me I was different from the other boys at school or on the playground. I just didn't seem to fit as part of their tribe, and I couldn't understand why.

In elementary school, I would often sit by myself under a large oak tree on the playground not feeling a connection with the other boys or wanting to join in on their games. And I wouldn't dare play with the girls on the playground as then I would be branded a sissy. I wasn't exactly sure of what being a sissy meant, but I knew it wasn't good. It all resulted in a lonely, isolated childhood.

By the time puberty began and I started feeling an attraction to other guys that I knew should have been for girls, I spent many years confused and became even more of an introvert. The other kids just thought I was odd, weird, strange, and every other word to mean someone who wasn't *like us*.

"Would you like to go one night with me?" he asked tentatively.

"I…uh…" I stammered.

What if I got caught somehow? What that would do to my family and Sally was simply unthinkable. I had already taken so many risks.

"I'd rather just spend time with you to be honest," I said.

He smiled, and it lit up the room like a Roman candle for me.

"I'd like to get to know you better, too," he said.

My heart practically skipped a beat.

"Do you have a big family?" I asked.

"Just my sister, Lily. She's sixteen. My mom and dad, of course. The rest of the family is in Seattle."

"How do you like college?" I asked.

He shook his head and chuckled.

"My parents have always expected me to take it over the restaurant one day. That was the only schooling my parents cared about at first. My culture is very traditional. We're expected to always follow our parents' wishes. It was a hard sell at first, but I convinced them of the new opportunities attending college would open up for our family," Hiro said.

"What about you? Big family?" he asked, changing the subject back to me.

"I have my sister Jane who is nine and a younger brother, Edward. I had another brother, too. John," I said, my voice growing quiet.

I didn't like speaking about John or what happened during the accident. It had been years ago, but every single second had been burned into my brain as if it had just happened. I often dreamed about the accident, and I could hear the moaning and crunching of the metal against metal as the Roadster crashed into our Ford Model B on the passenger side right where John sat. I could still vividly hear the shattering of glass, and the screaming of my brother, his blue eyes full of fear…until silence.

"What happened to him?" Hiro said, leaning so close to me I could smell his aftershave, a masculine woody scent.

I rarely, practically never, talked about the accident not even with Sally. My whole family didn't talk about it. I wasn't even sure if Jane realized she had had another brother.

The truth of it was that should have been *me* that died. I had talked John into changing seats with me mere minutes before the accident because I wanted to get a better look at the ocean since we were driving along the Pacific. He resisted at first, but then I told him he could play for an hour with the new guitar my parents had gotten me for my birthday. If I hadn't done it, that would have been me who died almost at impact. My parents, miraculously, were fine besides some bruising and cuts from glass. My leg got pinned under a piece of heavy metal. It took six firemen to free me and my leg had never been the same since.

Hiro must have noticed the distress on my face because he quickly added, "I'm sorry. It's none of my business."

The sad lyrics of longing in "Blue Champagne" began to play over the radio adding even more melancholy to the room.

"It's just that I don't talk about John or the accident much. It brings up a lot of memories I wish I could forget," I said, shaking my foot because of my nervousness.

"That's okay. You only need to tell me what feels right for you," he said, as I looked up and stared into his dark ebony eyes. They were eyes that made me want to open up and talk, which was so opposite of my usual personality.

"It's how I got my limp," I found myself saying.

Confused, his eyes widened a bit.

"Sorry?" he said.

"You probably noticed my limp when walking over. It's why I can't join the war effort," I quickly added, feeling like I needed to provide even Hiro with an excuse about my lack of military work.

"I'm sorry. I don't follow," he said, shaking his head.

I could feel tears burning at the edge of my eyes.

It can't be. I never cry.

All at once, I could sense so many emotions that I had buried deep within myself pushing their way up to the surface.

I had thought about the accident every single day, but I had also never shed a tear. To do so could open all sorts of floodgates I wasn't sure I could handle even now. Yet, here I was about to lose my firm grip on my feelings.

"There was a car accident. A man who'd been drinking too much hit our car along the Pacific Coast Highway. It killed my brother," I said, no longer able to stop the tears that had begun to pour out of me. "I was supposed to be sitting where John was, but I got him to move with me almost right before the car crashed into us. He died instead of me, and I got this limp from the accident."

The words had now begun to pour out of me.

"My other brother, Edward, wasn't in the accident. He had been spending the weekend with a friend's family."

My throat went dry, and I sucked in a breath.

"And every day I wonder what John's life would be like if I hadn't changed places with him. He could have been the son, the man my fiancée…" I saw a slight look of surprise on Hiro's face at the word *fiancée*.

"The type of man they all deserved. Instead, they've got *me*." Hiro reached out and gently wiped the tears from my face.

"It's not your fault…the accident, none of it. You are who you are," he said simply.

I shook my head.

"No. I should be able to do better, to be the type of man and have the type of life John would have deserved. He always looked up to me, his big brother, and I can't help but think he looks down at me and is disappointed."

"You Made Me Love You" came over the radio, and Hiro stood up and reached out a hand.

I didn't understand what he wanted me to do.

"What?" I asked, wiping my eyes with the cuffs of my shirt.

"Dance with me," he said.

"Dance?" I said, shocked at the idea of two men dancing together.

With a man? In the back of my parents' store?

The idea seemed silly and downright impossible to me, but Hiro took my hands and pulled me up and into him. Immediately, I felt a sense of warmth and protection that I had never felt before as he pulled me close to him and we swayed with the music. What had once seemed impossible, two men dancing together, suddenly felt like the most natural thing in the world to me.

"You're a sweet guy," he said, whispering into my ear as I found myself wrapping my arms around his lean, hard body as if I'd done it a thousand times before.

"You're...you're..." I stammered. "Something else."

I chuckled and buried my face in the crook of his neck.

"I hope that's a good thing," he said with a little laugh.

"It is," I said.

He pulled back until we faced each other again, and for a moment, I could have pretended the world consisted of only the two of us in each other's arms. All of my fears and feelings of shame evaporated.

Hiro's mouth opened slightly, and he looked on the verge of saying something. Instead, he suddenly pulled me even closer, tightly and determined, and before I knew it, his lips were on mine. Instinctively, I parted them, and I got the chance to taste his warm mouth. My body lit up with an awareness I had never experienced before as if every nerve in my skin was on high alert and experiencing even the faintest sensations tenfold what they normally would be.

I could have stood there all night with my arms wrapped around his sinewy body, but finally he slowly pulled away and broke our kiss. The grin on his face, though, told me that he'd been just as pleased as I had been.

What would happen next?

I had experienced a few hurried kisses with men that usually led to some sort of sexual encounter in the dark edges of the city. But undergoing this hormone-infused lip lock proved to be new territory for me.

I didn't know what to say or do next.

Finally, he took my hands into his and said, "I need to go home. I promised I'd help close the restaurant up tonight," he finally said.

"Oh, sure. Okay," I said, knowing that my voice was tinged with disappointment.

"Promise me you'll meet me tomorrow," he said, a new urgency in his tone.

"I will," I said, my heart leaping in my chest.

"On the Biltmore Hotel side of the park," he said.

"Where will we go?" I asked. "Back here?"

"Let me think about it," he said, looking around the room. "I like the privacy of here, but I don't trust myself."

"What do you mean by trust yourself?"

"If we just come back here, I'll probably end up just wanting to take my clothes off with you, but I want to get to know you more before. Is that okay?"

His voice sounded unsure now as if he couldn't be 100 percent sure we were on the same page with this.

"Okay," I agreed. "I'll meet you there. I can probably be there by seven."

He audibly exhaled and I could see him visibly relax.

"Great. Tomorrow night I'm off," he said.

We experienced a few seconds of somewhat awkward silence as I knew both of us wondered how to end such an unexpected evening.

Finally, I took the initiative and leaned in and kissed him on the cheek.

He blushed slightly, and it only managed to make him more handsome.

"See you tomorrow," I said.

"Tomorrow," he replied, giving my hand one more squeeze.

Hiro then exited the back door and closed it behind him.

I had to take a seat in the nearest chair and regain my composure.

So *that* had been what people meant when they talked about magical first kisses and developing instant crushes. All of these types of emotions had been buried deep inside me, and I hadn't even known I was capable of them. But this evening, when I didn't even have sex, with Hiro, I had managed to shift my whole outlook on life and awaken yearnings that were long dormant.

How could I possibly go on with Sally knowing that these types of feelings existed? Was that fair to her?

Suddenly, I found myself crying tears of happiness mixed with sorrow for the life I had felt the need to invent despite not being true to my heart. How could I go back to that world getting a glimpse of…knowing…and feeling…what I did now?

Chapter Three

The next day sitting in my teacher training class I should have been paying close attention to the review for the final exam. Instead, all I could think about was Hiro's touch, his smell, the songs that played in the background, and the taste of his lips. I may as well have been a thousand miles from that classroom as I couldn't have focused on one thing the professor said.

After class, when I met Sally at our usual lunch spot underneath the tree, I felt downright disloyal. I couldn't look her in the eye, and instead, I just focused on the roast beef sandwich sitting on the brown paper bag on my end of the table.

Could she see a difference in me and my body language?

How could I kiss her now knowing how a kiss with Hiro felt?

My world had been jumbled and then turned upside down, but it was also a world where it would be hard for one man to see a long-term romantic future with another. But I couldn't deny how Hiro had made me feel in such a short period of time.

"Are you worried about your finals?" Sally asked finally after many minutes of silence.

"Uh, no, well, maybe yes," I said, sounding completely confused.

I lifted my gaze to meet hers.

She scrunched her nose and eyed me curiously.

"Something's wrong. You're here, but you're not *here*," she said.

She pulled her hunter green box coat tighter because of the chilly air, and I realized we probably should have eaten inside. But my mind had been on much more than the weather.

"It's just finals, like you said," I offered with a shrug.

"No, there's more," she said, reading right through me. "You've got that ear scratch thing you do when you're worried."

"What ear scratch thing?" I said, immediately taking my hand down from my ear.

Sally rolled her eyes.

"We're engaged. Don't you think I know you pretty well by now?" she asked.

But you don't know me. Not really. There's so much you'd be shocked and appalled by.

"It's the war, too. I worry about my parents," I said, and it was true. "They've already lost one son. What if Edward doesn't make it back?"

Giving me a small reassuring smile, she reached out and placed her hand over mine.

"It...Edward...my brother...everything will be fine. You'll see," she said, on a confident high note.

I nodded, and sat what was left of my sandwich down. I had no appetite at that point.

"You want to go to the library to study?" I suggested, the wind picking up. "It's getting cold out here."

"Okay," Sally agreed quietly, and I knew she could tell that I was far from okay.

We threw what was left of our lunches away and began making our way to the library. I felt her hand wrap around mine as we made our way there, and she squeezed it. I wondered from the concerned look on her face if she had started to feel me really slip away from her. All I could think about was Hiro. Would he meet up with me tonight as he had promised and would the night be just as nerve-wracking exciting for me as the previous one?

Before that evening, I told Sally I needed to work extra time on my parents' books, and I told my parents I would be out with a study group. I did feel guilty about the lying, but oddly, it was becoming easier to do. I didn't think far enough ahead about what would happen if Sally and my parents ever compared notes somehow. I figured I would just come up with another story to cover the previous story.

My parents paid little attention, though, when I left the house. They were sharing some coffee and pie with Edward, and I knew they were both consumed with the thought that he'd be gone very soon. Any day now he'd find out when he'd be sent off to basic training. Edward and I had never been particularly close. I loved him because he was my brother, but we rarely saw eye to eye on things or shared any interests. I worried about him going off to the war, but my brother was a tough, bull-headed man if one had ever lived. I had to believe it would be that stubbornness that would get him through the war and would bring him home.

I had changed into my new dark red sweater Mother had knitted for my birthday the past November. I put on my best pair of black trousers, freshly polished black shoes, and my pea coat. My dark blond hair had been perfectly parted and combed with Murray's Pomade.

I noticed my mother gave me a slightly odd look as she watched me walk out the back door. She had to have been thinking I'd gone to a lot of trouble getting dressed up to meet a study group. I knew I must have looked ready for a big date, but she said nothing. She only eyed me curiously over the rim of her chipped coffee mug purchased during a day trip to Catalina Island.

On the streetcar ride to Downtown, I felt my heart rate quicken, and despite the increasing drop in temperature, I started to sweat. I grabbed an open seat when a family of five got off at a stop and sat next to an older lady busy knitting. She glanced up at me and smiled.

"Big night with your girlfriend?" she asked with a sly smile.

"Um, yes," I decided to say, hoping to end this conversation before it started.

She parted me on the arm and said, "She'll be very pleased. You look quite nice."

The lady then cleared her throat loudly and reached into her purse for a cough drop.

"So many of our boys are leaving now," she said, her voice drifting off at the end.

I sensed that maybe I reminded her of someone.

"Well, you two have a wonderful night," she said, pushing up her glasses and putting her knitting materials back in her purse.

"Thank you," I replied.

She got off at the next stop and looked back at me one more time with a mournful look in her eye that immediately sent a wave of sadness through me.

Despite all the Christmas decorations that lit up Downtown, a strong sense of melancholy had gripped the city now, and all we could do was put on our best brave faces. War nerves had officially taken over all of Los Angeles.

As the streetcar began to approach my stop, I got up and made my way to the door.

"You just watch," I heard one older man sitting near the exit tell another one. "First, Hawaii. Where do you think the Japs'll bomb next? Where's the closest target now? Los Angeles!"

A shiver went up my spine at just the thought. The war had seemed so far away from us, and then Pearl Harbor happened and everything became much more real. I thought about what Hiro said about feeling hostility toward the Japanese-American community and what it must feel like for some people to think you "look like" the enemy.

I got off the streetcar and made my way down Olive Street and headed towards the Biltmore Hotel and the park.

Will he really be there?

I had never had an evening with another man like the one I'd had with him. Not having had sex made me want to get to know him all the more, and I longed to be in his arms again.

I quickened my pace until I finally made it to the side of the park that faced the Biltmore Hotel and its imposing brick façade.

I looked right, left, and back again.

No Hiro.

I stood under one of the streetlights and stuffed my hands in my pockets.

He's not going to show.

Last night was just an odd one evening that wouldn't…that couldn't…lead to anything else. To try and tell myself otherwise was just plain stupid.

The only people on the street were some businessmen in suits in front of the hotel waiting for a taxi.

I felt like a fool. What did I expect really? A whirlwind romance with another guy? How could that possibly happen?

Just when I was getting ready to head back to the streetcar and forget about all this, I heard a familiar voice call out, "Jack!"

I turned to the right and saw Hiro quickly making his way toward me.

My heart leapt into my throat.

"I'm so sorry," he said, when he finally made it to me. His face was reddish and his breathing laborious. "I got stuck working at the restaurant for a few hours because my dad wasn't feeling well. Sorry I'm late."

"No problem," I said, feeling a great sense of relief.

He did show up!

"Where's your family's restaurant in Little Tokyo?" I asked.

I noticed just the slightest hesitation on his part.

"Don't worry. I'm not going to show up with a dozen roses," I said, reassuringly

He grinned and shook his head.

"I know," he replied. "It's close to First and San Pedro. It's a small place. Just ten tables, but my parents have owned it for a while now."

I noticed him looking me up and down.

"You look nice," he said.

I could feel the heat on the back of my neck from blushing.

"Thanks," I said, feeling awkward.

I had never been comfortable with compliments.

His dark hair had been slicked back, and he wore a navy-blue pea coat. His smooth, clear skin practically glistened under the light of the streetlamp.

"I didn't have time to change," he said, looking a little embarrassed.

He could've worn a potato sack and look handsome I thought.

"You look great," I said, meaning it.

"Thanks," he said, shifting his weight from one foot to the other. "So, any place you wanted to go?"

"Uh…" I stammered.

Where did two men go on something that felt sort of like a date I'd have with a girl?

"You might think I'm a little nuts, but…" he started to say.

"What?"

"I know it's a little cold, but I'd love to go to the ocean. I love smelling the salt air. Maybe we could get a hot chocolate on the Santa Monica Pier," he said, before quickly adding, "If you'd like, of course."

"Sounds like a plan," I said, but hot chocolate wasn't exactly what was on my mind at that point. Looking at his soft lips, I wanted to reach out, pull him to me, and repeat that magical kiss from the night before.

"Great," Hiro said, motioning toward the direction of the streetcar.

We began to head off and on the other side of the sidewalk, I saw a young couple. The guy couldn't be more than twenty, and his girlfriend looked a couple of years younger. They had that whole "love can conquer the world" look on their exuberant faces. Arms wrapped around each other, they made their way down the street. The fact that I wished I could do that very same thing with Hiro and I couldn't weighed on my mind. Instead of being able to enjoy any sort of physical touch, we both made sure to keep at least about a foot of space between us. But, unlike the previous night, we walked side by side. We had also both been cautious about who we might run into last night. I don't know if it might have been the power of the kiss, but tonight there was no talk about that. I'm not sure what I would have said or how I would have introduced him if we had run into a friend, family member, or God forbid, Sally, along the way. After all, I was supposed to be working on the accounting books.

Right before we passed the couple on the opposite side of the street, I saw the guy abruptly stop and stare at us.

"What is it?" I could hear the confused girlfriend say in a slightly whining voice.

"Hey! Jap!" the guy called out in an angry tone.

"Walk faster," Hiro said, picking up the pace.

I did so, but I worried the guy would start following us. He didn't, but when I glanced back, the guy was still frozen to the same spot and staring at us.

When we were finally out of sight, I could hear Hiro let out a slight sigh of relief.

"Sorry about that," I said when Hiro said nothing.

He shrugged and said, "It's not your fault."

"I know, but…" I stammered.

I didn't know what to say to make it better.

"Let's not worry about it," Hiro said, forcing a little smile. "I'm starting to get used to the stares or comments when I leave Little Tokyo. I can't change the way I look anyhow. Unless you might be uncomfortable being seen with me."

I could pick up on the hint of worry in his tone.

"Not at all," I said. "I don't care what other people think."

I wondered if believed what I said. After all, then why had I run off so quickly when my friend showed up on the night we met?

He nodded, but said, "Sometimes that's easier said than done."

Right then, we heard the *clang-clang* of the streetcar approaching.

"Sure you don't mind going all the way out there?" he asked.

"Not at all," I said. "I'm just happy we get to spend time together again."

His face lit up brighter than the Christmas decorations the city had placed on the streetlamps.

We boarded the almost empty streetcar. An older woman with a bag of groceries in her lap gave the both of us a disapproving look, but luckily she didn't say anything.

I don't know if Hiro didn't notice her stare or just pretended he didn't. Instead, he asked me about my classes at the university, and he told me that he wished he could also take some art classes as he had a passion for painting.

"There have to be some art classes at a local college," I suggested.

We sat along the back of the streetcar with one seat between us.

"The restaurant and my linguistics classes keep me pretty busy and now with the war…" he trailed off. "But I do make some time for it on Sundays usually. My aunt was a painter, and she shared some of her techniques with me."

"One day then," I said, with a hopeful smile.

"Yes, one day," he said, nodding wistfully. "What made you want to become a teacher?"

I thought about it for a moment. Ironically, no one that I could remember had asked me that question before.

"It seemed like something that would be stable," I said. "My parents, whose business held its own but still struggled through the Depression, always encouraged me to find a job that might be more secure. I did well in high school and managed to snag a scholarship making me the first one in the family to go to college."

"I'm the first in mine, too."

I nodded. I could pick up a bit of tension in his voice regarding the subject and thought he might feel a lot of the same pressures I did by being the first one in the family to go beyond high school. If I messed it up, my parents would be devastated. I think Sally, coming from a more well-to-do family, felt much less stress while in college.

"But you know what was unexpected?" I asked.

"What?"

"For one of my classes, I had to help tutor at a local high school, and I thought I just might actually be good at it."

"I'm not surprised," Hiro said. "You seem like a bright guy."

I couldn't help but stare into the dark pools of his brown eyes, and I lost my train of thought for a second.

"I don't know about all of that," I said finally. "But I do want to make a difference especially during these trying times."

At the next stop, a small in stature older man, maybe in his eighties, wearing a brown suit and carrying a newspaper, walked to the very back of the streetcar and sat right between us seemingly unaware of Hiro and me.

We shot each other amused looks. What was there to do?

The older man opened up his newspaper and all but blocked our view of each other.

Neither one of us said a word to him being respectful of our elders and all.

For the rest of the ride, I just stared out the window and occasionally caught holiday lights from homes and businesses twinkling in the night.

When the streetcar finally made its last stop with a thud and a lurch, Hiro and I practically had to step over the older man who kept reading his newspaper. As we exited the streetcar we heard the driver call back to the older man, "It's the end of the line, Pops. Just like I tell you every night."

"I wonder if that will be me one day," I said, as we walked toward the pier and the ocean.

"What do you mean?" Hiro asked.

"When I get old will I just do whatever I want and defy everyone. After all, when you turn a certain age what are people going to say to you?"

"It does sound a little liberating, but by that point most people have probably earned it."

The evening air was decidedly much crisper and salty at this location, and I crossed my arms for extra warmth. I could smell the salt water from the ocean, and I did find it comforting despite the frigid air. There had always been something so calming to me about the ocean with its utter vastness and crashing waves. It reminded me that no matter how much you worried about your life and whatever problems you had at the time, you were just a small part of something much, much larger.

When we made it to the corner of Colorado Avenue and Ocean, Hiro pointed to a small, ramshackle stand with window service near the entrance to the pier. Right next door a giant illuminated hand promised amazing palm readings.

"I know you must think I'm a fat-head for wanting to come all the way out here," Hiro said. "But this place has some seriously good hot chocolate! Come on. It's the red building over there."

He looked both ways on the Pacific Coast Highway and when the coast was clear, he placed a hand on the small of my back and said "Let's go!"

He darted across the street, and for a moment, I froze. Sure, there were no cars coming in either direction, but the "Don't Walk" sign was still illuminated. I had always been one to mostly follow what the signs, my parents, and society said and expected of me. The past few weeks of meeting men in the park and now going on this mini-adventure with Hiro was something I never would have imagined myself even doing a few months ago. It was as if now that I did the first thing not expected of me a whole dam of emotions and desires came rushing out in hard-hitting waves.

Once Hiro was across the highway, he looked at me expectantly.

And he was right. Why was I just standing there? Zero cars. No traffic cops. Yet, I stood there waiting for permission. Sure it was the law, but did it matter if I threw caution to the wind and crossed the road now?

"Come on!" Hiro called out to me. "The hot chocolate is real killer-diller. I promise!"

"Why the hell not?" I muttered under my breath, and I sprinted across the street even though no cars were still in sight.

"You're a real doo-gooder, aren't you? Waiting for the light to change and all," he teased once I made it across.

I thought about my limp and how much more pronounced it was when running, but Hiro didn't seem fazed at all or didn't seem to notice.

"I can't help it," I replied.

"It's okay," he said, elbowing me gently in the side. "I sort of like that about you."

"Sort of?" I said, cocking an eyebrow.

"I have a feeling there's a daredevil in there somewhere though," he said, before adding, "Come on. Let's get that hot chocolate."

I nodded and followed him to the little stand on the almost deserted pier. I was surprised the place was still open for the day. Apparently the kid who couldn't have been more than sixteen, who worked inside the stand found our presence unexpected, too. He looked to have been half-asleep, and his head snapped up straight when Hiro knocked gently on the window.

"Hey!" the kid called out. "What can I get you?"

I noticed his eyes narrow slightly once he focused in on Hiro.

"Two large hot chocolates, please," Hiro answered without missing a beat. "Whipped cream if you've got it, too."

The kid nodded and went to work on our order, but he certainly didn't jump to it. He made them like his whole body was inhabited by a slow-motion creature that had never worked a day in its life.

Hiro didn't seem to notice as he stood leaning against the small counter outside the stand and humming a song I'd never heard before.

I started to take out my wallet, but he reached out and stopped me. Our hands briefly touched, and once again I felt that electric spark from the night before.

"Nah, this is my treat. It was my crazy plan in the first place," he said.

I started to open my mouth to argue, but he held up one finger and said, "Nope. I insist."

I nodded, and said, "Okay. Next time is on me."

"Next time, huh, blondie?" he said with a twinkle in his eye and went back to humming his song.

Finally, the kid in the stand finished our hot chocolates. Hiro paid and handed me mine.

"Want to go down there?" he said, pointing to the empty beach.

A gust of crisp wind blew through where we stood on the pier. I could only imagine how frigid it must be right next to the water. He saw me hesitate.

"Come on," he said, encouraging me. "Just for a minute."

"Lead the way," I finally said.

He motioned for me to follow him toward some wooden steps that led down to the beach.

Besides the cold air, I also thought about all the sand that would end up in my shoes, but I decided to trust him on this mini-adventure.

He took a sip of his hot chocolate as we walked through the heavy sand and toward the waves.

"Ah, just as great as I remember it," he said fondly.

I tasted mine, and I had to admit that he was right. For what I would've assumed would just be some generic instant hot drink, the thickness of the hot creamy chocolate liquid mixed with the whipped cream proved to be quite good. Ironically, the bitter wind blowing in off the waves really did help emphasize the goodness of the hot chocolate.

"It is tasty," I agreed.

"See I told you," he said, grinning, his coal black hair whipping in the wind. "Come on. Just a little further."

Just when I began to wonder if he would crazily walk right into the water, he stopped a few feet from where the tide would come in on the beach. There were no other people around this night, and it almost seemed as if the beach were there just for the two of us.

Hiro didn't say anything. Instead he just stood there with his eyes closed with the salt air hitting his face.

"Here, for a moment, you can almost forget about everything else in the world, can't you?" he said.

"Yeah, you can," I agreed, starting to feel almost invigorated by the brisk wind.

There on the dark, moonlit beach I felt his free hand reach out for mine, and there we stood for what I wished could have been forever.

Just the two of us, together, with the vastness of the Pacific Ocean in front of us, all of our worries, all of our family expectations, and all of society's rules didn't matter. The warmth of his hand intertwined with mine filled me with a peace I had never experienced before. For the first time, I felt as if I were truly…me.

After about an hour, we both decided maybe we should head back. What neither of us mentioned, yet it seemed to be a given, was that we both knew the night was far from over. On the streetcar ride, we didn't say much, but every now and then our gaze would meet. A feeling of understanding appeared to connect us.

We got off at a Downtown stop, and we started to head in the direction of my parents' store.

"Do you have to head back home yet?" I asked, seriously hoping we were on the same page.

"I've got a little time," he answered.

I nodded, and we made our way down the near-empty Broadway Street.

My pulse quickened, and I realized that despite the air temperature I had begun to sweat from nervousness.

Both of us picked up our stride almost as if being in a race and knowing what the prize at the finish line would be.

Even though we didn't speak, I felt an undeniable connection to Hiro like an invisible string had tied us together in the most pleasurable way as if we belonged to each other now. It was a deep feeling I had never felt with Sally despite how much I often prayed that I would.

Finally, we turned down the alley leading to the back entrance to my parents' shop, and once we were at the door, my hands slightly shook. I had trouble unlocking the door due to my excitement. I just couldn't seem to steady my hand enough to get the key in the lock.

Suddenly, Hiro reached out and placed his hand on mine.

"It's okay," he said in a half whisper. "Is this what you really want to do?"

"Yes," I said, my voice raspy from the holiday evening air and my nerves.

His touch steadied my hand, and the key slid into the lock and unlocked the door.

Each time I did this, I prayed that nothing had brought one of my parents back to the shop. Maybe they forgot something or decided to do some extra preparation work since it was the holidays after all.

But once I opened the door the room was dark and empty. I reached over and flipped the switch on a small table lamp on a shelf near the door, and then I closed the door behind us.

For a moment we just stood there looking at each other. It felt like both of us were waiting to see who would make the first move.

Without hesitation, Hiro wrapped his strong arms around me and pushed me against the door. He began to kiss me, first gentle and sweet, and then his kisses became more urgent, more deliberate.

I grew weak and submissive at the feel of his hard body. I wished I could just melt into him and yearned to somehow manage to be even closer to him.

His tongue parted my lips, and he pulled me in even tighter for the type of toe-tingling kiss I had only heard about but never experienced.

He pulled back just slightly and said in a husky voice, "Do you want me to stop?"

"No," I pleaded. "Don't stop. *Please.*"

His hands began to roam down the front of my chest, past my belly button, and then lower to the point where he knew just how badly I wanted him.

Instinctively, I knew I'd been changed forever by this man's smile, light touch, and complete acceptance.

■ ■

Afterwards, I was physically and emotionally closer to him than I had been to any other man. We lay on the floor on a frayed thin blanket that had been stuffed in a supply closet. It didn't matter though. I would have made love to him on a bed of nails and not noticed anything but the feel of his smooth muscular chest against my furry blond one. He smelled clean and masculine, and the warmth of his body was more pleasurable than any wool blanket I had ever had on top of me. I could have stayed just that way for the rest of the night.

He placed a gentle kiss on my lips, and then rolled over on his side. He pulled me closer into a tight cuddle with him.

"That was amazing," I managed to say once I could collect my thoughts. "I don't think I've ever felt something like that in my life."

"Me, too," he whispered in my ear.

I could hear a slight twinge of sadness in his voice.

"What's wrong?" I asked.

He snuggled his face into the crook of my neck and said, "My grandmother in Seattle isn't doing well. My whole family is traveling up to see her."

"I'm so sorry to hear that," I said, squeezing his knee.

"Thanks," he said, his voice growing a bit quiet.

"How long will you be gone?" I asked, immediately realizing how self-absorbed that must have sounded. Here Hiro was with his grand-mother sick, and all I could think about was when I'd see him again.

It had taken me so long to experience *this* with another person, and the idea of losing it…losing him…was enough to send me into a slight panic.

"I'm not sure. She has cancer, and at this point there's nothing the doctors can do. It's just a waiting game. My whole father's family is going. We're even closing the restaurant, but it's been so slow lately I'm not sure it really matters anyway."

"I'm so sorry," I said already missing him.

"Thanks," he said, running his fingers over the hair on my chest. "I wish I knew when I'll be back."

"You could write to me while you're gone," I suggested, craving the idea of having some sort of contact with him.

"What will you tell your parents if they get the mail?" he asked.

"I'll just say you're a buddy from college that moved," I said. "Besides, I'm usually the one that checks the mail."

He nodded and said, "I will then. It'll be hard to be without you after *this*. It was so unexpected. The day I went to the park I never thought I'd meet and get to know somebody like you."

"I never thought I'd meet somebody like *you*, "I said, pulling him tighter to me.

How I wished I could make time slow down.

"Are you still going to marry your fiancée?" he asked, sounding sad but resigned to what might be inevitable.

"I don't know how to handle that," I said. "I've never felt the combination of emotions I've felt with you in just the little bit of time we've spent together. I know I haven't given that to her, either. She deserves it. She's a good girl."

"And you're a good guy," he said, placing a small kiss on my lips. "I wish it didn't have to be like this. So complicated."

"I know," I said mournfully.

Where could this possibly go? We were both well aware of the conventions of society, but our hearts weren't following those rules.

The past two nights with Hiro had profoundly changed me, and I didn't know how I could go back to my regular world knowing, feeling what I'd experienced with a man like him.

Chapter Four

I barely slept the whole night after returning home. My mind and my heart were entirely with Hiro. It felt like I had been transported into a new world by the time I spent with him. How could I go back to my regular life knowing what kind of emotions and what kind of sensual touches could exist in life?

When my alarm clock went off and jolted me back to the present, I felt like I had just fallen asleep. I groaned when I looked at the clock and saw I only had a couple of hours before my exam.

Wiping the sleep out of my eyes, I stumbled downstairs and started to come around when I smelled a pot of my mother's eye-widening coffee brewing.

The tension in the air practically slapped me across the face when I walked into our kitchen. I noticed the grim look on my mother's face as she fried eggs. Edward stared down at his plate and chewed his breakfast methodically. My father read the newspaper and shook his head at the headlines. Even Jane, usually filled with early morning young girl chatter, remained uncharacteristically silent and just moved her bacon around on her plate with a fork.

"What's wrong?" I asked.

My father folded his newspaper and put it on the table.

"Your brother received his notice for basic training. He's leaving on the twentieth of this month," my father said, giving Edward a hard pat on his back. "He's going to make this family proud."

Edward smiled, but it didn't look genuine.

"Before Christmas?" I said, thrown by how quickly everything was happening.

"Yep," my father said, before taking a long sip of his coffee. "But we'll all be together in spirit, and that's what counts."

Mother sat a plate of eggs for me at the empty seat.

"Eat before your eggs get cold," she said, her voice void of emotion. I knew all of this was hitting her hard. I'm sure she never expected any of it to happen so early especially around the holidays.

I sat down and poured myself a glass of orange juice from the pitcher on the table.

"When did you find out?" I asked Edward.

"I got the news last night," he said. "I'm going to Keesler Field in Mississippi."

"Mississippi!" I exclaimed.

It sounded so far away, so foreign.

Mother finally sat down, and I noticed her plate was still empty. The woman who often said breakfast was the most important meal of the day just sipped on coffee. Her eyes narrowed and focused on me.

"Sally stopped by last night with a casserole her mother had made for us. She appeared surprised to find out she was supposed to be with you," Mother said, giving me an accusing look.

I felt a rush of heat course through my body and knew I was blushing. Why did I have to be so transparent all the time? But I couldn't help but become flustered at just the thought of Hiro and the intimacy we'd shared the previous night.

"I know," I finally said. "I ended up deciding I just needed some time to think by myself."

"Where did you go?" Edward said, and I knew he wouldn't believe my story.

"The beach in Santa Monica," I said, hoping a half-truth would help me get through the situation.

"The beach!" Mother exclaimed. "It must have been cold as ice there last night. What a strange place to go!"

I just shrugged and said, "I just needed to get away a bit. I needed a study break."

Father grunted, and I could tell he knew there was more to the story.

"Edward has to leave. He's joining the Army," Jane said to me as if I hadn't been in the room the past few minutes.

"I know," I said, reaching over and smoothing down her golden hair.

Sally would certainly be angry with me when she saw me on campus. I couldn't believe I had been so naïve not to come up with a better cover story.

What would I tell her? It certainly couldn't be the truth.

But my memory of Hiro putting on his coat, kissing me sweetly on the lips, and promising to write before he left the storeroom last night dominated my thoughts above all else. Inside, I felt so undeniably changed as a person, like someone who'd just gotten out of prison after a long sentence.

How could I possibly navigate the world I'd been living in now that I knew an undeniable truth about myself?

When I arrived on campus to take my exam, I kept an eye out for Sally since we shared this specific class. In my head, I had been going over what to say to her, and I decided to stick with the story that I told my parents. Any more lies and I would become hopelessly confused. But what would I tell her after today if I continued to see Hiro? How long could I go on like this and maintain a secret life?

I waited outside the building that housed our class and watched as the other students filed inside. I glanced at my watch and saw there were only three minutes until the class would begin. Sally was never late. In fact, she usually arrived at least ten minutes early for everything, even places she didn't want to go.

A bell rang, and I knew I had to go inside. I made my way into the auditorium classroom and picked a seat on the lower right side where Sally and I usually sat. She couldn't miss this exam. It was one of the last ones we needed to take before starting our student teaching in the spring.

The professor, a man who always wore the stereotypical tweed jacket and glasses, began to pass out the exam. I heard the back door open and slam behind us. Everyone turned around and saw a breathless Sally standing there and looking disheveled. Her hair was pulled back in a half-hearted ponytail, and her usually freshly pressed clothes were instead wrinkled.

She made eye contact, and instead of sitting next to me, she chose a seat in the back of the room.

Before I could talk to her, the professor announced, "Begin!"

It proved to be quite hard to focus on the test, yet I did my best. Being one of my last classes before student teaching, I knew that this was one of those exams that had the past three and a half years riding on it. I still couldn't get my mind completely off Sally and what I would say to her.

I ended up being the third one finished with the test, and when I exited the building, Sally was in the middle of scribbling down the answer to one of the essay questions on student learning styles.

Outside, I picked a bench under an oak tree, sat down, and waited. I kept glancing at my watch to determine how much time was left on the exam. Finally time ran out, and students, mostly wearing relieved looks, began pouring out of the building.

Peering through the crowd, I saw no Sally. Just as I started to get up and go inside the classroom to find her, she walked outside clutching her books to her chest. I got up and immediately rushed toward her.

"Where were you? You're usually early," I said.

She rolled her eyes slightly, avoided my gaze, and kept walking.

I began to walk next to Sally and matched her long, quick strides.

"Look," I said. "I'm sorry. I know I told you I was going to help my parents last night and…"

She suddenly stopped and turned to face me.

"Why did you lie to me, Jack?" she asked, her voice almost disturbingly calm.

We had rarely argued and never really had what I would call a fight, so this tension between us could be described as new to both of us.

"I just needed some time to myself," I said. "There's a lot going on. Edward's going off…"

"We're all dealing with the war," she said, cutting me off. "Do you think I'm not worried about my own brothers going off and never coming back?"

"Of course you are," I said. "I was just having a bad day."

That was nothing but a lie. I had had the most amazing evening with Hiro, but I certainly couldn't tell my fiancée that.

I became consumed with feelings of guilt now that I stood in front of Sally. She'd always been nothing but upfront with me. That had been one of the things I liked about her most. She deserved better than I could or had given to her. She was worthy of a man who had the kind of feelings for her that I had the previous night with Hiro. But how could I tell her that I wasn't or probably couldn't be the man she merited? Sally would be a catch for most men. Just her luck she ended up with me, a guy who didn't understand why his heart never leapt for joy in her presence until another man showed him what that felt like.

"We're engaged, Jack. We're supposed to be each other's best friends and tell each other everything, but lately it seems like you're becoming more and more distant from me."

She furrowed her brows, and I could tell she fought back tears.

"I'm…I'm…" I struggled to answer.

What could I say? It certainly couldn't be the truth, and when I saw the pain in her eyes my heart did break. She deserved so much more than this, but I still couldn't seem to bring myself to end it. After all, marrying Sally is what everyone expected of me, including Sally.

"You're what? Say it!" she challenged me.

"I don't know what's going on with me right now," I said, averting my gaze and staring out at the open campus lawn.

"What is that supposed to mean?" she asked, sounding very 81rustrateed.

"I don't know. Like I said, there's the war. We student teach next semester. There's just so much going on right now. I should have told you I just needed a night to myself, but I didn't want to hurt your feelings."

I glanced over at her and could see the hurt and confusion in her eyes.

"Not to mention we still haven't set a date for the wedding. People are beginning to ask and wonder if things are all right between us," she said.

"Let's talk about that once we all get through the holidays, okay? Then we'll talk about it," I said solemnly.

"Promise?" she asked, her green eyes lighting up just the tiniest bit.

"Promise," I said, buying some time for all of us.

She leaned in next to me and laid her head on my shoulder, and I realized I had done the exact same thing with Hiro the night before.

The next few weeks went by in a blur of exams, getting ready to say good-bye to Edward, and holiday preparations even though none of us were in a very celebratory mood this year. Sally and I were on better terms. However, a cloud hung over what relationship we had, and I was the only one who knew the true reason why.

Hiro.

He was all I could think about.

Every day I anxiously waited for the letter he said he'd write. I had the delivery of the mail almost perfectly timed and often greeted the mailman when he arrived.

"Waiting for a big Christmas package?" he asked me one day.

"Something kind of like that," I answered.

We had sent Edward off with a stoic good-bye. My father repeated how proud he was of Edward for fighting for our country in these troubling times. My mother kept a stiff upper lip and made him swear to write as often as he could. She had buried a brother in World War I, and I knew her well enough to know that the thought of having to do so with a son terrified her.

Sally and I spent more time together now that we were out for the holiday break. We saw a few movies, and I helped her family decorate their tree. Her house was even more filled with even more anxiety than mine since her brothers would be heading off to Basic Training right after the New Year. The two of us talked but never about our feelings now. We'd both gotten student teacher positions at nearby schools. I would be teaching social studies, and she'd be teaching elementary.

I knew once we were finished with our student teaching, we'd probably get jobs soon after. Everyone would be looking for us to finally tie the knot. At that point, we'd really be full-fledged adults, and there would be no good reason for us not to start our own new family. I didn't know what I would do when the time came, but I kept procrastinating having to come up with any sort of a plan.

The night before Christmas Eve, feeling lonely and longing for Hiro, I found myself at Pershing Square Park again. There appeared to be a whole new crop of men, especially college-aged, roaming through the greenery on the lookout for any possible temporary distraction. The whole situation made me even sadder and lonelier for Hiro. I ended up just leaving the park and heading home.

"A letter came for you today," my mother said, when I walked into the kitchen.

Of course, the one day I wasn't the one that checked the mail!

She stirred a large pot of beef stew.

"I didn't know you knew anyone in Seattle," she said.

I prayed she hadn't opened the letter.

"Seattle? How do you know it's from Seattle?" I demanded a little too roughly.

She looked slightly taken aback but regained her composure. She wiped the sweat off her brow and ran a hand through her graying medium brown hair.

"I saw the return address," she said, eying me curiously.

"Oh," I muttered. "Where is it?"

"I sat it in on the desk in your room," she replied.

"Thanks! Just a friend from school home for the holidays," I called back leaving the kitchen and practically dashing to my room.

When I got there, my heart leapt when I saw the letter on the desk. The return address had the name listed as H. Narita.

I tore the envelope open and took out the letter.

Jack,

I hope all is well with you and your family. I know many people are struggling with the holidays this year as war seems to be on an unstoppable march through our world.

My grandmother is still very ill, but she's surprisingly holding on quite well. The doctors are frankly shocked she's still with us. She's always had a lot of grit and determination though. So, it's not a complete surprise. I'm not sure how long we'll be here, but my father is determined to be with his mother if she is going to pass soon. My little sister, Lily, misses her friends, especially this time of year. She just listens to the radio and reads movie magazines.

Everything seems off-kilter these days. Everyone seems to be looking at each other...at us...as possible enemies.

I'm so glad we had the time to become friends before I left on this family trip. You were a boost to my morale before I left. I can only hope that our friendship will continue to grow once my family returns.

I noticed how vague a lot of the wording was at this point, and I instinctively knew he'd written the letter in such a way that if someone had stumbled upon it or opened it before me, they wouldn't be privy to the real nature of what happened between us.

I continued reading.

I'll be sure to send word when it looks like we may be returning home for Los Angeles. I look forward to hearing how your holidays went and if you found out about your student teaching assignment. I know you'll be a great teacher.

Your friend,
Hiro

I exhaled deeply. He was still thinking about me just as much as I couldn't get him out of my head.

"Dinner is ready!" I heard my mother call out.

I carefully folded the letter and placed it in the bottom of my sock drawer. I couldn't wait to write him back. Just as he had been careful in his word choice, I would be, too. But I would let him know somehow through some careful prose how much I had been missing him and how I couldn't wait for him to return to Los Angeles. Then, we could see if there was perhaps a remote possibility that something could continue between us. I couldn't think of anything in this world that could possibly make me happier.

At dinner and over my mother's meatloaf, my parents discussed our traditional drive down to San Diego to see my paternal grandparents and Aunt Carol. I knew it would be strange taking that drive minus Edward. I had to admit that out of all of us he probably got the most excited for the holiday. Rough and tumble Edward turned into a softie when Santa would be coming to town. For Jane, he even wore the red hat and made ginger cookies. I couldn't imagine how hard it would be for him to be so far away from us this year.

"Maybe we should just stay here this year," my mother said, more pushing her food around on the plate versus eating it.

"Nonsense," my father snapped. "We have to keep up traditions as much as we can. Otherwise, we're letting the Japs and all the others win."

"Don't argue!" Jane exclaimed, on the verge of tears.

I reached out and put my hand on her shoulder. I could tell with Edward gone she had started to worry a great deal, her nine-year-old mind having to deal with emotions and concerns a child her age shouldn't be having to go through.

"No one's arguing," I said, shooting my mother and father quick looks.

My father just sighed and picked at his food, and mother took a sip of water and cleared her throat.

"I had one of them come in today," my father said, chewing on a bite of carrot.

"One of what?" I asked.

"A Jap," my father said, shaking his head. "Can you believe that? He had the nerve to come in and say he wanted to buy an engagement ring. I told him that we didn't serve his kind."

My mother's eyes widened, and I knew she was much more concerned about the badly needed sale than a potential customer being slighted.

"They got their own stores," he said. "I still can't believe they're allowed to just walk around like nothing's going on."

"Not everyone of Japanese ancestry is the enemy," I said, challenging my father which was something I rarely ever did.

Growing up, I had thought of my father as a tough but overall fair-minded man, but his consistent lashing out against the Japanese community in Los Angeles startled me. He seemed to be taking for granted that one person of Japanese descent was just like any other.

"What the hell do you mean?" he came back at me, his eyes narrowing.

"Howard," my mother said to him in a pleading tone. I knew she was in no mood for a family argument.

"I want to hear what he's got to say," my father said.

He put his knife and fork down and looked me dead in the eye.

"I just mean…" I started to say, choosing my words carefully. "A lot of them here are American citizens, too, or they have children that are American citizens."

"That doesn't make any of them *real* Americans," he said.

I noticed little Jane had started to wring her hands. She had so much stress at an early age, but I just couldn't let this one go…not after getting to know Hiro.

"I've never heard you say that about the Hofmanns," I said referring to the family that owned a clothing store next to our business. "They're German. First generation. You know…Germans…Hitler."

"That's different!" my father snapped back in a harsh tone.

"Why? Because they're white?" I replied in a cold voice.

"Now, you just listen here!" my father said, suddenly standing up.

"Stop it!" Jane blared in a high-pitched scream.

It proved enough to stun both my father and myself. Jane could be a talkative little girl, but she never yelled like that and in such a way that revealed how tormented she was inside. Edward's leaving for the war had really impacted her.

"Please. Stop," Mother said in a half whisper.

Jane got up and ran down the hallway to her room.

I could tell Father was about to say something, but Mother shot him a "not now" look.

Instead, he got up and said, "I'm going to get a smoke."

He went out the back door and let the door slam behind him.

"Was all that really necessary?" Mother asked, shaking her head.

"I only spoke the truth," I said, standing my ground.

"Narita," Mother said, refolding her napkin.

"What?" I responded.

"*Naaarita*," she said slowly to add emphasis. "That was the last name on the return envelope you got. That's a Japanese name, right?"

I nodded and answered, "Yes. So?"

"Just do me a favor and don't let your father see the letter. That's all we need right now," Mother said, standing and picking up her and Jane's plate. She then added dryly, "Merry Christmas to all."

I sat there by myself for a few minutes processing everything. Part of me wondered if my mother suspected anything. Nah she wouldn't. The thought of their son being intimate with another man would never cross their minds. If they knew some of things I had done in that backroom of the shop, I was sure they'd never want to go inside there again.

***

Later that night and after everyone had gone to bed, I sat at my desk, took the letter from Hiro out, reread it, and then began to write my letter back.

Dear Hiro,

I was very glad to hear from you. My thoughts are with you and your family during what I'm sure is a trying time on many levels. I'm glad you're getting to spend this time with your grandmother. Families should be together right now. I think a lot about my brother, Edward, right now. It's very strange not to have him here for the holidays. Although, I know he's here with us in spirit.

What could I say to reveal what really had been going through my mind since the evening we spent together? I wanted to tell him how I longed to feel his strong arms wrapped around me again and how his kisses practically sparked a new sense of life into me. Of course, part of me still felt guilty for even having these thoughts. I shouldn't be having these feelings for another man. However, they were undeniable even if I still didn't fully understand what to do with these emotions.

I pondered it for another moment or so. Just by the receiving the letter he'd know he had been in my thoughts, but I'd longed to say more.

Finally, I thought I'd come up with what to say.

When you return home, there's a place in Santa Monica that makes the best hot chocolate in the world! Real killer-diller! I discovered it while on a date. We should go when you get back to LA I know what a sweet tooth you have.

I read back over the sentences to judge how they might sound to an outsider, and finally, I decided they sounded innocent enough but would tell Hiro what I thought of that night.

I signed the letter.

Your friend,
Jack

I took an envelope out of the desk drawer, addressed it, and slid the letter inside. I'd drop it off at a mailbox around the corner in the morning. I didn't want it sitting in our outgoing mail in case my father decided to take a peek at what was there.

I glanced at the clock and saw it just turned midnight.

Christmas Eve.

For the first time, I wished that we could just speed through the holidays as I longed for Hiro's return. At that moment, I knew that if this between us...whatever it was...continued, I couldn't go on with Sally. I knew I couldn't announce the real reason why. It just wasn't done in those days, but maybe Hiro and I could find a way to make some sort of relationship work.

I don't think I had even spent twenty-four hours with him combined at this point, and I could've been accused of just having a schoolboy crush. But that's how Hiro made me feel, swept away in a sea of long-dormant desires.

Chapter Five

Christmas and then New Year's went by in a melancholy blur, and yet every day I worked to beat my mother to the mailbox hoping for a reply from Hiro. But each day my hopes were dashed. I worried for him and his family. Anti-Japanese sentiment grew exponentially every day in the news and also what I heard in the streets. I wondered if his family might be too scared to even return to Little Tokyo.

Sally and I were kept busy starting our semester of student teaching. So far, it had gone fairly well for both of us. We got along with the other faculty at each school, and the students were somewhat engaged. However, you could sense that the students' minds were preoccupied by some very daunting things. I knew many of them probably had a family member fighting overseas at this point. Also, a number of the senior boys found themselves in the position of possibly getting drafted right after they graduated, and girls worried they would lose their boyfriends to the war. It took what was supposed to be one of the most exciting years of their lives and turned it into one that put them on a daily march closer and closer to possible personal crisis. Of course, most people supported the war effort and saw it as a just cause, but it still didn't take away the fear and anxiety about losing loved ones.

One day in early February, my curiosity about what could have become of Hiro got the best of me, and I took the streetcar to Union Station and walked over to Little Tokyo. If I thought the mood was gray in my part of the world, there it proved to be downright depressing and frightening all at once. The Japanese-American residents walked around in ghost-like trances. They seemed to be looking nowhere and everywhere at the same time. Many times I received suspicious looks from people as I made my way down First Street to where I remembered Hiro said the family restaurant was located. Everyone seemed to be on edge and wondering if I was about to start some trouble. Mothers took their children to the other side of the street as I made my way down the sidewalk. I noticed a small grocery store had a "We're Proud Americans Too!" sign hanging in their window.

Finally, I made it to what I assumed was the Narita family restaurant. The door was locked, and I could barely see inside, it was so dark. A handwritten sign had been taped to the inside of the front door. It read "Closed for Family Emergency."

Part of me had wondered if Hiro's family had come back to Los Angeles, and maybe he'd thought better of continuing any sort of contact with me. But this confirmed that they were probably still in Washington. His family could still be taking care of his sick grandmother. But I began to ponder, what if they never came back especially with all that was happening. His lack of response added to my fear that that instant special connection I felt with someone had slipped through my fingers like fine sand on the beach.

In the meantime, Sally and I were still officially engaged, but I could sense now that she knew things had shifted, too. We hadn't talked about setting a date recently and she stopped pushing the subject. Valentine's Day resulted in a stilted dinner at an Italian restaurant near Downtown in which we talked *around* instead of *about* things. Most of the conversation focused on our student teaching, the weather, or the latest movies. What we really felt and should have discussed just hung in the air around us suffocating what remained of our relationship.

We just sort of went along with the usual motions such as meeting up with our friends for hamburgers and movies and going over to each other's houses for Sunday dinners. But we also begged off many times on other activities claiming we had a lot of lesson planning or grading to do. It was as if we both knew we were on a slowly, sadly dying horse, but neither one of us could conjure up the nerve to pull the trigger and end it.

Then on February 19, 1942, Executive Order 9066 from President Roosevelt happened, and I feared for Hiro and his family even more. The President had ordered that all people of Japanese descent, foreign-born or not, be forcibly relocated to some vague places where they would be contained and thought of as less of a threat. After all, there had to be some Japanese sympathizers out of the 120,000 or so Japa-nese-Americans was the supposed reasoning. So the shocking, to me, train of thought seemed to be that in order to stay safe we should just remove all of them from their homes even if nothing connected them to a crime.

I remember being quite stunned when I saw the headline on my fa-ther's newspaper when I came home from a day of teaching. I stared down at the paper as it lay on the kitchen table and tried to make sense of it all.

"'Bout time," Father said, rapping his knuckles on the table as he walked by me. "Get 'em out of here."

"But…" I started to argue, but then stopped myself. Lately, when my father made up his mind about something, he refused to look at the nuances, the gray between the black and white. Everything and everyone was good or bad. There was very little room for variance. Growing up, I had never thought too much about his attitudes. But then I lived in an all-white neighborhood and went to all-white schools. It was much easier to see other entire groups of people as just bad or good when you didn't actually have to face them, talk to them, and actually get to know their personal lives.

Instead of waiting for dinner, I just grabbed an apple from the fruit bowl on the kitchen table and headed to my room to supposedly work on the next day's lesson for class. My mind couldn't be further from anything that had to do with work, and I could feel my heart break just a little more.

As of February twenty-second, I still had not received a response back from Hiro, but I still checked the mailbox religiously and hoped I would. Yet, with each passing day I lost a little hope and began to think of the time we spent together as a brief window into something, something true and joyful I would never have in my life. But with President Roosevelt's order, I couldn't help going back to Little Tokyo one more time to see if his family might have returned to their restaurant. Nothing could prepare me for what I saw upon my arrival.

Where the last time everything had appeared frozen and on edge, there was now a flurry of desperate activity going on everywhere I looked. As soon as I arrived in Little Tokyo, I found people rushing about everywhere in a frenzy. Some of them, wearing what looked to be their finest clothes, carried or dragged suitcases and duffel bags behind them. Some people hurried about with a look of intense determination as if the whole neighborhood was on fire and they needed to get out what they could.

Shops had signs in the windows that read things such as "Closing Soon. Everything on sale!" "Thank you for your business. We hope to see you again soon." One cleaners had a sign that read, "Pick up your dry cleaning now. We can't take it with us!"

When I made it to the location of Hiro's family's restaurant, I was shocked to find it not only closed but completely empty inside. There was nothing left, not a table, a random chair, or a menu board. A "For Rent" sign hung in the window.

His family must have come back at some point since I'd been there to clear the place out, I reasoned. I couldn't imagine what he and his family must be going through as I observed the desperate chaos surrounding me. If only I had a way of getting some answers; I just wanted to know what had become of him. But I certainly couldn't ask around without raising extreme suspicions.

Defeated, I continued walking. Last time I visited Little Tokyo, I had gotten more than my share of suspicious looks. This time people appeared to be in too much of a rush to notice me at all, and I saw a high number of well-to-do looking white people walking about, some with smiles and laughter. They seemed oddly oblivious to the frantic Japanese population. I wondered what had brought them to Little Tokyo that day. But when I turned down a residential street, it all became clear. I saw what appeared to be one huge neighborhood yard sale that went on and on as far as the eye could see. All the houses had items of furniture, kitchenware, art work, and just about anything else you could think of sitting out in their yards. Many people, mostly white, were filling up trucks with all sorts of things I assumed they had just purchased. Most people were moving at a rapid speed as if they were in a race against a clock and someone might beat them to a good deal.

I saw one Japanese man sitting in a living room chair in his front yard. He looked lost and stunned as he stared straight ahead while two women debated over the quality of a set of dinnerware that sat on a wooden radio, also I assumed for sale, in the yard. I kept walking and had to practically push my way through the crowds.

Part of me hoped that maybe, just maybe, I might find Hiro somewhere in this unruly mass of a crowd. Even if I didn't get the chance to speak to him, seeing that he was at least alive and okay would have meant a great deal to me. But then the more I thought about it, could any of these people who appeared to be selling everything they owned be *okay*?

Out of nowhere I heard a piercing guttural scream come from one of the front yards. I turned and saw a housecoat-wearing, disheveled

Japanese woman, maybe mid-thirties, throwing and shattering what looked like fine china against the sidewalk in front of her house while two stunned Caucasian men wearing suits watched and appeared too caught off guard to move.

"Five cents apiece!" the woman yelled. "I'd rather destroy it all than sell it to you vultures!"

"Mama, stop!" a young boy, around nine, pleaded with her.

The woman, who appeared to be on an adrenaline rush, ignored everyone around her now as she continued to destroy plates before moving on to porcelain collectibles and later picking up a large shiny new radio and smashing it on the ground.

The two men who'd been standing in the yard must have finally decided there were no deals to be made here today backed up and scurried off.

The little boy who'd been pleading with his mother noticed me staring, and our gazes met. He looked so frightened, so lost, and he stared at me with a pleading, haunting look as if maybe there was a slim chance I might know what he should do in this situation.

"Vultures!" his mother repeated one last time before turning and heading back into the house.

I stood there for a moment still locking eyes with the little boy. I don't know what I possibly could have said to him to make some sort of sense of what was happening around him. I'm sure he wondered why his family had to go through this. What had they done to deserve it?

In defeat, his shoulders slumped, and he turned to head back into the house where I could hear his mother throwing more items against a wall taking out her frustration in the only way she could probably think of doing.

Somehow I knew that I would remember that moment. Those brief few seconds in time would always stick with me. I would forever recall the boy's face and his desperate look for someone to help him.

I would see similar facial expressions many, many more times over the coming months.

I gave up on possibly finding Hiro that day, and the more I thought about it, the more I began to wonder what I would've said to him anyway. After all, I had never gotten another letter from him. Maybe with his community being pulled apart at the seams, he had much more to worry or wonder about than a guy he spent time with for only two evenings.

I had to come to the realization that no matter how special those hours had been for me, nothing else was going to happen. Everyone around me was making sacrifices, and I realized I needed to get back to my life. As much as it hurt, I had to face the fact that those special moments I had shared with Hiro were just that...moments.

Walking out of the chaos, I made my way back to the streetcar. But instead of going home, I got off a stop before and walked to Sally's to see if she was home. Our relationship had remained strained with neither of us seemingly willing to face our issues. On my end, I'm not sure what I would've told her about my level of distance. It certainly couldn't be the truth. But now that I accepted the fact that Hiro was lost to me, I felt the need to confront things head-on with Sally. It was something she'd deserved for a long time.

When I walked up to her house, her mother was out in the yard, bent over and digging and working in her garden as if it were the middle of spring and not the still-chilly winter. Sally had told me numerous times that her mother threw herself into gardening whenever she got anxious.

Sally's mother, Martha Jenkins, was a kind woman who never had a bad thing to say about anyone. Slightly plump, she tended to wear floral dresses, and she kept her graying mousy-brown hair wrapped up in a bun on her head. The only nod to vanity she displayed was the bright red lipstick she applied to her otherwise natural complexion. What she wore more than anything else though was her smile that had immediately put me at ease the first time I met her. Today though, even from a distance, I could see that her welcoming smile was absent.

I knocked on the front gate of the white picket fence in front of her house.

"Knock, knock," I said, as I tapped the wood.

Startled, she jumped slightly and turned around.

"Jack Henry! You almost gave me a heart attack," she said, hand to chest.

"I'm so sorry. I didn't mean to," I said. "Just wanted to get your attention."

She visibly relaxed and her smile returned, albeit for a brief moment.

"Sally didn't say she was expecting you today," she said, grabbing a rag off a wheel barrow and wiping her hands.

"I just thought I'd take a chance and stop by to see if she was here," I said, starting to feel increasingly nervous about meeting with Sally. Our time together had become more and more strained, and I had grown increasingly anxious. I had begun to realize that if I couldn't be for Sally what she really needed perhaps the best thing I could do for her was let her go which I knew would be hard for both of us. She had essentially become my best friend, and even though our relationship hadn't been the best for a good while, I still counted on her support in many ways.

"She's inside planning for some of her classes," Mrs. Kemp said, wiping the sweat off her brow one more time. "I'll go get her for you. Why don't you have a seat?"

She motioned to the swing on the porch.

"Thank you," I said.

I took a deep breath to steady my nerves. This would positively be the hardest conversation of my entire life.

Mrs. Jenkins opened the creaky screen door on her porch and went inside.

I sat in the swing and kicked it off to a slow back and forth. There would be no good way to say what I needed to say. I didn't know what life could possibly be like for me after Sally. Our lives and our families had been so intertwined the past few years. There were so many expectations of both of us. Marriage. Babies. Growing old together. And when I thought about what my life would be like in the future without her, I had no idea. The men at the park, and especially Hiro, had shown me I didn't even know that a major part of my life was missing. But what future could there be for a man like me if I didn't have a wife and children? Was I doomed to be alone?

As I contemplated my fate, Sally, wearing a black wool knit sweater and gray skirt, finally walked outside carrying two mugs of coffee.

"Hi," I said.

"This is unexpected," she said, handing me one of the mugs. "Two sugars and a drop of cream."

"You always remember," I said, gratefully accepting the hot beverage.

We neither kissed nor hugged at seeing one another.

Caffeine and sugar probably wouldn't do a lot to help calm my nerves, but I welcomed the bit of a distraction for a moment.

"How's the lesson planning going?" I asked since I struggled to come up with a way to bring up the topic to be discussed.

She pushed a few loose strands behind her ears and shrugged, and we both placed our mugs on a small table in by the swing.

"Okay. It's all easier and harder than I thought at the same time. Keeping their attention is the most challenging. God knows I can't sit down for a second or the whole class goes out of control. The kids have so much energy," she said, sighing.

She cast her eyes downward, and when I looked down I saw one of her hands trembled slightly.

"What's wrong?" I asked, instinctively placing my hand on top of hers. Old habits were hard to break.

"Jacob and Steve," she said, a tremble making its way into her voice. "They'll be gone to Basic Training within weeks."

"Both of them at the same time?" I said, surprised.

"Yes," she said, a tear trailing its way down her right cheek. She immediately reached up and wiped it away with her free hand.

"I'm so sorry, Sally," I said, squeezing her hand.

"My mother is putting on a brave face, but I know how shook up she is."

"The same thing with my mother and Edward. I know she spends most of her days worrying about him."

"If I lost one...or both of them, I'm not sure any of us would be able to make it through that," Sally said, the tears now falling too fast to wipe them away individually.

Sally had always been close to her brothers, and they'd always kept a protective eye out on her, too.

"Don't even say it," I urged. "They'll both be okay. Just wait and see. They'll be home before we know it."

She shook her head and said, "Do you really think that? Seriously? You see what they're doing with the Japanese. They're rounding them up and sending them away."

A knot twisted in my stomach when I heard her say it.

Hiro.

But I pushed it out of my mind. I would drive myself crazy if I kept thinking and worrying about where he went and what happened to him, but I couldn't stop myself.

"And then there's us," Sally muttered.

The proverbial elephant in the room had just been acknowledged.

"We haven't been so close lately," Sally said, meeting my gaze. "Why, Jack? Why?"

"I...uh..." I stammered.

I thought I had built myself up for this moment, but now that it was there and Sally was right in front of me, it proved to be much harder than I thought. I did love her. I had just begun to realize that I hadn't been *in love* with her. But that didn't mean I didn't have strong feelings for her or care a great deal about her. She was one of the people in this world that I never wanted to hurt.

"I can't lose you, too, Jack," she said suddenly. "I know things have been off between us, but I really think if we work at it we can get back to where we were."

Where we were? Where was that?

I opened my mouth and began to say what I knew she really needed to hear, but when I looked into her eyes I just couldn't do it. I couldn't break her heart any more than it had already been broken by her brothers being sent to war.

"Things *have been* off lately," I agreed, my strength starting to dwindle.

"We've both been stressed about student teaching and the war," Sally said, hurriedly. "All this was bound to take a toll on us. But you remember the good times, don't you, Jack?"

A tone of desperation began to sink into her voice, and I knew I just didn't have it in me at that moment to end things with her and add to her sorrow.

"I do remember," I said.

And there had been plenty of good times spent just together and with our friends. Even though I never experienced the same spark with Sally that I had in that brief time with Hiro, what if I never felt that way again for anyone else? Would I always regret letting someone as special as Sally go?

"We can get that back. I just know it," she said, squeezing my hand.

"Okay," I finally said, exhaling.

A look of intense relief instantly spread over her face, and she leaned over and placed a soft kiss on my lips.

"I don't know what I would do if I lost you, too," she said. "You mean so much to me."

"You mean a lot to me, too," I said, honestly.

"Let's work on us. Spend some time together. Just the two of us, and maybe once we finish our student teaching and get jobs in the fall, we can finally set a date."

Setting a date?

I felt my pulse quicken in concern. How could I go through with a wedding knowing my true feelings? But sitting there with her and knowing how much Sally depended on me, I didn't see any way out of it that would make sense to other people. My bum leg and injury had ironically made others more dependent on me as those without a disability got sent to war.

"Please? Let's do it. I know we can make each other happy again. I just know it," Sally said, leaning into me and wrapping her arms around me.

I pulled her in close and said softly, "Okay."

We stayed like that for a good twenty minutes rocking softly and just holding each other, and I resigned myself to the fact that maybe a life with Sally was my destiny after all.

Chapter Six- August 1942

"Wait. What? Where is she going?" I asked, not sure I heard right.

"Manzanar. You know. The relocation center," said Frank, another teacher who had been in some of my classes at USC. "The *Jap* camps. Joan from class got a job teaching there. It's in the middle of nowhere, but the pay is supposed to be good, and she says she feels like she's doing something to help out the cause."

We sat at the soda fountain at a local drugstore drinking vanilla Cokes on what felt like a rare free afternoon. Frank, who so far had not been drafted, had just accepted a job at Los Angeles High School teaching shop class, and he was in the middle of catching me up on where others in our graduating class found jobs.

"They're hiring teachers to work at these camps, really?" I asked, surprised. Although, admittedly, I knew little about where the Japanese-Americans had been sent. The only thing I knew for sure is that Little Tokyo had become a ghost town and was now in the middle of switching demographics as a number of black residents were moving there.

Anti-Japanese sentiment had reached a new level of heightened fury in the months since Pearl Harbor. The boiling point had been achieved at the end of the previous February with the infamous Battle of Los Angeles where a runaway weather balloon had been mistaken for a Japanese warplane and the whole city went into a panic over the course of a night. The fear that night set into the hearts of the residents of Los Angeles cemented the idea of Japanese-Americans being the enemy.

"Well, yeah," Frank said. "They have to have schools for the kids. When I ran into her she told me some of the teachers were Japanese, but they didn't have enough of them. So, they're hiring white teachers to come help out."

"I never would have thought of that," I said, mulling the idea over for myself.

At the moment, I had almost signed the deal to teach at Hollywood High School starting in just a few weeks. Sally had already signed her contract for the elementary school and was again excitedly bringing up the idea of finally setting our wedding date. The ice between us had thawed for the most part, and I tried to put on my happy face. Inside though, my nerves were raw as I knew I couldn't put off the wedding for much longer. It was going to happen. *It had to happen.* Most people had begun to question what was taking us so long. I had run out of ideas of how to put off the inevitable for just a bit more. I saw no other path, but if I could just buy myself a little bit more freedom, maybe it'd be enough to help me figure it out.

I had started visiting the Pershing Square again. Although, my efforts to meet and be intimate with other men had remained half-hearted since Hiro. I guess part of me kept hoping and dreaming that another Hiro would appear in my life and somehow save me from what appeared to be my destiny. Instead, all I got were more brief, nameless encounters and fears of being arrested.

Then what Frank said about Joan feeling like she was helping out the cause stuck in my head. When my brother left for the war, I couldn't help but feel guilt-ridden, almost ashamed, that I got to stay behind where it was safe and peaceful. Maybe this would be my chance to do my part, and, admittedly, buy me more time before having to marry Sally.

I also thought of Hiro, and others in his community forced into uprooting their lives and going off to some secret location. I'm ashamed to admit it now, but I kept those opinions to myself at the time knowing how strongly many of those around me, especially my father, viewed the situation.

Before Frank and I left the drugstore, I asked, "Do you have Joan's number?"

"Hey! Aren't you engaged?" Frank asked, cocking an eyebrow.

"Don't get any ideas," I replied. "I just want to get some information from her on how she got that job at the war camp."

"I thought you were about to sign a contract for a job here!"

"Yeah, but if I can do something to contribute to the war effort, maybe this could be the thing for me," I said, as we slid off the stools at the soda fountain.

Frank didn't look convinced as we left the drug store and walked out on the busy sidewalk filled with workers heading home from long days.

"How would Sally feel about that?" he asked, looking more than a little skeptical.

"I'm sure she'd understand. After all, it's to help the war effort."

A mere few days later I found myself needing to tell Sally of my sudden change in plans.

"You want to what?" Sally exclaimed, her face turning crimson from a rush of intense anger. We had just started walking home after seeing a screening of "The Talk of the Town" with Cary Grant, an actor who had always left me a little spellbound while watching his films. At that point, I had a much better idea of *why* he did so for me.

Sally stopped on the corner of the street in front of a coffee shop and crossed her arms in a moment of complete and utter bewilderment.

"I just want to do my part," I argued. I knew that the right level of conviction was absent from my voice and that this flew right in the face of the plans we had been talking about all summer. "Sometimes it feels like I'm one of the few that's not doing...I don't know...something to contribute to the war effort. This is my chance."

I picked the moment Sally and I left the Los Angeles Theater on Broadway as the moment to tell her the news since she was often in a great mood after seeing a picture, whether it had been good or bad. I told her that Joan had put me in touch with the hiring person for the schools at the camps, and I had been offered a position almost immediately.

Arms still crossed, Sally turned away from me and started swiftly walking down Broadway and away from me. She didn't speak, but the loud click-clacking of her heels as they pounded the pavement spoke volumes. I had to run just to catch up with her.

"And I'll make extra money. It'll give us a better start. It's only for one school year, and I'll come back home all the time to visit you. The camp, Manzanar, is only a few hours from here," I said, trying to reason with her, but even I knew my argument was barely paper-thin.

When we reached a crosswalk, she stopped but kept looking away from me. She lifted a hand to her face, and I knew that she wiped a tear away.

"Whatever you want to do, Jack. Whatever makes you happy," she said, her voice turning raspy.

"Sally…" I started to try to comfort her even though I didn't blame her for one second for how this must have made her feel.

It had been me who had dragged along this engagement, and it had been me who seemed to come up with one excuse after the next to prolong it. Yet, here I was doing it once more.

The light changed and the walk sign came on. Sally took off across the street without looking back, and I, not knowing what to say that would make any sense to her, just stood there and watched her. I knew from the dejected look on her face at that moment Sally had reached the proverbial breaking point. She'd hung on, hopeful and optimistic. But now, I knew she had to admit to herself that this relationship would probably never be what she needed it to be.

***

When I arrived home, I walked into our modest living room with its sturdy but inexpensive Gingham print furniture and found my mother knitting and my father reading one of the drugstore paperback Westerns he enjoyed so much. A few months ago, I would have been quite surprised at finding them up past ten. But ever since Edward had left for war, my parents went to bed later and got up earlier. Their eyes always looked just a tad bit bloodshot with dark circles underneath them.

Letters from Edward always sat in a neat pile next to a family picture on our fireplace mantle. We never talked about our worries for Edward, but instead my father would read his letters out loud, usually over supper, as if Edward were on some vacation and great adventure. His letters sort of suggested the same as they were never anything but positive. But I knew my brother. He hated to admit any weakness or fears or the thought of worrying our parents. I knew we might never know exactly all the hardships he faced while off at war.

Both of my parents looked up, and I steeled myself for the conversation that would soon happen. I had no idea what my parents would say about me leaving to teach at Manzanar. Would my father see accepting the job as helping the enemy? Would my mother read it as just another way for me to postpone the wedding to Sally? I already could see in her eyes that she had doubts that my engagement would actually end in a marriage, and I assumed that she wondered why I was dragging things out.

"I need to talk to both of you," I said, still standing near the door.

My father sat his novel down on the side table next to his favorite chair, and my mother put her needlepoint on the coffee table. Both sat up straight at attention and looked to be readying themselves for some sort of horrible news.

"Are you going to sit to tell us or just stand there?" Father said suspiciously.

I nodded and sat just a couple of feet from Mother on the sofa.

"What is it, Jack? Tell us," Mother pleaded in a voice that suggested she really didn't have much capacity left for extra anxiety.

"It's nothing bad," I said. "Just a change of plans."

I saw them both visibly relax just a tad but not completely. They both sank back in their seating just a little more and took a few breaths.

"What do you mean change of plans?" Father asked.

"Does this have to do with Sally and the engagement?" Mother asked, raising her eyebrows slightly.

"A little but not completely," I answered.

My parents, more confused than ever, looked at each other before turning their gazes back to me.

"Get to the point, Jack," Father said in his no-nonsense tone.

"Okay," I said, sucking in a breath and readying myself. "I've accepted a job to teach at one of the relocation camps for the Japanese."

"Why would you do that?" Mother said, crinkling her nose and shaking her head. "You and Sally had everything planned out already. Why would you want to go teach *there*?"

"What's this really about?" Father said, crossing his arms.

"Look. Sometimes it feels like I'm one of the very few men my age that isn't off at war and doing his part. All because of this bum leg," I said in disdain.

My parents rarely, if ever, brought up my injury because all it did was also bring up questions and sadness regarding the other son they could have had. I knew that they didn't consciously blame me for the accident, but I suspected they both held some deep resentment somewhere in their hearts and minds. After all, John had been the baby at the time, and he always had the pleasing type of personality that made everyone gravitate toward him even at a very young age. I, on the other hand, had often been the cranky teenage son who was mostly withdrawn and distant.

"I want to contribute to the war effort, and this is one of the best ways I can think of doing so."

"By teaching Japs?" Father said. His voice rose on the term *Japs*.

"Have you talked to Sally about this?" Mother interjected. "My God, Jack! You've put the girl through so much already. She's waited and waited for you. Do you really think she's going to wait for you forever?"

No, I wanted to say. I knew this very well could be the final straw for her. Part of me hoped it would be in a passive-aggressive way that I wasn't very proud of, but I couldn't think of another option.

"I told her tonight," I answered.

"And?" Mother said. She folded her hands in her lap, and her eyes narrowed.

"She's not too happy about it," I admitted. I scooted to the edge of the sofa and called upon my inner strength to give me a boost to continue. "But I've made up my mind. This is how I'm going to do my part."

"Hmmmm," Father grunted, far from sounding convinced. "Don't get me wrong, son. I admire you wanting to do something to help the effort. I'm proud of you in fact. But teaching Japs? There's got to be another way."

"Look, Father. I know we disagree about what's happened to the Japanese in America these past few months, and I don't even want to take the time to argue about it now," I said. In fact, Mother tried to change the subject every time my father appeared to be bringing up the topic. "Many of those people are just as American as us."

Father shook his head and rolled his eyes in contempt.

"And their children deserve to be educated. Those kids have played no part in the war that's raging. They deserve a good teacher, and dare I say, I think I might be a pretty damn good one."

Mother bristled at *damn*. She wouldn't even watch *Gone with the Wind* because of its infamous use of the word in the film.

"I can't say I understand much at all what you're doing, Jack. I don't know why you want to risk everything you've been building with Sally to do this, but…" Her voice trailed off.

Could she possibly be seeing some of the situation from my eyes?

"I agree that children shouldn't be punished. They deserve an education. So, if you're going to be stubborn about this…"

"So, you'll support me?" I asked, my voice filled with hope.

"As much as I can, given the circumstances," she said.

Her shoulders slumped and she sank even deeper into the sofa.

"Father?" I asked, turning to him. "And you?"

Father exhaled loudly, and I could look at him and tell he was choosing his words carefully.

"You're right. We don't agree on this issue. Not by a long shot," he finally said. "But like I said, I'm proud that you want to do what you can *in your mind* to help the war effort. So, if this is what you want to do, then do it, but I'd be lying if I didn't say I wished there was another direction you'd go in. And, just like your mother said, I don't think Sally is going to wait around forever."

I nodded, and decided not to say anything about my issues with Sally. At least I had their half-hearted blessings to buy me some more time to try to make sense of my life, and maybe, just maybe, I could do some good along the way.

"When would you leave?" Mother asked.

"Next week," I answered.

"That quick?" Mother sighed. "Jane's going to miss you so much. She already feels like she's lost Edward."

I knew my little sister would miss me, especially when I helped her with her homework or listened to her stories about her friends at school. But, knowing my mother, she was speaking more of herself than my little sister. She had one son already deceased, one at war, and now the third one would be leaving for what she considered questionable reasons.

"I'll be home a lot. You'll see," I promised, although I couldn't be sure this would be the case.

"It's time for me to turn in," Mother said abruptly. She stood up and smoothed down her simple navy checkered dress. "I'm opening the store in the morning."

"I'll head up, too," I said, standing.

"Be there in a bit," Father said, picking up his book once again.

I couldn't help but wonder how much of his mind could possibly be on that Western novel for the rest of the night.

I silently followed Mother down the hall.

We passed Jane's room, and, by instinct, Mother briefly stuck her head in the doorway to check on her.

"Good night," she said to me before entering my parents' bedroom.

"Night," I said, walking into the room I shared with Edward.

I shut the door behind me and looked at Edward's twin bed, once again left untouched.

Still in my clothes, I collapsed on my bed.

Some doubts about what I was deciding to do creeped into my mind, but I tried to disregard them. For reasons I couldn't entirely explain, I felt more and more drawn to this idea the more I spoke about it.

As often happened late at night before I fell asleep, I thought of Hiro and wondered where he was and what he was doing at that moment. Had he been sent to one of the camps, and what was life at these "camps" really like for the people there? I would find out soon enough.

I wondered if Hiro would possibly be at the same camp at which I would teach. How much of this hope I had was leading me down this path to find a man I had shared only two evenings with? From what I knew, there were quite a few camps quickly thrown together by the government and thousands of people had to leave their homes and were forced to relocate. And even if he was there, what would be the chances of running into him or him actually wanting to see me at this point?

Eventually, still fully dressed, I drifted off into a fitful sleep full of dreams about an uncertain future.

I spent the next couple of weeks preparing for my move to Manzanar. I had been given a list of things to pack: toiletries, a variety of seasonal clothes, and teaching resources. The man from the War Relocation Office who hired me told me not to expect much in terms of accommodations.

"Very, very basic," he warned.

My rent and board would be cheap, so I should be able to save a nice amount of money if I spent carefully.

Sally and I only saw each other twice after I told her of my plans. The first time was at a mutual friend's birthday party where the tension hung in the air like a heavy wool blanket. The second time was by accident when I walked up on her sharing a sandwich with one of her girlfriends on Larchmont Boulevard while I was running an errand to the bank. There she greeted me with a thin smile and said she would call. Her expression dared me to press the subject.

I called her house a few times hoping to...I don't know what exactly. Part of me knew as I had for a long time that I wasn't what she really needed, but she didn't know the reasons why. Plus, she'd been my confidante, my companion for so long. I couldn't help but miss her.

The next day I was almost packed and set to leave. I had my train ticket that would take me to nearby Lone Pine where I would be picked up by one of the camp managers. Reality hit me hard that day, and I began to second-guess the whole idea. I had barely been out of Los Angeles. My parents had never been big travelers since someone had to run the jewelry store six days a week. They didn't believe in hiring extra help when they could do the job. This didn't leave much time for travel as a family. My longest trip was a week during sixth grade Spring Break spent with my two brothers at our aunt's in San Diego. We spent almost the whole time on the beach playing volleyball, turning tan, and eating almost endless sticky and sugary shaved ices my uncle would buy for us.

I found myself in many ways suddenly nervous about leaving home, and I thought of Edward. He'd been just as sheltered as I had been. How had he dealt with being sent to the other side of the world into a war zone? I would only be traveling a few hours away, but it still seemed like I was taking off for a completely different world.

Just as I packed my last pair of socks, I heard a knock on my bedroom door.

"Come in!" I called out.

Mother and Father both walked in, and I immediately worried that something bad may have happened.

"What's wrong?" I asked.

"Nothing's wrong," Father said. "But we want you to come out to the front for a moment."

My interest more than piqued, I followed them through the house and out the front door.

Jane skipped ahead of us while repeating, "Jack has a surprise! Jack has a surprise!"

I couldn't imagine what to expect, so I found myself especially confused when I walked out the front door and saw nothing out of the ordinary and just our regular front yard.

I turned to my parents in confusion.

"You wanted to show me…the plants outside?" I said.

"No," Father said, reaching into his front pocket.

I saw a slight smile on my mother's lips. It was the first one I'd seen in quite a long time.

Father pulled out a key ring with one single key on it, and he held it out to me.

"Go ahead. Take it," he said.

Not knowing what this meant, I hesitated at first, but I took the key. I studied it for a moment and then recognized it as the key for my father's old 1932 black Ford pickup that had sat idle and broken for a few years.

"The pickup key?" I said, confused.

Father motioned to the truck parked in front of the house.

"Your mother and I discussed it, and we want you to take it with you. I had it fixed up and got it running again. It'll hopefully make the next year easier for you to get around and do what you need to do."

I had rarely been so shocked.

"Really?" I said. "Are you sure? Won't you need it?"

"We have the family car, and if we need to, we can take the street-car," Mother said. "We want you to be able to come home whenever you want, too."

I knew what a sacrifice this was. Money had remained tight through the Depression and now the war. But I also knew what a sign of support from my parents this gesture was despite the misgivings I knew they probably still harbored about my decision. I could feel myself starting to tear up. I choked the tears back though and said, "Thank you. I promise to take really good care of it."

"You better," Father said, playfully slapping my arm.

"Promise me you'll take care of *yourself*," Mother said, and I could tell she was holding back her own tears.

"I will," I said, trying to assure her.

We'd never been much of a hugging type family, and both my parents were often stoic with their emotions. Little Jane hadn't quite picked up that habit at her age yet, though. I felt a tug on my sleeve and looked down to see my young sister staring up at me with her deep brown eyes with a look of fear mixed with sadness on her tiny face.

"Do you really got to go, Jackie?" she said, using her nickname for me.

"I'll be back to visit all the time. I promise. And each time I come back I'll bring you a little something," I said, tousling her long dark hair.

She rewarded me with the tiniest of smiles, and I realized just how much I would miss her and her innocence. She was still young enough not to completely understand all that was happening around her, and I couldn't help but envy that. I had already decided being a grown-up wasn't always as much fun as you thought it would be when you were a child.

I planned to leave first thing in the morning, so that night my mother prepared steaks, an extremely rare luxury during those days, au gratin potatoes, corn, and her homemade biscuits. My parents, Jane, and I sat around the table enjoying the food and listening to some big band music on the radio. We all tried to just enjoy the evening and not think about things too much even though I had deep down started to become a little bit excited at just the thought of seeing and experiencing something new.

I had continued to try to call Sally to speak with her, and I even stopped by her house once. Mrs. Jenkins said she was out with some friends, but I could tell by the way she refused to meet my gaze she wasn't telling the truth. Sally told me her mother always did that when she wasn't being completely honest. I truly felt bad at how things had gone the last time we saw each other. We still hadn't even officially broken up.

"So, are you engaged or what?" Frank had asked when I met him at a bar, ironically not far from Pershing Square, for a beer to celebrate my new job.

"She won't talk to me. I don't know what to say," I told him that night.

And now here I was less than twelve hours from leaving, and I still had not properly sorted things out with her. I couldn't blame Sally for not wanting to see me. The more I thought about it the more I realized that in a way I had stolen precious time with her as I tried to figure out what my life could or would be. I knew many of the men I met at the park had wives, evident from their wedding rings, but as time went on, I just didn't think I could do that to Sally. I knew people would start to wonder what was "wrong" with me as time went on, but I decided I would deal with that later. I knew taking this job so far from home would give me more time to try to sort myself out.

We had just started to clear the table when my father, who had walked out to the front yard to sit on the steps and smoke a cigar as he often did after meals, walked into the kitchen and said to me, "You've got a visitor."

As soon as he said it, I knew it.

Sally.

"Thanks," I said, heading outside.

I noticed my father didn't follow me. He obviously knew we would need some time to ourselves. This wouldn't be just any drop-by or social call.

When I walked outside, I found Sally leaning against the front window. She wore a green pencil skirt and a rose knit sweater. Her hair had been loosely curled at the ends, and I noticed her cheeks looked rosier than usual. She looked…well…beautiful.

"Hi," I said. "I've been trying to talk to you."

"I know," she said, standing up straight. "My mother gave me the messages."

A few beats of awkward silence went by as we just stood there for a moment. I could tell from the look on her face she was readying herself to say some important things.

"You look nice," I offered, trying to defrost the chill in the air between us.

She looked down at what she wore as if she just became aware of it.

"Thanks," she said. "I'm meeting some of the girls from the teacher's college out. We're having a night on the town before we start our new jobs."

"That sounds nice," I said, motioning to one of the front lawn chairs.

"No thanks. I can't stay. Besides, I can't wrinkle this skirt that took an hour to iron," she said, with a bit of a chuckle. "You leave tomorrow, right?"

"Yes," I said. "First thing. I want to try and get there by lunch. Father's letting me use his truck."

She nodded and said, "That's nice of him."

"I'm glad you stopped by," I said. "I hated the way we left things."

She nodded, reached into her purse, and pulled something out. She walked over to me and said, "Hold out your hand."

I did as she asked, and she placed the engagement ring I'd given her in the palm of my hand.

Even as bad as everything had gotten, I was still a bit surprised by this.

"I think we both know this isn't going anywhere at this point," she said.

"Sally, you don't have to give back…" I started to say.

"No, no," she said, shaking her head. "It's only right. Whatever we had is over, and I think you should have it back."

Reluctantly, I accepted the ring and slipped it into my pocket.

"I'm so sorry how this all turned out," I said. "This is not how I thought things would go."

"Join the club," she said, with a bit of a forced laugh. "I don't know why or exactly how things started going wrong between us, Jack."

Suddenly, she looked like she was about to cry and her words might choke her. She took a deep breath and avoided looking me in the eye. Instead, she let her gaze focus on my mother's rose bushes, wild from my parents' lack of gardening skills.

"Sally..." I began.

"No, please. Let me finish," she pleaded. She sucked in a sharp breath and then looked back up at me. "I loved you, Jack Henry. We had some really wonderful times together. I'll always care about you. And you don't have to say it. I already know it. What I feel for you is not what you feel for me. I waited and tried a long time to see if it could be, but I have to accept it now. I need to go on with my life and find someone who will feel that way about me."

"You're so special, Sally. I wish…I wish…" I wished that I could be honest with her about why I didn't or couldn't feel the same thing as her, but I knew there was no way possible I could do this. Hell, I was still trying to understand it myself.

"Please know that I did really care about you. A lot. I hope you find someone who makes you happy. You deserve it."

She nodded, but I knew that every word I said came with a sharp sting no matter how I phrased it, and I hated knowing I caused this pain.

"Well, maybe tonight," she said, putting on a false cheery smile. "Hope springs eternal."

I nodded.

Any man would have been lucky to have her, and I wished that I could have been the type of man who could appreciate her in the way she deserved.

"Drive safe, Jack," she said softly. "And good luck."

She walked over and placed a single, soft kiss on my cheek.

"Thank you, Sally. That means a lot," I said.

She nodded, and without another word, walked away, down the street and away from my life.

Early the next morning, just as the sun had begun to peek through the night sky, I made my way into the kitchen to brew some coffee, but I found Mother had already beaten me to it. She poured a mug of the piping brew and set it on the table.

She wore her worn pink bathrobe tied in the center and greeted me with a smile.

"Good morning," she said. "Don't think you're leaving without me fixing you one final breakfast."

"You're acting like you're never going to see me again." I laughed.

"Well, who knows how long it will be?" she said, motioning for me to take a seat.

I sat down, and she took some eggs out of the refrigerator.

"Is everyone else still in bed?" I asked.

"Your father was still snoring when I checked on him a few minutes ago," she replied, cracking two eggs into a cast iron skillet. "And Jane is still sound asleep of course. I made you a thermos of coffee to take with you and wrapped up some ham sandwiches."

"You didn't have to do all that," I said, although I definitely appreciated the sweet gesture.

I had kind of hoped to sneak out and be gone before everyone got moving as I hated good-byes, but I guess Mother wasn't going to let go one last chance to "mother me" before I left slip by.

As she flipped the eggs, she glanced over at me while I sipped the strong black coffee.

"Jack?" she said.

"Yep?"

"Are you really sure about this? Is it what you really want to do?" she asked.

"For now, yes. I'll be back to visit before you know it though."

She nodded, looking somewhat satisfied by my answer.

"Well, then. We better get you fed and on the road," she said, sliding the eggs onto a plate.

She sat the plate in front of me, and before she could sit down, I reached out and grabbed her hand.

"Thank you, Mother. For everything," I said, suddenly feeling nostalgic.

As excited as I was to see someplace new, the thought that I wouldn't see my family for a long period of time hit my heart.

Mother squeezed my hand, sat across from me, and poured sugar into her own coffee.

My father and Jane, all sleepy-eyed, had barely wandered into the kitchen before I gave Jane a quick hug, shook Father's hand, and took the thermos of coffee. I wanted to leave before they woke up too much, and I'd have to go through a round of good-byes.

"I'll write soon," I promised, grabbing my luggage. "Thanks again for letting me use the truck!"

"You're welcome," Father said, just sitting at the breakfast table.

I walked outside and was greeted by the chill of the morning air and made my way to the truck I still couldn't believe Father was going to let me borrow, knowing how he felt about the war and the Japanese. However, I remembered the look in his eyes as he handed me the keys

I slung the luggage into the back of the truck and turned around to take one more look at my childhood home. Even though I hadn't even started on my journey, I had a deep feeling inside me that I was about to truly start on a new chapter in my life.

Father's truck may have been a little old, but it ran smoothly now thanks to him having it worked on. It felt a little bittersweet as Los Angeles grew smaller and smaller in the distance as I continued down the highway.

This was really happening. I was leaving home for something completely unknown.

The drive went by fairly quickly as I made my way north and could feel the anticipation building inside me. Radio stations went in and out as I drove the long stretch down the highway. I had never seen this rural area of California before. It seemed like being in a completely different world than the one I had come from. I thought about what it must have been like for the Japanese who were born and raised in Los Angeles to be brought to this undeveloped land.

The farther north I went the windier and dusty it got, and the landscape grew more and more barren with a background of snow-covered mountain ranges. You couldn't get any more different from Los Angeles than this place, and I really began to wonder what I had gotten myself into. It all had seemed like a good enough escape plan from my predetermined life, but what would I do here besides just work?

I thought about Hiro and how much he loved the ocean. I could only imagine how he must have felt if he had been brought to such a barren, dusty place.

When I stopped in a small town called Lone Pine for gas and the restroom, I noticed that the truck had already been covered in a thick layer of dust which was only a small preview of things to come. I didn't know at the time that I'd spend weeks and months battling dust storms and frigid nighttime temperatures constantly at my new home.

The cashier at the gas station counter told me I was already much closer than I thought.

"It's only about ten more miles up the road," she said, a cigarette hanging out of her mouth while she spoke.

I thought she had one of those weathered faces that could put her in the age range from thirty to over fifty depending on how difficult her life had been.

"What should I keep an eye out for? How will I know I arrived?" I asked.

She cocked an eyebrow and looked at me curiously.

"Trust me. There's no way you can miss that place," she said, before turning her attention back to the issue of a movie gossip magazine she had spread out on the counter.

After about another fifteen minutes on the road, I found out that the cashier had been correct. There was no missing Manzanar. On the other side of the highway and out of seemingly nowhere, I saw a high fence and guard towers sticking up. As I got closer, I saw the fences were barbed wire, and I saw row after row of rudimentary wooden buildings. An American flag at the top of a pole whipped around in the unforgiving, ceaseless wind. My throat grew dry just looking at what I saw. The place without a doubt resembled a prison and not so much a simple "relocation center" as the news outlets had referred to it.

I turned into an entrance and pulled up to a guard entrance. An armed officer in full uniform held up his hand to stop me.

"Yes?" he said.

"I'm one of the new teachers for the school," I said, digging into my pocket for a piece of paper on which I had written my contact's information. "I'm supposed to meet one of the managers. A Mr. Sanders."

The guard gave me a skeptical look and asked, "What's your name?"

"Jack Henry," I answered.

My palms began to sweat, and I could feel my heartbeat quicken with my nerves. Just sitting outside the place strangely made me feel as if I had done something wrong.

"Wait here," the officer commanded, as he went back into the booth.

I saw him pick up the phone and make a call.

A couple of minutes later, the guard came back and pointed to a building that looked slightly nicer than the ones lined up in endless rows.

"Drive through that gate and park next to the building. Mr. Sanders will meet you there," he said.

"Thank you," I said.

The guard gave me a slight nod and walked back into the booth.

I slowly drove down the gravel driveway through the high barbed wire fence and more guards and parked as I had been directed.

I hopped out of my truck and immediately regretted putting my luggage in the back of the truck. Sand and dust covered everything. I hoped it hadn't gotten into my bags.

I heard the crunching of gravel and turned around to find a gray-haired man wearing khaki-colored pants and a button-down dark green shirt. He carried himself with a confident swagger, and I wouldn't have been surprised to find out that he was ex or current military.

"Henry? Jack Henry?" he said, before spitting on the ground.

I noticed the tobacco bulge in his mouth.

"Yes, sir. The new social studies teacher," I said, reaching out to shake his hand.

He shook my hand all the while giving me a long stare as if to size me up.

"Sanders here. I work in Internal Security. What in the hell brought you out here, Jack Henry?" he asked.

The question threw me off guard.

"I…uh…" I stammered, not sure what he wanted to hear from me.

He finally slapped my arm and smiled.

"I'm just shittin' with you," he said. "But you gotta admit…" He gestured all around us.

"Guess I'm here because I want to do my part in the war effort. I'm not able to take part in active duty."

Sanders shrugged as if he'd instantly already lost interest in my story.

"Grab your stuff. I'll take you into the dorms for teachers. Hope you ain't expectin' the Ritz," he said, turning around and heading back inside before I could even get my bags.

"No, sir," I called after him.

"You'll meet the principal and other teachers later," he said.

I was anxious to see Joan from college to get the details on the place and what to expect.

I reached down in the back of the truck and pulled out the dusty bags. That's when I noticed. A group of about five Japanese teens eyed me curiously from behind another layer of barbed wire fence. Despite their youth, they already looked world weary and tired as wind storms whipped around them. I knew these teens could very well be my students.

I, feeling a little stupid after, gave them a little happy wave from my side of the fence. They all just continued to stare at me blankly except for one young girl, maybe sixteen, who had a red ribbon in her hair providing a pop of color in an otherwise drab environment. She, out of the sight of the others, lifted her hand by her side just a little and gave me a tiny wave back, but I didn't read an ounce of friendliness on her face.

"Home sweet home," Sanders said, walking me into a room that could be described as sparse at best. Yet, I already figured these accommodations might be luxury compared to those of the detainees. The room contained two small twin beds with thin mattresses, two desks, and two chairs. A metal lamp sat on each table. Each side also had a small closet.

One side of the room had a smattering of personal belongings such as a stack of paperbacks on the desk, a few clothes hanging in the open closet, and what looked like a couple of family photos tacked on the wall.

Sanders pointed to the bare side of the room.

"That one's yours," he said.

"Thank you," I said, trying to shake a little more dust off my bags before putting them on the bed.

"You'll get used to it," he said.

"To what?" I asked.

"The dust. That and the wind and the crappy food," he said, obviously not trying to sugarcoat things.

At that moment, a guy around my age and height with ginger hair and a smattering of freckles walked into the room.

"Speaking of lunch…" Sanders said.

The guy stopped in his tracks when he saw me. He blinked as if to clear his eyes and make sure that what he saw was correct.

"Jack Henry, meet Donald Washington," Sanders said. "Washington'll be your roommate, and he can show you around. Chow's being served now."

"Yum," Donald said, his eyes still fixated on me. "Lunch."

"I'll let you two get on with your day," Sanders said gruffly before turning around and leaving us.

"Hi," I said a little shyly.

Donald, who I now noticed had the greenest eyes I'd ever seen, continued to stare at me and made me a little uncomfortable.

"Where you from?" he asked.

"LA. You?" I said, sitting on the bed. I realized just how thin the mattress was when I felt a spring poke me in the rear.

"LA, too. Mid-Wilshire. What part are you from?" he said, leaning against the door and folding his arms.

His stare made me uncomfortable, and then all of a sudden, I recognized a certain look in his eyes, the same one I saw in the gaze of men from Pershing Square.

"Larchmont," I answered.

"You look familiar," he said, in a slightly teasing tone.

"Hmmm," I said. "I don't know. Maybe I just have one of those faces."

"Uh, huh," Donald said with a sly smile. "Maybe."

He then stood up straight, raked a finger through his fiery hair, and said, "Well, let's go to lunch, and then I'll show you what are going to be the classrooms. You can meet some of the other teachers and the principal. I hope you like eating a lot of canned food and teaching with few resources. It's the name of the game around here."

"I suppose I can get used to it," I said. "Don't have much of a choice."

"Tell me about it," Donald said in an almost dreamy voice that suggested that he wished he were anyplace but at Manzanar. "Let's go."

Donald walked me over to a loud, crowded mess hall where I saw some more guards and Caucasian workers. Besides the kitchen staff, there were no Japanese anywhere. Since I was the new guy, a lot of eyes were on me, and I could practically feel the stares.

"The food can be pretty damn bad, but I'm still too lazy to cook anything on my own. Each meal is 35 cents or you can pay a dollar a day," Donald said.

"Hey there," a pretty young woman who resembled Joan Crawford said as she sashayed by me carrying a tray of food that all appeared to be close to the same color.

"Be prepared," Donald told me.

"For?" I asked, as we got in line and grabbed trays.

"You're new meat," Donald said, grabbing a coffee cup.

"Excuse me?" I said.

He shot me a bemused look.

"Are you married?" he asked, and I realized he had a small dimple in his left cheek when he smiled.

"No," I said, feeling a crimson blush making its way up my neck and to my face.

Donald jokingly elbowed me and said, "Don't' worry. I'm just warning you. With the shortage of men our age these days, and here in the middle of nowhere, you'll be a hot commodity here at the camp."

"Well, I'm not looking," I said, avoiding his eyes.

I wondered if he could see my truth with just a glance, and it embarrassed me. I don't know why for certain. After all, I got the same feeling from him. But Donald struck me as someone who wouldn't mind playing with some danger…and his reputation…at times. I still had to go back to Los Angeles eventually.

"Just giving you the background on your new home," he said, lifting his plate and handing it to the older Japanese man with a whisker of a beard.

The worker took a huge serving spoon and plopped a bunch of…well…something onto his plate.

"What is that?" I asked.

He shrugged and said, "Some kind of stew. Do yourself a favor and don't think about it too much."

I nodded.

"Hi, Dottie!" he exclaimed when a middle-aged woman walked by us to get in line. "Meet the new teacher. Henry, right?"

"Jack actually. Henry is my last name," I said.

"Dottie McKenzie. I teach math. Save me a space at the table, Donald?" she said.

"Sure, hon," he said, with more than a little sugar in his voice.

It surprised me that Donald didn't seem to be doing much to hide on which side his bread was buttered.

As we made our way with our trays of "stew" and cups of pale coffee, Donald leaned toward me and said, "That Dottie has to have a story. Why's a middle-aged woman deciding to come out here by herself? And she's quite evasive with answering any personal questions. But I guess it's none of my business. After all, what are any of us doing here?"

We sat down at a wooden picnic-style table in the back.

"So, what's going on with the school and the start of the term?" I asked.

Donald looked positively disappointed that I didn't want to continue the gossip, but he took a long slug of the coffee, grimaced at the taste, and said, "Well, there's been some makeshift classes already, but the school is starting its official term in the next few days. Dottie, some other teachers, and I have been doing some setup. Well, there's not much to work with, but we're doing our best. I'm teaching high school English, and I'm still waiting on enough books."

"Where are all the Japanese?" I asked looking around the room.

Donald chuckled and said, "Separate from us, even the Japanese teachers. There's little mixing between the two sides. Sometimes a baseball game happens and everyone joins in, but besides that...the two groups stick to their side of the camp for the most part. We'll probably have more interaction with them than most of the staff since we're teaching."

"Hmmmm," I said, mulling over how to phrase my next question. "Do you know..."

Donald's face perked up as he could tell I had something I wasn't sure how to ask.

"Yes?" he said.

I just had to know if it was possible.

"Is there a way to know if a certain Japanese man is here?" I asked finally.

"Why?" Donald said, avoiding answering but digging more information at the same time.

"Just a friend from LA. I don't know what happened to him and his family. I'm pretty sure they were sent to a camp, but I don't know which one."

"Is that why you came here?" Donald asked in a half whisper. "To try and find your *friend?*"

"What? No. I came here to teach and help the war effort in a way I could," I said.

Donald looked on the verge of chuckling.

"If you say so," he said, rolling his eyes. "As far as your friend...I'm sure someone in one of the administrative offices might know something, but if you start asking for specific people, don't be surprised if you raise some suspicions."

"It was just a thought. That's all," I said quickly.

Dottie arrived with her tray and sat next to Donald.

"You should see the math books I got. I might as well take them outside and use a stick in the dirt," she said. Her perfectly round hairdo of brown curls didn't move a bit as she shook her head.

"I guess something is better than nothing," I offered up.

They both looked at me slightly bemused.

"You better eat your stew," Donald said. "Once it gets cold you won't be able to choke it down."

"Do you know a teacher, a Joan…" I started to ask.

"Jack Henry!" I heard a familiar voice behind me.

I turned and saw Joan Johnson from my teacher classes at USC. She had light curly brown hair, a ruddy complexion, and a slightly plump figure. She'd always been one of the more outgoing people in our classes.

"Joan!" I said, standing up.

"You made it. I heard you got the job," she said, pulling me in for a quick hug.

She pulled me a little to the side, while a curious Donald and Dottie looked on at us.

"So, what are *you* doing here?" she asked, raising an eyebrow. "Last I heard you and Sally Jenkins were engaged to get married."

"Yeah, well, things didn't go as planned," I said, trying to be vague.

This seemed to captivate her attention even more.

"Well, there's a story there," she said.

I turned the tables on her and asked, "What are *you* doing here?"

She stiffened and answered, "I just had to get out of my parents' house. But what are any of us doing *here*?"

"Well, I'll show you the school, or what they're calling a school, after lunch," she said, before leaning in and saying, "Watch out for your roommate. He can be a bit of a gossip."

I nodded, and she said, "Let me go grab a tray, and I'll be back."

"Sure," I said, as she hurried off to the chow lane.

I knew she must have her own reasons for running away to Manzanar and the unknown.

The next few days were spent working with the handful of other teachers, including some Japanese ones, to get the new classrooms set up and ready to go. It felt so strange at the end of the day when the white teachers were able to head back to our much nicer quarters. The Japanese teachers lived in the same ramshackle buildings as anyone else. It turned out it didn't matter who you were: teacher, doctor, or engineer. All the Japanese lived on one side and the Caucasians on the other.

Donald and Dottie hadn't been joking that resources were scarce. I tried to plan out lessons as best I could. The rooms weren't well insulated and the temperatures tended to be downright cold to start the day and stuffy by mid-day. And with winter coming, I had the feeling I should have brought even more warm clothes. One thing every classroom had prominently displayed was a United States flag, and we were told we should start each day with the Pledge of Allegiance.

The Japanese teachers I met were very polite, but I didn't really get to know any of them personally. It felt downright weird. Here were two groups of people, including thousands of Japanese-Americans, sharing cramped living spaces on this plot of dusty land with the Sierra Nevada Mountains in the background, and yet they barely interacted just as Donald told me the first day.

It still shook me up a little every day when I walked outside and saw the armed guard towers and the barbed wire. At night, the white staff often gathered to play cards, listen to records, and drink cheap beer. Sometimes we went to a small bar in Lone Pine that Joan especially liked and drank.

I quickly realized another stark difference between us and our Japanese internees and coworkers. We could leave. They stayed within the confines of the fence, and as a result, even though we lived so close, I didn't have much idea about life on the other side. I wondered about it often after I arrived. What was life in this ramshackle barracks like for those forced to be there?

I also went back and forth about visiting one of the administrative offices to find out if Hiro was one of the thousands who lived there. If he wasn't at Manzanar, maybe I could still find out what camp he'd been sent to just to know what happened to him. I was still scared of raising suspicions on many levels. Instead, as I walked in and out of the barracks and the school and passed groups of internees, I always discreetly scanned the crowd looking for his handsome face. Of course, I also realized the awkwardness of the situation if I did happen upon him.

What would I say to him if I did?

"How have you been?"

It didn't seem appropriate considering the circumstances.

"Why didn't you write back?"

He could tell me it was because his family was in the process of losing everything and being sent to a glorified prison. In other words, he'd been very busy to say the least, and who did I think I was to believe taking the time to write a letter to me trumped all that?

I quickly began to realize how much I took for granted being able to come and go as I pleased. Every time I drove out of the camp in Father's truck, I felt a huge sense of relief as if I had just gotten out of prison myself. Some of the other Caucasian employees seemed to be able to almost ignore the barbed wire and the armed guards and go about their day. I, on the other hand, couldn't shake the feeling of being locked up and not in control. If I felt that way, what must the internees feel?

Donald had been right about my being "fresh meat" as I had numerous flirty advances made to me by female staff, including Joan. Each time I just smiled and played ignorant as if I didn't know what they were doing. Most got frustrated and moved on, except a tiny young blonde woman who couldn't even be five feet tall and had a bit of what sounded like a Southern twang. Each night, she'd eventually make her way over to me in the recreation areas and try and strike up a conversation. I always remained polite, and Donald would give me smirks from across the room.

Donald and I had yet to bring up our "connection" that went beyond life at Manzanar even though I knew it had become quite obvious to the two of us. Donald had danced around the subject a few times.

"Spend much time Downtown back in LA?" he asked one day as we hung posters of US presidents on the wall of a classroom.

"Some. My parents have a jewelry store there," I replied.

I knew this was *not* what he meant. But instead of pushing the subject, he gave me one of his knowing half smiles and continued his work.

At night, when we were alone in our room, I avoided talking about anything too personal with Donald. Even though I suspected we had quite a bit in common, I still felt extremely uncomfortable discussing anything more with someone I worked with every day. All of it added up to me feeling lonelier than ever.

I came so close to going home and telling the Manzanar administration they could have their job back before I even started. Days were long and mostly boring. I missed the hustle and bustle of the city. I longed just to go out and see a simple movie or have more choices for food besides something that came out of a tin can. I found myself quickly becoming homesick.

One day, Sanders allowed me to use the phone in his office to call home for a few moments. It was the middle of a Thursday, so I called the jewelry store number. Mother answered.

"Ring It Up," she answered with the store's name.

"Hey. It's me," I said.

"Jack!" she exclaimed, and I could hear a sense of relief in her voice, too. "How are you?"

"I'm good," I said, trying to sound upbeat. "How are you? Am I calling at an okay time? Is the store busy?"

"No one's here right now. Perfect timing. How is it?"

"It's…well…" I struggled for the right words.

I wanted to tell her I felt miserable and wanted to head back home before I taught a single class. But I remembered what a big deal I made about coming to Manzanar in the first place and needing to do my part.

"It's okay," I finally said. "Dusty. The food is sometimes unrecognizable. It really is the middle of nowhere."

"Homesick?" she asked, the concern in her tone.

"Maybe a little," I admitted.

"Look," she said, "You can do this, Jack. Even if I don't completely understand, you said you wanted to go there and help educate these kids that needed the help. I know it's got to be hard, but I know you have the strength to do what you set out to do."

I let out a breath and some tension along with it. I guess I just needed to hear those words from someone who believed in me even when I didn't believe in myself.

"You think?" I asked.

"I know it," she replied, before adding with some humor, "You're my son after all."

"Thanks, Mother," I said. "I'll write soon, too. I promise. Have you heard from Edward?"

"We just got another letter from him the other day," she answered. "He says he's doing okay, but as always, he can't say much about where he is."

"As long as you're hearing from him," I said. "That's what's important."

Sanders walked back into his office carrying a huge cup of coffee and a donut. He gave me a look that told me my time was almost up. He'd been reluctant to let me use his phone in the first place. He only agreed because I told him I would find out if the nurse he had a crush on had a beau.

"I gotta go," I said. "Give Jane a hug for me, and tell Father I'll be fine."

"Will do," she said.

I hung up the phone and told Sanders, who now sat at his desk with one of his legs propped up on an old chair, "Thanks again for letting me use the phone."

"Remember our deal," he reminded me. "Find out if Nancy is taken."

"Promise," I said.

I walked out of his office with a sudden burst of renewed energy from my brief conversation with Mother. I needed to believe in myself just as much as she did. I had come here for a reason, or really many reasons, and now that I was here I owed it to myself to try to do the best job I could.

I headed back to my room to put the final touches on my first lessons.

"I pledge allegiance to the flag of the United States of America and to the republic…"

I listened to my class repeat the Pledge of Allegiance in an almost uniform monotone voice. Finally, the first day of school had arrived, and the teachers had been instructed to begin the day with the pledge. I couldn't help but feel conflicted as I watched and listened to my students stare at the flag and repeat the words.

"…liberty and justice for all."

It almost seemed cruel to me, even then, that the students were made to recite this every morning. After all, where was their justice and the respect for their liberty? These were just kids. What crime had they committed that forced them to live like this?

Despite their circumstances, the freshman year students were polite and dutifully took notes as I discussed the separation of powers within our government. I drew a diagram to illustrate the main points on the chalkboard at the front of the room and tried to make my discussion as lively as I could by involving the students in completing parts of the diagram and having them work in small groups. As I went through the day and taught other high school social studies classes, I found the most satisfying part of the classes was when I could help the students perhaps "forget" where they were for a few minutes and get them engaged in learning. I wanted them to just be able to be kids, not kids locked up for dubious reasons.

As my last class of the day made their way into the room, I recognized the girl with the red ribbon in her hair who had waved at me the first day I arrived. She wore the same ribbon that she used to tie back her hair into a high ponytail. She was at the tail end of a line of students who entered the classroom in an orderly fashion while I stood at the front of the room. I caught her staring at me as she made her way to a seat in the back. Her stare was so intense, so focused, that she almost ran into a student desk.

I became unnerved. I had gotten used to curious stares during my short time at Manzanar, but this young teenage girl was different. She looked at me like she might *know me*.

"Please take out your notebooks and copy the timeline I have on the board while I call roll," I said, picking up a handwritten roll sheet that had been given to me that morning.

I made my way down the list and when I called "Lily Narita," the girl with the red ribbon raised her hand and in a barely audible voice said, "Present."

When I finished roll, I started a world history lesson on democracy in Ancient Greece. I split the class up into various city-states and told them they'd work in groups looking up information on their city-states in some encyclopedias and their meager textbooks and presenting it to the class.

"Plan on giving at least a five-minute presentation. I want everyone in the group to speak, and you'll tell us what's special about your city-state," I said, walking around the room, the whole time feeling Lily Narita's eyes on me.

All of the students were staring at me, but for the rest of them, I took it more as a first day sizing up the teacher sort of look. Not Lily. Her stare almost seemed to be silently accusing me of something.

Lily's group had been assigned Sparta, and as her classmates worked together, I would catch her still taking peeks at me.

I heard one of the other girls in her group, Emily Soto, say to Lily, "Geez! Pay attention. I'm not doing all of your work for you!"

"Any questions?" I asked, stopping by Lily's group.

The lone boy in her group said, "No questions, Mr. Henry."

Lily looked down at her paper and absentmindedly doodled.

She was the only student in the class who appeared to be off-task, but her stares made me feel so uneasy that I didn't confront her about it. Instead I found myself moving nervously around the classroom while I spoke. I wondered if the other students could pick up my discomfort.

Why did she keep stealing glances at me every chance she got? I wasn't vain enough to think it could be some sort of schoolgirl crush. There was something much more to it. I could sense it in my bones.

During her group's presentation she softly added a few tidbits about Sparta.

"Sparta's constitution focused on military training and excellence," she said, half-heartedly.

Finally, the bell rang, and I couldn't have been more relieved that the end of the first day had finally arrived.

"Class dismissed," I said. "Don't forget your homework."

A few students responded.

"Yes, sir."

"Yes, Mr. Henry."

"Okay."

I noticed Lily hanging back and slowly gathering her belongings.

Would she say something to me? Tell me why she'd waved at me that first day she saw me and now seemed to have trouble keeping her eyes off me?

Emily Soto gave Lily a small shake of the shoulders.

"Come on. We're going to be late!" Emily said urgently.

I had no idea what they'd be late for, and I continued to gather my materials and then erase the board.

Emily and Lily were the last two out of the class, and as they walked out the door, I said to them, "Have a good evening, girls."

"Thank you, Mr. Henry," Emily said, all smiles.

There was a wannabe teacher's pet if there ever was one, I thought to myself.

And just barely above a whisper and with a flash of anger in her eyes, I heard Lily say, "Good night."

When the room had finally emptied out, I took the time to straighten up the chairs that the students had haphazardly tried to reorganize after their group work. That's when I saw it, a composition notebook sitting on the floor.

I reached down to pick it up and saw written on the front "Lily Narita. Block 15."

She'd forgotten her notebook when Emily hurried her up. I flipped open the cover and saw a few pages of notes from different classes. It looked like all of her day's work was in this notebook. She'd probably be unable to do any homework without it.

Clutching the notebook, I hurried outside to see if I could catch the two girls. Maybe they were still outside the school talking to each other or some of their classmates. But by the time I made it outside, all the students were gone. I could see a few in the distance making their way home.

I wanted to try to connect with these students and to do the best job I could. Many of my professors in college kept warning us that our days would go well beyond the last bell. There'd be more lessons to plan, paperwork to be completed, grading to be done, and many, many other things that would pop up. I looked down at the notebook. Lily had made me anxious with her dark piercing eyes stealing a glance at me every time she could.

What *was* that about?

I looked at the notebook again and knew what I had to do. I would take it to her barracks so she'd have the materials she needed for her homework. And maybe, just maybe, I'd get some sort of idea on what was going on with Lily Narita.

I dropped off some books in my barracks beforehand and found Donald spread out on his cot. His legs dangled over the foot of the bed, and he had one of his arms lying across his face and over his eyes.

"Those kids like to have killed me today. They had so *many* questions," he moaned without even saying hello first.

"Well, sir, you are the teacher," I said, sitting my papers and roll book on my desk. "I'll be back later."

"Where are you going?" Donald asked, sitting up suddenly and excitedly added, "Dottie got a bottle of whiskey to celebrate our first day. Thought we could all have some before going to the mess hall."

"As fun as that sounds, I'm going to take a student her notebook she left in class," I said, heading back to the door.

"Wait!" Donald exclaimed. "You're going...*over there*...where they all live?"

"Well, yeah," I said. "I can't return it any other way."

"I've never been over to where *they* all live," Donald said.

You would have thought I suggested I might take a trip to Mars.

"It's about time I saw more than our little corner over here," I said, before adding in a teasing tone, "I'll let you know if I survive."

I made my way to that *other* side of camp to the row after seemingly endless row of barracks so hastily put together I could see cracks in the walls as I walked by. I could only imagine how the wind must send an endless amount of dust in these people's homes, not to mention the cold fall air. At times, I thought I might even choke on the dust-filled air.

As I continued on my way, reading the signs for the block numbers, I saw many of the Japanese standing outside the barracks smoking, watching children play in the dirt, or trying in vain to plant some sort of plants in the rocky soil.

Many people did a second take as they saw me walk by as if astonished to see a Caucasian who wasn't in a military uniform in their area. I saw one of the teachers, a Mr. Tanaka, watching a small boy and girl playing with a ball outside a barracks' door. I waved, and he responded before quickly looking away as if I'd caught him doing something he shouldn't.

"Do you know where block fifteen is?" I asked a couple of people as I walked around.

One older man with a cane and a shock of thick gray hair, dumbstruck, just pointed in a general direction to the left.

"Thank you," I said, although it left me just as lost as before.

I passed a small building that had a sign on it that read "Latrines" and a line of women waited outside. They all looked surprised and ashamed to see me and quickly looked away as I walked by.

I found one of the kids I remembered from my class that morning sitting on a front door step. He had a lanky build, baggy clothes at least a size too big, and a sharp crew cut.

The teen looked just as surprised to see me as everybody else.

"Hi there," I said.

I didn't remember his name yet.

His eyes widened.

"Hello," he replied, tentatively.

"Do you know where block fifteen is? I have a notebook one of your classmates left behind," I said, holding up the notebook as a way to explain my presence "on the other side."

"Two blocks straight ahead and take a right," the kid answered.

"Thanks," I said. "See you tomorrow."

The kid, still in shock at my presence, just nodded and watched me walk away.

I wasn't used to receiving such a large amount of attention just by being me.

I turned the corner, and was pleasantly surprised to see that flash of red-colored ribbon and Lily Narita standing outside one of the barracks.

"Hi, Lily!" I called out.

Her mouth dropped open when she saw me, and then a man in a pair of rough brown wool pants and a light blue cotton shirt walked outside.

I stopped on a dime.

He appeared to be just as thrown as me to see him.

Hiro.

After all this time, there he stood right there before me. I turned and looked back at Lily, and I noticed a flash of anger across her face.

"Hello," I managed to croak out.

A stunned Hiro stayed frozen to the spot. He hadn't taken his eyes off me from the moment he saw me.

"Who are you?" a feminine voice demanded from behind Hiro and Lily.

Chapter Seven

Standing in the doorway of the barracks, I saw an elegantly dressed woman in a smart looking, dark A-line skirt, and green sweater. Like Lily's splash of color of her hair ribbon, this woman had the same color lipstick, and her coal-black hair was swept up in a bun.

"Can I help you?" the woman demanded in a terse voice.

"I'm sorry. I don't mean to bother you," I said, my stomach twisting in a tangle of knots now that I had Hiro standing in front of me. He looked a little worn and weary but just as handsome as ever. He still had the striking bone structure, smooth porcelain skin, and piercing eyes I remembered from almost a year ago. So much time had gone by, but just one gaze from him proved to be enough to stir up all those feelings he had managed to pull from the deepest part of my heart before.

"Yes?" the woman in the doorway said, obviously running out of patience.

But it was hard to pull my thoughts into something coherent with Hiro in front of me. I had gone back and forth about trying to find out if he had by chance made it to this very camp, but I hadn't gotten the courage to do so. And now, as if by some sort of destiny, I was brought right to him at that very moment.

It all started to come together for me. Lily must be Hiro's younger sister, but it still didn't explain her strange behavior toward me. And after taking a look at the woman in the doorway, I noticed facial features that were similar to both Hiro and Lily. She had to be their mother.

"I'm Lily's social studies teacher," I finally managed to mutter while all three looked fixedly at me. "She forgot her notebook in the class-room. It has her homework notes. I thought I'd bring it by."

The mother's face softened just a tad.

"Oh, thank you," she said.

She smoothed down her skirt, and turned to Lily.

"Lily, you must be more careful. You can't waste your teacher's time like this," she chastised.

"Yes, Mother," Lily said, her face turning crimson.

"It's no bother," I said, walking forward and handing Lily her note-book which she timidly took.

I turned to Hiro and stretched out my hand to be shaken.

"Hello. I'm Jack Henry," I said, hoping that I wasn't giving us away.

At first, he looked slightly taken aback, but then he quickly gathered himself.

"Hiro Narita," he said. "Lily's brother."

I felt a quick shot of electricity from his touch. I so badly wanted to pull him to me, and tell him how happy I was to see him again. But I stayed professional.

"Nice to meet you," I replied, reluctantly letting go of his hand.

I had a hard time reading his face to see what he felt besides shock at seeing me. Did he feel the same mix of swirling emotions that I did? Or did he wish he'd never seen me again?

"I'm Mrs. Narita," the woman said, still standing in the doorway. "Thank you for bringing my daughter's notebook. Lily won't forget it again. Will you, Lily?"

"No. I won't," Lily said, gazing down at the dirt ground.

"No problem," I said.

A few seconds of awkwardness went by before I quickly added, "I hope you had a good first day at school, Lily. I'll see you tomorrow in class."

"Thank you," Lily said in a monotone.

"Have a good evening," I said first to Mrs. Narita before turning to Hiro and nodding.

He nodded back.

It took all the strength I had to turn around and start to walk away. I so badly wanted to embrace Hiro and tell him how much I had thought about and worried about him over these months. But I knew this was an impossibility.

So I headed back to the worker's mess hall with my mind running a million miles a minute.

He's here.

Hiro.

The one person who ever showed me I might be capable of the feelings of falling in love.

Here we were at the same place, but distanced by society and a tall barbed-wire fence.

"If I'm served hot dogs one more damn time," Donald said, pushing the sausages around in a thick sauce with baked beans in a tin pie pan. "This is the fifth time in seven days. Can't they get anything that's fresh or not from a can?"

We sat in the very back of the packed mess hall. All of the other teachers must have beaten us to here or they were sick of hot dogs since we were the only staff from the school at the meal, and we all tended to eat together. I had also been seeing less and less of Joan, and when I asked about her, another teacher said she tended rushed off to her barracks after work.

I sat silently and methodically chewed without tasting any of it.

"Jack?" Donald prodded. "You there?"

"Yeah," I said, still startled at seeing Hiro.

"What happened to you when you took that notebook? When you got back you looked like you saw a ghost," Donald said, shaking his head. "You should be relieved to make it through our first day of teaching. And you missed whiskey with Dottie. Let's just say she's not the best at holding her liquor as she passed out before the rest of us even left."

I debated how much to tell Donald. I had worked so hard to keep my real feelings, my real truth, from people for so long that it proved hard to let anyone get to know me or to reveal much about my inner thoughts. But after being thrown by seeing Hiro, I felt the need to at least get some of what happened off my chest. Even though I figured Donald had the same types of desires as me, fear kept me from letting him into my life completely since we worked together.

"Remember…" I started to say, trying to come up with the proper words.

Donald sat straight up in anticipation of a good story.

"Go on," he urged.

"Remember how I mentioned if I could find out if a particular friend from Los Angeles had been sent here?"

"Yes," Donald answered expectantly.

"He turned out to be the brother of the student whose notebook I went over to return," I said.

"Really? What are the odds? A *friend*, right?"

"Kind of, yes," I said. "It was a shock to see someone I know. It's not very nice over there to say the least. It's like we live in Beverly Hills on this side of the camp. It's all hard to wrap my head around."

At that moment, the whole mess hall found itself startled when two of the Japanese employees, a young guy probably no more than twenty and a middle-aged one, in the food line started arguing and yelling at each other in Japanese. All eyes turned and widened at the increasingly tense scene.

"What are they arguing about?" I said to Donald.

"Who the hell knows?" he answered. "But it must be something big."

Suddenly, the younger guy picked up one of the huge metal pots off the food line and slammed it into the floor before storming out.

"Jesus Christ," Donald muttered.

Armed guards quickly appeared and began to question the middle-aged man.

We could hear the various guards firing off questions to the cook.

"What happened?"

"What were you two fighting about?"

"What block does he live in?"

"Back to work!"

"That's been building," Donald said to me, once the situation calmed down.

"What do you mean?" I asked.

He shook his head and said, "I can tell you in the time I've been here I've felt the tension in the air growing thicker by the day. Sanders was mentioning how some of the Japanese are turning against each other. There's the side that says they should just go along with this *arrangement*, for lack of a better word, and others who think they should fight against it."

I nodded. I could understand how such groups could form and divide the population in a situation where there was no good answer and things didn't make sense.

I wondered which side Hiro was aligned with, and, of course, I wondered how I could see him again. That was if he wanted to see me. I couldn't tell much more from his expression besides sheer surprise.

I thought about what would happen when Lily returned to my class the next day. Would she say anything? Would she still give me the cold stares that so unnerved me?

Between everything that had happened, I lost my appetite, and Donald and I headed back to the staff dorms.

"Some of the staff, including Joan who's finally come out of hibernation, are hosting a poker party in the administrative office? Wanna come?" he asked. "But watch out. I played with Dottie before. She's a card shark. Don't let the innocent face fool you."

I chuckled and said, "Thanks. But I think I'm going to just go over my lesson notes for tomorrow and turn in early."

Really I just needed some more time to let it sink in that Hiro, the man who caught my attention as no other had at Pershing Square, was being held as a war prisoner in the very camp I worked. Sure, I knew it had been a possibility, but I never expected for us to come face-to-face through his sister.

I wanted to talk to him so badly, but I had no idea how to get the message to him or if he'd want to see me.

That night I had trouble sleeping, and I tossed and turned on my hard cement-like mattress. Sleeping in the dorms was difficult enough, but now all I could think about was Block 15 and Hiro being there and would I get to see him again somehow. Then that fight in the mess hall had reminded me yet again we were not simply off at a camp where people voluntarily signed up to spend some time. All of it together added up to be a restless night.

I heard Donald's voice booming in the hallway as he made his way to our room. I turned to face the wall so I could pretend to be asleep. The last thing I wanted was to hear Donald's gossip from the poker game after the emotional sucker punch seeing Hiro had proved to be.

The dim light in the room came from one of the guard towers and a full moon, and I could see Donald's shadow on the wall.

Donald opened the door, and I could hear him stagger toward the bed. He then fell onto it with a loud flop. I didn't turn around, and in a few minutes, I heard him snoring lightly.

I closed my eyes tightly and covered my ear with part of my pillow to try to drown out the snores.

I wondered what the next day could bring, and if I'd finally figure out a way to speak to Hiro once again after all this time.

Chapter Eight

Eventually, I must have fallen into a fitful sleep, and I awoke with the morning light streaming into the room. I reached over and grabbed my watch and saw it was 6:30. I wasn't sure when I fell asleep, but it must not have been more than a few hours ago. I sat up in bed and rubbed the sleep out of my eyes.

I saw Donald had passed out on his bed fully clothed.

He's going to have fun today in class, I thought.

I dragged myself out of bed, walked over to Donald, and shook him gently.

"Rise and shine. School starts soon," I said.

"*Ughhhhh*," Donald moaned.

His eyes fluttered open as I stood by his bed and looked down at him.

"Christ. What time is it?" Donald said, shielding his eyes from the light.

"It's six thirty. Class in an hour and a half," I said.

"And you already woke me up?" he groaned, turning over and burying his face in the mattress.

I chuckled, grabbed my toiletries, and headed off to the shower.

I passed a couple of other staff already dressed and headed to breakfast.

Despite the cold, bare concrete floor in the shower, I did have a little more pep in my step once the lukewarm water hit my body. I quickly showered, dressed, and headed back to my room to drop off my things before breakfast. Donald still lay in bed and groaned when I shut the door behind me.

"I don't think I can do this today. I drank way too much last night," Donald said, running a hand through his unruly red hair. "My mouth is so dry."

"You can't miss the second day of school," I told him, dropping my toiletries on my desk.

Donald sighed loudly and said, "I hate when other people are right about things."

"You'll be fine after some of that fine coffee in the mess hall," I replied with a wink.

"You mean that cold brown water they tell us is coffee?" he said, finally pulling himself up into a sitting position.

"Better than no coffee at all," I reasoned. "Meet you over there?"

"I'll be there in ten," Donald said. "So, are you going to try and see your *friend* on the other side again today?"

I knew Donald suspected there was a lot more to the story.

"Who knows what the day will bring?" I answered, knowing I'd just flamed the fire of his curiosity.

The school day seemed to drag toward the last period of the day, the class with Lily Narita. We started the morning yet again with the Pledge of Allegiance without speaking of the irony of the situation, and I did the best I could to deliver engaging lessons even though my mind had more than just a little trouble focusing. I found most of the students again to be very cooperative and polite overall. Only a couple appeared to be shell-shocked for lack of a better term.

As the students for the last class filed in, I greeted them at the door.

"Hello. Hello," I repeated.

Most of them greeted me back or shyly nodded at me. All except Lily. She tagged behind her friend, the more gregarious Emily. With her head down and her books held tightly to her chest, she made her way to the back of the classroom.

This time I tried not to stare at *her*.

"Please take out your homework," I announced, as I made my way around the room and checked off names of the students once I saw their work was completed.

"Thank you. Thank you," I said, as I made my way around the room.

The students quietly chatted away as I did this. Since it was the last class of the day, I knew they were tired and restless, so I was perhaps a little more permissive than my professors in college would have advised me to be.

When I got to Lily I looked down at her notebook and saw a blank page. For the first time since she came into the class, she looked me dead in the eye. But her stare was a blank. I didn't know what to make of it. I didn't say anything to her but kept making my way around the room until I walked back up to my desk.

"Please open your books," I said, clapping my hands to get everyone's attention. "Page twenty. We'll continue to talk about Athens, the birthplace of democracy. From what you read in your homework, what can you tell me about democracy in Athens?"

"Women couldn't vote!" Emily piped up.

"Correct, Emily. Anyone else?" I said, making a list on the board.

I heard a few rustles of papers being turned as students went through their notes.

Surprising me, Lily's hand popped up despite not doing her homework.

"Yes, Lily?"

"Non-landowners. Like my papa here. He's not allowed to own land in this country because he was born in Japan," she said. Her voice had a tinge of anger coming through.

"That's correct, Lily," I said.

"So, it wasn't a *true* democracy, right? Like here. We're American citizens, but we didn't have a choice in leaving our homes," she said.

"You're right," I concurred.

Some of the other students began to shift uncomfortably in their seats. Again, I could see the tension between those who thought it best not to make waves as a way of survival and those who were willing to let their discontent show through.

In my teaching courses, my professors talked about how students, especially in the higher grades, might question some of the thoughts or ideas present in a lesson. But they didn't really prepare us for what to do if we *also* agreed. As I looked around the room, I might have been looking at teenagers with Japanese relatives, but they were American teenagers in the way they spoke, dressed, and carried themselves.

"I guess you could say the Greek version of democracy and our own today was far from the ideal," I said. "There's still a lot of work to be done to bring everyone to the table just like in Ancient Greece."

Lily stared back down at what I knew to be her blank paper for the rest of the class as I struggled to bring students into a discussion about democracy. I don't know why I didn't think before about why this would be an uncomfortable, emotionally charged subject for them, and I felt stupid for not realizing this before.

The Ancient Greek democracy ideas were not inclusive of everyone, and the ones we had in the US in 1942 apparently applied to whomever the government wished for it to at the time.

And there I stood in front of the class not sure of where to go from that point. My mind, the whole lesson I had planned, the words that had been on the tip of my tongue, all turned into a blank.

The whole class waited for what I would say next, and as I looked around the room, I could feel the tension hanging thick in the air like a morning fog.

What could I tell these kids for things, for their lives, to make more sense?

"Tell you what," I began. "Why don't all of you take out your journals, and let's spend a few minutes writing about how you feel about democracy in America."

Once again, the students looked uncomfortable and restless. This time it was almost as if I had just thrown a live grenade their way and no one knew where to run.

"It's okay. I don't have to read it if you don't want me to," I said, trying to encourage them.

Finally, a few students, including Lily, began to scribble in their notebooks at first slowly and then furiously. Part of me wanted so badly to move about the room and see what thoughts my students were letting loose from the depths of their minds. But I resisted. I didn't want to stop their flow. If nothing else, I hoped it gave them the chance to unburden their souls at least a tiny bit. After twenty minutes, they were still writing, and I let them continue.

In the back, Lily Narita appeared to be writing faster than anyone else.

At the end of the class, the students hurriedly gathered their materials as soon as I said, "Class dismissed." Most were gone before I could even finish my sentence. Once again, Lily lagged behind.

"Come on, Lily!" Emily called back from the door.

"I'm on my way," Lily said, hesitating a bit.

Did she want to talk to me? Did she have anything to say about Hiro?

I closed my books and erased the board while Lily gathered her belongings.

"Did you have any trouble with your homework, Lily?" I asked. "I noticed you didn't complete it."

She walked up to my desk, and pushed a few stray dark hairs behind her ear. Gone was the red ribbon. Her shoulder-length hair hung loosely but had still been nicely combed with a part in the middle.

"I didn't have time," she said. "Sorry. My mother didn't feel well. I was trying to help her."

"I'm sorry to hear that. I hope she feels better," I said, wiping the chalk off my hands with a tissue.

"Yes," Lily said. She stares at me hard. "Who are you really to my…"

"Lily!" a voice called from the doorway.

Lily and I, both startled, turned to see Hiro standing in the doorway. He wore dark cotton canvas pants and a matching shirt. In his hands, he held his hat and a brown paper bag.

"Hiro!" Lily exclaimed, obviously taken off-guard.

"Hello," I managed to squeak out.

Ever since I had laid eyes on him the day before, I had wondered how and if I could arrange seeing him again. Now here he stood before me, and the only way I could be described was too tongue-tied to say anything beyond a general greeting.

"Mother needs help with the laundry," Hiro said to Lily. "I need to talk to your teacher."

Lily raised an eyebrow and said with a skeptical tone, "Really?"

"*Now*, Lily," Hiro stated in a stern but forceful voice.

Lily glanced at me once more with an ever increasingly suspicious eye.

She started to speak, but then must have thought better of it.

"I'll see you at home," she told Hiro as she walked past him and out of the room.

Once we heard her footsteps grow distant, Hiro started to walk toward me, and my heart began to beat faster. After all this time, here we were the two of us…alone again. In his arms, I had never felt so at peace, and I so longed to feel that way again.

"Hiro, I…" I started to say.

He held a finger up to his lips to tell me not to speak, and held out the bag.

"My mother wanted me to come and thank you for last night. She apologizes for being curt, but, well…we've grown suspicious when strangers show up at our doorstep."

"That's okay. I understand," I said.

I could feel the sweat on the back of my neck and my body temperature rising.

"This is a gift she sent me to give you," he said, holding the bag out toward me.

"I don't need a gift," I said. "I just wanted to help out a new student on the first day of class. There's no need…"

"*Please*," he said, looking down at the bag. "This is our thanks."

I felt guilty taking any sort of gift from people who obviously didn't have much to give at this time in their lives, but Hiro looked extremely insistent.

"Thank you," I said, finally taking the bag.

I cleared my throat.

I had to ask.

"Did you receive…"

"Please open the bag. Your gift." he said.

"Okay," I said, placing the bag on my desk.

I opened it, reached in, and pulled out a beautiful cotton cloth with cherry blossom trees on it.

"It's what we call a *tengui*," Hiro said. "It's sort of a multipurpose cloth. We use it to wrap things or as a decoration. Many different things."

"It's beautiful," I said, holding the soft fabric in my hand.

"Please open it so you can see," Hiro said, motioning to the cloth.

The gift was nice and very unnecessary, but I had to admit finding it strange that Hiro focused on it so much.

I caught Hiro looking back and over his shoulder.

I unwrapped the cloth and a small piece of paper fell out and landed on my desk.

Hiro's eyes met mine, and then he looked down at the piece of notebook paper.

I picked it up and read what was written on it.

And then it all made sense.

Chapter Nine

Lying in my bed later that night, I glanced at my watch in the moonlight streaming through the window and saw that it was fifteen past midnight. I held the letter from Hiro tight in my hand. My heart pounded in expectation, and my throat felt dry and scratchy. I hadn't felt such a swirl of emotions since the last time I met up with Hiro, and we ended up in Santa Monica. Now, after all this time, I finally had the chance to speak with him again, and to see if, maybe, he harbored some of the same thoughts and emotions for me.

Earlier in the classroom when I picked up the note it read:

Meet me at the garden between the elementary school and block fifteen, next to the Protestant church, at one in the morning when most people should be asleep. If a guard asks where you're going, tell them you couldn't sleep and are going for a walk. I'll wait until 1:30 to see if you're able to make it.

I had looked back up at him, and he gave me a pleading look and a nod.

"Thank you again for bringing my sister's book, Mr. Henry," he said, before mouthing. "See you later."

Hiro then walked out of the classroom.

I had to pull out the rickety wooden chair behind my desk and sit for a moment after that. I couldn't help but read the note again a few times.

After all this time since last December, I had begun to think that what happened was an anomaly and not something I would likely feel again for another man. Yet, here we were meeting up in quite an unlikely, and let's face it, even more inhospitable place.

I finally managed to compose myself, headed back to my barracks, and then met the other teachers for dinner. It was Tuesday, slop suey night. I didn't have any appetite anyway. All I could think of was the anticipation of what would happen that night and if I could make it to the meeting point without drawing unwanted attention. Joan kept teasing Donald about two kids falling asleep in his class while sitting straight up.

I tried to feign attention, but it was hopeless.

"Where's your mind tonight?" Donald asked, cocking his eyebrow like he did when he thought there might be a story.

"Just tired. Hey, at least my kids didn't fall asleep!" I teased.

Later, after we went to bed, bundled up under rough wool Army blankets, I waited to hear Donald's snores, and then I kept taking a look at my watch. I had casually, but very much on purpose, left my heavy coat lying on my desk next to a pair of pants with my shoes by the bed.

Luckily, Donald had proven to be a very heavy sleeper. I would still, as quietly as I could, slip on the extra clothes and sneak out of the room praying no one else would be up and about. I would use the story Hiro suggested. But how many people would want to go out for a middle of the night jaunt in freezing temperatures?

So, now all I had to do was wait, with each passing minute seeming like five. I went over and over in my head what I would say when we finally had the chance to speak. How was he holding up under these stressful circumstances? Could I help in any way? I knew this last thought to be naive. After all, what could I possibly do for him when our country had basically declared him and his whole family possible enemies to the country?

Finally, it turned 12:40, and I couldn't wait any longer.

I carefully and slowly got out of the bed and began to get dressed. When the sole of one of my shoes made a loud squeak when I started to walk, I froze in fear that Donald would wake up and wonder what the hell I could be up to at this time of night. But, if Donald was consistent on one thing, it was sleeping like the dead. He never even stirred.

Still, I slowly opened the door and walked out into the hallway which was dimly lit by one light, and I made my way outside. Ironically, the staff housing for the Caucasians had been painted white, a stark contrast to the brown tarpaper barracks for the Japanese, and the brilliance of the shiny white paint shone in the full moon.

I didn't see anyone out and about. Although, I knew there was a guard posted nearby in the tower to the south-west of the administration area. The only sound was the bone-chilling wind as it whipped around the various buildings and through the streets. In the distance, I thought I heard a coyote yelping.

As swiftly as I could without causing a disturbance, I walked past blocks one and eight and near the high school. My eyes kept darting back and forth, but the only person I saw was a stooped over older woman with a cane making her way to the women's latrine. Despite her age, she seemed to be on a focused mission to her destination and didn't notice me at all. I had heard from some of the staff that the Japanese women, especially the older generation, who often prided themselves on proper appearances and discreetness, were utterly horrified by the lack of real privacy in the latrines. As a result, some of them waited late into the night in the hope of not having to face anyone else there.

I continued past block fourteen to fifteen and finally made it to a tiny park that had been built by the residents. I marveled at what they had done with probably very few resources. A small rock garden and some carefully tended plants and trees had been planted. A tiny cement pond next to a wooden bench held frozen water. If by some miracle they had gotten some koi fish for that pond, I'm sure the fish were shivering in this bitter cold as much as I was.

I looked around and saw no one. I glanced at my watch and it showed 12:50. I was early. I pulled my coat in tighter and wrapped my arms around myself to try to get as warm as I could. The longer I walked around the tiny garden the more amazed I became at the details that had been put into it from the obviously meticulously tended plants and small trees to the floral carvings someone had added to the wooden bench. There had been so much care and time spent making a piece of this land, surrounded by barbed wire fence, into something beautiful. If it had been me living in one of these poorly constructed barracks and forced to leave my real life behind, I'm not sure I could have gotten focused enough on creating something of beauty, something that required great care within my confines.

"Jack," a voice said in a hush tone behind me.

I turned around and Hiro stood just a few feet behind me. He had been so quiet I hadn't even heard him walking up.

"You made it," he said, his breath practically freezing on the exhale. He wore what looked like an old Army issued jacket with his hands stuck deep in the pockets.

"Of course," I said. "I had to see you."

"Did you get stopped on the way?" he asked, his eyes darting to see if anyone might be around.

"No. It's pretty dead around here," I said, wanting to wrap my arms around him right there but holding back.

"Everyone's in their barracks struggling to stay warm. There are holes and cracks and crevices in all the floors and walls. It's practically impossible to stay warm no matter how many scratchy blankets you pile on top of you. I didn't know if everyone would ever get to sleep. My mother half woke up. I told her I had to go to the latrine."

"It's so good to see you, Hiro," I had to tell him. "I didn't think I would ever lay eyes on you again."

"Good to see you, too. I've thought about you a lot," he said, walking towards me and getting so close that I could feel his breath on my face.

Despite the cold, my heart practically melted at his declaration.

"You have?" I said, hearing the words I had longed to hear from the moment he walked into my classroom.

"Yes," he said. "Every day."

His hand came out of his pocket, and he reached out and barely touched my fingertips with his. Their warmth immediately gave me a much needed jolt in the bone achingly freezing weather.

"Look, I know how to sneak into the church," he said, motioning to the Presbyterian church nearby. "The back door doesn't lock well. Just give it a little push. We can get warmer in there and *talk*."

"Warmer sounds good," I said.

"Come on. Let's go quick," he said, suddenly grabbing my hand and pulling me into the direction of the church.

I let him lead me.

"How do you know about this?" I asked.

"I briefly worked as part of the clean-up crew," he said, as we made our way to the back of the church. "This place was on my list of places I had to tidy up each day."

He pressed all of his weight on the door, and just like magic, the door popped open.

"Come on," he said, pulling me inside.

We walked into a small back office. In the dim light I could make out a crucifix on the wall, one small desk with what looked like sheets of music sitting on it, and a stack of Bibles.

Hiro shut the door and locked it behind us.

"I don't want to turn on any lights or light any candles just in case someone sees," he said, my hand still in his.

"I understand," I replied.

He led me to the front of the church, and we sat down on the creaky first row pews. It was still cold within the thin walls of the church, but at least they blocked some of the bone-chilling wind.

He sat right next to me, and just having him that close made me momentarily forget the cold. I could feel the warmth of his body just mere inches from mine.

My eyes finally began to adjust to the small bit of light that came through the windows at the front of the church.

There was a moment of awkward silence, but then we looked into each other's eyes and let out a short chuckle.

"You sure know how to surprise," he said, smiling. "When you walked up carrying Lily's notebook, I was more than just a little shocked."

"Me, too. I couldn't believe she was your sister," I said.

Our hands intertwined and our faces got closer and closer until our lips were mere inches apart, and then, wondering if I could be dreaming all of this, his soft lips touched mine and he gave me a gentle but eager kiss.

I felt myself falling into him as I wrapped my arms around him and pulled him close.

Our kiss grew more urgent and intense.

Despite the setting, despite the winter temperature, I could have kissed him forever. If someone were to tell me I could have only one memory to take with me when I was old and dying, I would say this one right here because no other one had made me feel so alive as if every nerve in my body had been put on full alert.

Finally, we broke our kiss and pulled back just a little.

"Hiro," I whispered.

"Yes?" he asked.

"I can't tell you how happy you made me those days last year."

"I felt the same way."

"I never heard from you again though," I said, referring back to the lack of response to my letter.

He slumped back a little in the pew but kept his fingers intertwined with mine.

"I thought I didn't hear from you again," he said. "I thought you never wrote back to me until the other day."

"What? I don't understand," I said, shaking my head.

Hiro seemed to be struggling for the right words. Eventually, he just uttered, "Lily."

"What about your sister?" I asked. "I noticed she acted strange around me before I even knew she was your sister."

"She…well, she sort of knows something is going on between us," he admitted.

"What?" I said, sitting straight up. "How?"

"It's complicated, but when we met up and took the train to Santa Monica, Lily followed us. That's why she recognized you."

"Why? I don't understand."

"She was upset because I wouldn't take her to a movie that night. Our parents had gone out to a neighborhood meeting to discuss what they could do about the rising anti-Japanese sentiment. So, when I told her I was going out to meet a girl for a date she followed me…us…that night. She saw us standing near the shoreline in Santa Monica before she went back home."

"What did she say to you?" I said, the situation with Lily becoming clearer but dangerously so.

"It…" his voice trailed off.

"What—tell me," I pleaded.

"It hadn't been the first time she followed me. She did one night when I went to the park before I met you. She saw me…*meeting*…a guy there and heading down an alley."

I tried to wrap my mind around all of this. I wasn't sure how to respond.

"Did she understand what was going on?" I finally asked.

"Not at first. I think she was just confused as to who these secret 'friends' of mine were. But the next day after we went to Santa Monica she confronted me and demanded to know who I was with when I said I was going on a date. She asked if you were the date. I think she just meant it as sarcasm, but when I struggled to respond for a second, she started accusing me of doing something 'unnatural'. I told her she could never mention any of these ideas to our parents and how much it would upset them."

"Oh, my God," I uttered, shocked.

"Luckily, Lily loves me a lot. I took care of her many times when she was younger and our parents were working at the restaurant. When we went to Seattle, she took it upon herself to check the mail for my grandmother every day. She saw the letter from you, and put it together from your Santa Monica comment in it...and you mentioning you had taken someone on a date there."

"I'm so sorry, Hiro. I never would have written that if I had known. I tried to write everything in...code," I said, fear building inside me.

What if Lily decided to tell people what she thought...and what happened to be...true?

Hiro shrugged.

"Don't worry about it. I understand. But Lily kept the letter and never showed me. Eventually, things got back to normal between us. But last week, she started to act strange and almost angry again. I didn't know what was going on."

Then I figured it out.

"She saw me!" I exclaimed. "Before I headed into the camp. She was in the group of kids who were staring at me. She stood out because she gave me a little wave, and she had a red ribbon in her hair."

Hiro nodded and said, "Red's her favorite color. After you left and our mother went back into the barracks, Lily confronted me again saying she saw the way we looked at each other and it wasn't right. That's when she told me that you'd written me a letter, what was in it, and she burned it. I'm so sorry."

"Don't be. I understand. I can't tell you how much it means to me to find out that that was the reason I never heard from you," I said. "Do you think Lily will say anything?"

"I really don't think so. Our mother has just been hanging on, and Lily doesn't want to upset her. The past weeks here have been, well, more than difficult."

"I can't even imagine what you and your family have gone through," I said. "I went to Little Tokyo and saw your family's restaurant empty. I saw people selling off all of their belongings."

Even in the dark, I could see the tears forming in his eyes, and he looked away.

I reached up and tenderly touched Hiro's cheek, and he turned around to face me.

"What happened?" I asked. "What have you been through all these months? Tell me, Hiro."

He shook his head and pulled back a little from me.

"It would take more than the hours left until morning to tell you everything that's happened in these past months. I can't even believe it all myself. It's sometimes like I'm watching some movie where horrible things are happening to the people on the screen and I keep waiting for things to turn around for them. I keep waiting for the happy ending where everything comes together for them and life becomes good for them again. Just a few months ago our lives were…normal. Lily and I helped out at the restaurant. I went to my classes. My mother would make our favorites like *manju*, red bean cakes, and *mochi* once a week. Now we eat these weird concoctions like can peaches served over white rice."

He shook his head and his expression changed a bit.

"How the hell did *you* end up here?" Hiro asked. "Why aren't you teaching at a school in Los Angeles?"

"I almost did, but I knew I needed to get out of Los Angeles to figure some things out."

"Like?"

"I knew I couldn't marry my fiancée, not when I thought so much about you after just those couple of nights we spent together."

He looked very pleased and gave me a smile, but then he turned serious.

"You broke it off with your fiancée?" he asked.

"Let's just say me postponing the wedding again and saying I was moving hours away to teach here proved to be the straw that broke the camel's back. She told me she couldn't wait on me anymore. And to be honest, that's what I kind of hoped for. I know it was passive-aggressive, and she deserved better. One of my friends from college knew a mutual acquaintance who'd gotten a job teaching here. So I used the excuse of wanting to contribute to the war effort."

Hiro let out a short chuckle that definitely couldn't be taken for finding something funny but rather thinking it ironic.

"Supposedly, that's why we're all locked up here, you know? We're helping the war effort by staying out of sight and doing things like making camouflage nets and such," Hiro said, his gaze drifting off, and I knew heavy thoughts must be weighing on his mind.

"I think I'd be even more bitter over this situation if I were you. You haven't done anything wrong."

"Yes, I have," he said dryly.

"Wait. What could that be?"

"I have Japanese heritage. That was the only requirement for any of us here to be taken from our homes and brought out to the middle of nowhere. Do you know there are people who were brought here just because they had one Japanese great-grandparent or that orphans with Japanese heritage were brought here, too?"

"I heard from the other teachers that there's what's called a Children's Village," I said. "Those are the orphans, right?"

"Seriously, what threat would a five-year-old pose?" he said, his face turning red from anger.

I squeezed his hand, and all I could think to say was, "I'm sorry." I could see his facial muscles relax a bit and his shoulders fall.

"It's not your fault," he said.

"I kind of feel like it is in some ways. Maybe that's one of the other reasons I came here."

"What do you mean?" he asked

"All that's been going on, all the things I've heard people say on the street, I've let a lot of it go and haven't spoken out against it. When I think about that and when I think about my brother signing up for the military without being drafted, I feel like...like a coward."

Hiro shook his head and reached out and ran his fingers through my hair.

His touch had a way of making me feel like everything was actually okay with the world no matter how much it wasn't.

"Don't say that. You're a good man, Jack Henry. That's the thing about war. It makes good people do all sorts of things they otherwise wouldn't. We're all caught up in a lot of unfairness now."

"But I can leave this place if I want to do so. You can't. That breaks my heart."

"That's reality," he said somberly.

"What about the rest of your family?" I asked. "How are they?"

Hiro looked away, but even from the side of his face I could see the pain that swept over him.

"Right when we came back to LA from Seattle, the FBI showed up and arrested my father," he told me. "And before they took him away they practically tore our house apart piece by piece looking for what I'm not sure."

"Why would they arrest him?"

"He belonged to a Japanese business owners group. All the members were arrested without an explanation."

"How long did it take for him to get released?"

"He never has been, and we don't know where the government sent him," Hiro said, the tears beginning to flow. He couldn't hold back any longer.

I pulled him closer to me, and he buried his face in the crook of my neck and continued to cry until he ran out of tears. During this time, I just held him and let him release his emotions.

I'm not sure exactly how long we stayed like that, and I think he may have actually drifted off to sleep for a bit. I didn't, however, I just sat there on that pew holding him close to me.

I was content to spend the next few hours with us just holding one another and keeping each other warm in the frigid temperatures. I had been made incredibly happy by seeing Hiro again but saddened by how much he'd had to endure. As the first bits of morning light made their appearance, I nudged him.

"I think we have to head back. Morning will be here soon," I said.

He sat up and rubbed his eyes.

"Thank you," he said.

"For what?" I possibly wondered.

I thought I should be thanking *him*. Despite our surroundings and circumstances, he'd managed to once again awaken feelings in me that I thought were at least dormant if not dead.

"I feel so alone here," he admitted. "Sure, I'm with my mother and sister and the other family that got assigned to my barracks. But I can't talk to them, not about *everything*."

"I feel the same way," I told him, running my fingers through his coal-black thick mane of hair.

He glanced at his watch.

"We've got to get moving," he said, standing up. "They'll be getting breakfast ready at the mess hall soon, and then I have to work at the net factory. I have to get back to the barracks. Hopefully, my mother and sister are still asleep."

"When can we meet again?" I said, taking his hands and letting him pull me up.

"Maybe someplace that's not a church," he said with a laugh. "I think I might have an idea. Can you meet me tonight again? At one?"

"Of course," I answered.

I would have met him anywhere, anytime it could be arranged.

"Meet me outside the net factory back door," he said.

I nodded. "I'll be there."

"Great," he said, putting his arms around me one more time and bringing me in for one more kiss.

We could have kissed a thousand more times, and I still wouldn't have felt like it had been enough.

Before we parted, leaving the church five minutes apart from each other, he said, "Can I ask you something?"

"Of course."

"What was it like on the way here?"

"What do you mean?"

"Did you drive?"

"Yes."

"What did the countryside look like on the ride?"

"There wasn't much. There's just the little town, Lone Pine, a few miles from here. I drove stretches and didn't see much. Why? Didn't you see?"

He shook his head and said, "No. They pulled the blinds so we couldn't see where we were going. So, I've often wondered just whereabouts they've sent us. After Los Angeles, the next thing I saw was when we exited the train here, and most of what I saw looked empty, as barren as most of us felt after being brought here."

Chapter Ten

The next day I was exhausted from a lack of sleep, and it took multiple cups of lukewarm coffee to get through teaching a full day of classes. But my heart was full of joy after once again spending time with Hiro, so I had no complaints. I had the students work on group presentations on checks and balances in our government.

As always, the school started with saluting the stars and stripes first thing in the morning, and I underwent an even greater sense of conflict now that I knew more about what the citizens on the other side of the camp had gone through.

With liberty and justice for all.

Well, not quite.

With liberty and justice for some.

Those words would be a bit truer.

Knowing Hiro and working at the camp got me thinking of the world in all sorts of new ways. Seeing all the Japanese-Americans behind the barbed wires where I worked and lived with much more freedom than they enjoyed, got me thinking of other groups of people where liberty and justice didn't always apply such as the segregated neighborhoods and schools for the non-whites back in LA, and people eating at different lunch counters, or entering businesses from the back door versus the front. Most of my life, I had to admit, I hadn't really thought much about this and just accepted it for life as it was. Even with my family's working class roots, I had begun to realize more and more the advantages and conveniences I had from simply being white. And for this reason, I found myself growing more and more uncomfortable in my work and living space in Manzanar. What made me special that I got to be warmer at night or have a better quality of food given to me for some of my meals?

In my last class for the day, Lily Narita walked in with a small group of other girls. Now I finally had insight into why she acted the way she did, and I wondered how she would continue to behave in class. I wondered just how much knowledge she really had regarding the type of relationship I had with her brother.

Lily walked to her seat in the back of the class and sat down.

"Good afternoon, class," I said lively, trying to interject some enthusiasm.

It had turned a truly bitter temperature for this time of fall, much colder than the students were used to this time of year back in Los Angeles where most of them came from. They all looked tired, stressed, and distracted.

"Does anyone have any questions from the homework?" I asked.

Silence.

"What was something new you learned?" I asked.

More deafening silence. It was one of the moments teachers dread, a totally unresponsive class.

"What about voting rights?" I asked, trying to fish out some answers.

I suddenly noticed that Lily had her red bow back in her hair. It tied her shiny dark mane into a tight ponytail. She also wore a light pink sweater, white bead necklace, and a black skirt. Just like most of my other students, they always presented themselves in a well-dressed, or at least cared for, manner when it came to dressing. You would never guess they were living in less than ideal surroundings that many farm animals might not be subjected to.

Finally, a voice piped up, and it turned out to be Lily's.

"Women were granted the right to vote in 1920. I learned that," she said.

"Correct," I said, excited she was participating. "And what amendment gave women the right to vote?"

"The nineteenth," she answered, making direct eye contact with me.

Something was different than the other times she had looked my way. She appeared more relaxed and less on guard.

"Thank you, Lily. Very good. Now everyone open up your books to page seventy-three," I said, cracking open the extra-large teacher's edition of the text.

After school ended, I went back to my barrack to clean up a bit for dinner.

Donald sat at his desk, chain-smoking and frantically grading a stack of essays. He leaned back in his chair and gave me a sly look as I gathered up some toiletries.

"You look like you're in quite a chipper mood after work. Those must have been some amazing classes," he said in a tone that suggested he thought my mood had zero to do with teaching.

"It went okay," I said, grabbing my towel. "I'm going to clean up before dinner."

"Better hurry! I heard there's actual beef that didn't come out of a can tonight," Donald said.

"Anything has to be an improvement, huh?" I said, heading to the door.

"Could I ask you a question?" he said, crossing his arms. "And you can tell me it's none of my business. I won't be offended. Promise."

I stopped, turned, and looked at him.

"Okay," I said, bracing myself for anything.

"I usually sleep like the dead, but last night I woke up in the middle of the night and couldn't go back to sleep. I don't know maybe it's the scratchy Army blankets."

I tapped my foot waiting for him to get to the point.

"Yeah, they're not the best," I said.

He gave me a Cheshire grin and said, "I noticed you were gone...for a long time. And you weren't at the latrines. I know. I had to piss. And there's not exactly a lot of other places for someone to spend time around this place."

I looked at him and thought about it for a moment. I still didn't know how much or if I could trust him, especially with his love of gossiping about other staff members.

"I couldn't sleep either, so I went for a walk. It helps me clear my head," I answered. "That's all."

"Kind of cold for a walk last night," he said, obviously not convinced.

"Yep, but that seems to be what does it. I guess I just can't stop thinking about lesson planning these days. You know, wanting to do a good job and all."

He nodded and then raked a hand through his red hair.

"Sure," he said, nodding with a grin. "If you get bored later, you can always help me correct some of these essays."

"You look like you're having too much fun with that. I wouldn't want to take any of it away," I said, with a wink.

I then quickly made my way out of there and to the latrine before he could ask any more questions. Of all nights for him to wake up, I thought. But it wouldn't keep me from sneaking out to see Hiro again that night. Nothing would.

For the second night in a row, I lay in bed impatiently waiting for the time to meet up with Hiro. The camouflage net factory was located due north of the staff housing, so I hoped it would decrease my chances of being seen out and about that late at night. I wondered how dangerous the meeting would be for Hiro traveling from where his family's barracks was located.

Once again, Donald settled into his rhythmic snore. We hadn't said much to each other at dinner with the other teachers or when we returned to the room. Dottie, with a new bottle of whiskey she'd managed to sneak in, had invited us back to a room she shared with a recently arrived young female teacher, Sarah, from San Diego. She would be teaching science classes, and Dottie thought we should celebrate the new arrival. When I saw Sarah at dinner, the tiny meek young woman with mousy-brown hair and thick Coke-bottle glasses looked downright shell-shocked at her surroundings. I wonder what had made *her* decide to come teach at a place most people wanted to flee. Besides the Army soldiers who weren't given a choice to be stationed here, I had come to the decision that it took a certain type to willingly come to work at Manzanar, ranging from some sort of sense of helping the war effort to, like me, running from something back home.

I declined to help finish off the bottle of whiskey by saying I had a headache.

"Don't be a fuddy-duddy," Dottie pouted, batting her heavily mascaraed eyes.

"I think he had a rough night last night," Donald said, sounding halfway sympathetic and half-way gossipy.

For a couple of hours, I read a dog-eared copy of Steinbeck's *The Moon is Down* and found myself wondering if the residents of Little Tokyo had felt like they were being invaded like the fictional small town characters in the novel.

At eleven, I finally switched off the light and hoped that Donald returned back to the room and went to sleep before I needed to leave. The next day was Friday, the end of our first week of teaching. I couldn't imagine he'd stay out too late.

It must have been right after midnight when I heard him finally stumble into the room, obviously three sheets to the wind, and collapse onto his bed and into a snoring slumber.

I checked my watch and saw it was time to meet Hiro. I should have been exhausted after staying awake much of the previous night and then working another day. But just seeing him gave me the spark of energy I needed to keep awake.

Again, I slipped on my clothes and shoes and made my way outside into the icy cold.

"Where you goin', Henry?" a haggard voice said behind me.

I turned around to find Sanders in a heavy winter coat and hat with a cigar hanging out of his mouth. He leaned against the building and exhaled a puff of tobacco-tinged air.

"Oh, hi," I said.

I stuck my hands in my pocket and tried to put on my best casual late night in the middle of nowhere walking face.

"Little late to be out and about, isn't it?" he asked, taking another long drag on his cigar.

"I could ask the same about you," I said, throwing it back at him and, hopefully, the subject off me.

He shrugged his shoulders and lifted his hat to scratch the top of his crew-cut scalp.

"Can't sleep," he shrugged, walking toward me.

There was something in the way his gaze fixed on me. It reminded me of…the men of the park. But then I thought it couldn't be. Sanders had that man's man military thing about him, but I swear the way his eyes began to survey me from head to toe I started to wonder.

Before I knew it, he was maybe only a foot away from me.

"Anything that helps you sleep?" he asked, in a slight drawl.

Where was he from? Texas, maybe?

I hadn't spoken to him much since my arrival, and to be honest, he carried himself in a way that sort of intimidated me like a father who might get pissed at you any second. So I had sort of dodged him.

Hiro was probably waiting on me at this point, yet I couldn't figure out how to remove myself from this situation.

The way Sanders looked at me made me nervous, not the good romantic kind of nervous that Hiro brought out in me, but in a scared nervous.

Sanders stepped even closer toward me until I could smell the cigar on his breath.

"You likin' it here so far?" he asked.

"It's fine. I'm learning a lot…about teaching…and such," I said, pulling my coat tighter around me as if it were a shield.

No. I wasn't just reading into the situation, I decided.

"This can be a cold and lonely place," he said, dropping his cigar on the ground and then grinding it out with his boot. "Sometimes…you need something to help keep you going around here. If you think about it all, it can be too much."

He scratched his rough cheek, and I noticed a wedding ring.

"You have a wife?" I asked, hoping Hiro wouldn't give up and go back to his barracks.

"Yeah. Twenty-five years. Two boys. One in the Army now. I don't see her much though. She stays with her family back in El Paso. So, I'm sort of *on my own* most of the time."

He gave me an awkward smile that didn't make me more comfortable in the least.

Sanders was doing what he could to make his desires known. The guy was old enough to be my father. Not to mention he was my superior. I had no interest, but I knew rejecting him after he'd put himself out there like this could have its own consequences.

I had to make a quick exit before he got even bolder.

"Well, have a good night," I said, trying to sound cheery. "I'm going to take a brisk walk and try and calm my mind."

"Need some company?" he said, clearing his throat.

Even in just the light from the front of the building, I could see his eyes were wide and a little hazy. Another whiff of his breath and I smelled whiskey. Maybe he'd been at Dottie's party, or maybe he drank alone.

"Thanks, but I think I might go to the Presbyterian church. They leave it unlocked sometimes for people to come in and pray. I want to go…you know…pray for peace. It helps me feel better about things."

He shot me a look that said he couldn't tell if I was feeding him a line of shit or not, but it turned out to be enough for him to back off a bit.

"Well, be careful out there. It's full of Japs, you know," he said, cocking his head, laughing and still sizing me up.

"I'll keep that in mind," I said, producing a weak chuckle.

Unexpectedly, he reached out and put his hand on my shoulder.

"If you ever get down or lonely around here, you come talk to me, okay? I'm here for you," he said, before quickly adding, "For the whole staff that is."

"Okay. Thanks," I said, stepping back.

His arm fell back down by his side.

"Night," I said, heading in the direction of the church to keep up my part of the story.

"You, too," he said.

Without looking behind me, I quickly headed off as fast as my shoes would take me over the gravel terrain. Once I figured I was out of Sanders's sight, I cut over and headed toward the net factory. I glanced at my watch and saw I was fifteen minutes late. I hoped Hiro didn't give up on me showing up.

But when I got there, my breath labored after practically running in the cold, there he stood in the same heavy coat from the night before outside a back entrance and under a very dim light. He looked a little worried with a frown when I first saw him, but then his face lit up a bit once he saw me.

"I'm so sorry I'm late," I said. "I got caught up with…" I thought about how much detail to give over my odd meeting with Sanders, but I decided to just say, "a guy from administration who was outside and couldn't sleep."

He nodded and said, "That's okay. I actually just got here myself. I thought I might have missed you, too."

I noticed he seemed tense and his eyes kept darting back and forth.

"Are you okay?" I asked.

But instead of answering, he grabbed my arm, opened the back door of the factory with a key, and pulled me inside. The room was dark, and I could barely see him. He reached over and flipped on a small light on a desk that was covered in paperwork. There was another door leading out to what I assumed was one of the main parts of the factory.

Even though the light from the lamp was dim, I could see he still looked worried.

"What's wrong? Do you think we shouldn't have come here?" I asked, reaching out and taking one of his hands into mine.

"I'm sorry. I'm just a little shaken up. One of the guard towers spotted me and followed me with the spotlight. So, I headed to the latrine. He kept the light there until I walked out and then had it follow me all the way back to the barracks. I had to wait a few minutes once the light was gone and sneak out again hoping he wouldn't find me and keep the light on me again," he said.

I could tell his breathing was heavy and labored.

"Jesus Christ," I said. "He followed you all the way to the latrine with the spotlight! That must have been scary."

"Especially when you remember he has a loaded gun pointed at you."

I took his other hand in mine and said, "It's okay. You're safe now."

"I don't know if I will ever really be *safe* again," Hiro said, leading me to a small, worn, slightly torn sofa in the office.

We sat down, and a few moments of awkward silence went by. Honestly, I couldn't think of anything to say that would make things better.

"I'm so sorry," I said finally.

He nodded, and he gave me a little smile.

"I know," he said, with a loud sigh. "I don't think this is what either one of us had planned for our lives."

"True. But you have much, much more to deal with," I said.

"I feel better after seeing you," he said.

I leaned in and began to kiss him. At first, it was gentle and sweet, but then our physical contact became more intense, more fueled by pure desire and perhaps the need to forget the present for a few moments.

Between kisses that were getting deeper and deeper, we both haphazardly pulled off our coats. I began to frantically unbutton his shirt until I was able to pull it open. I ran my hands over his hard, smooth chest. I had longed for many months to get to touch him like this, and now that it was happening, it was a little hard to believe. Sure, once again the unromantic setting of a shabby office environment served as our place to connect. But I could have met up with him anywhere, and my heart would have overflowed with joy.

I pressed and leaned him back into the sofa until he was lying underneath me. My kisses started at his mouth and made their way down his neck, collarbone, and to the space between his pectoral muscles. Once again, I marveled in his beauty and the surprise that he had similar feelings for me.

My mouth traveled lower and lower to his belly button, and then to his belt buckle. His caressed my hair, and when I looked up at him he said to me, "Please take me away from this place, Jack. For tonight. Please."

I pulled myself back up and kissed him on the mouth again. The feeling of the skin-to-skin contact of our bare chests made me want to melt into him.

I pulled back and looked down at him below me and ready to give himself to me.

"I will. I promise," I told him.

Afterwards, we lay in each other's arms only in our underwear and using our coats as blankets.

"How much time do we have left?" Hiro, holding me from behind, whispered into my ear.

I looked at my watch and saw it was after three.

"Maybe a couple of more hours," I said, pulling his arm closer to me. "I wish we didn't have to go back out there."

"I know," Hiro said, his breath hot on the back of my neck. "Can I tell you something though?"

I turned around on the couch so I could face him.

"What?" I said, running my hands through his dark hair.

"I was about to give up," he said, looking away.

"What do you mean?"

"The day you showed up at our barracks…I was…I felt like I was on the verge of giving up. I'm not proud of it, but it's what I felt."

"What do you mean give up?"

"Ever since my father got taken away I've tried to take his place in the family and look after my mother and sister, but I feel like such a cheap replacement."

"Why do you say that?"

"I can't do anything to make our situation better. We're trapped, and I can't think of any way to get us out of it."

"Many families are like yours," I said, placing my hand under his cheek and bringing his gaze back up to me. "All that's happening, a war between all these countries, is not your fault."

"True, but my father always found a way out of a tough situation or came up with a way to make things better. He *would* figure something out."

I gave him a peck on the lips and said, "I think you're being really hard on yourself."

"A couple of hours before you showed up at our doorstep, I had been sent home from work here at the factory. I was just doing my normal tasks, and suddenly, it was as if I couldn't breathe and my heart rate quickened until I thought it would burst out of my chest. I must have looked really bad because one of the other guys on the assembly line ran to get one of the soldiers. They said I looked as pale as snow and sent me home for the day."

"That sounds frightening," I said, placing my hand over his heart. I could feel its steady beat beneath the skin. "What was wrong?"

"I don't know," he said, shaking his head. "But I really thought I might be going crazy and what would my mother and sister do after that. I was standing outside trying to catch my breath when you walked up."

He smiled.

"Of course, then I lost my breath again for a few seconds," he half joked. "But seriously, seeing you gave me hope that somehow things would get better and that something good could happen again. I had thought of you so often since those nights we spent together. I didn't think I'd ever set my eyes on you again. But, then, like a miracle, there you were. It gave me a boost of strength that I needed."

"I know what you mean," I said, pulling him closer to me and wishing that somehow this moment didn't have to end.

Before full light broke, we gathered ourselves together, and Hiro told me to leave first. He'd follow a few minutes later so we weren't seen together.

"When can I see you again?" I asked, as we pulled our coats back on.

"We have to be extremely careful," Hiro warned. "As much as I would like to, we can't do what just happened every day. We have to space out the times and locations to avoid suspicion. I'll think of our next place we can meet."

I must have looked saddened because he pulled me in for another kiss and said, "Don't worry. We'll figure it out."

"Okay," I said. "I'd be happy just getting to see you even if we can't get alone time."

He looked like he was pondering a thought for a moment and weighing its pros and cons.

"What are you thinking?" I asked.

"I'm helping work on the garden around Block 22 this Saturday in the afternoon if you want to stop by and see. Maybe you can use the excuse that you were heading to the hospital to see a doctor. Not many staff come over, but I'll be there. At least we can see each other. Maybe I can think of another plan for us to meet in private by then, too."

"Block 22. Saturday afternoon. I got it. I'll be there," I said.

With one more quick peck on the lips he said, "You better go."

"See you soon," I said, before sticking my head outside to make sure the coast was clear.

I turned around one last time and whispered, "Bye."

Hiro mouthed "Good-bye."

I dashed out and headed quickly back to the dorms hoping that Sanders wouldn't still be out there hours later.

I didn't even think much of the risks of being caught being in an intimate situation with an internee, especially a *male* one. Instead, I quickly made it back to the staff barracks and held my breath that I wouldn't attract any attention.

Luckily, I didn't come across anyone on my way back, and Sanders was nowhere to be seen. I still wasn't the least bit over how uncomfortable that encounter made me, and I hoped it would never happen again.

The hallways in the barracks were empty. As quietly as I could, I opened the door to the room I shared with Donald and tiptoed inside. I stood next to my bed and began to undress. Maybe I could still get a couple of hours of sleep, I hoped.

Unexpectedly, the lamp next to Donald's bed switched on, and he sat up and looked at me wide-eyed and awake.

"So, are you finally going to tell me the real story about what you're up to?" he said, a devilish look in his eye.

Chapter Eleven

"I don't know what you're talking about," I said, feeling my heartrate quicken.

Donald raked a hand through his red hair, pushed it out of his eyes, and viewed me with an almost amused look in his eyes. He reached over and grabbed a pack of cigarettes and a lighter off his nightstand.

I continued to undress and ignore him as if I had no clue what he could be referring to even though it was quite obvious I'd been out doing something during the night.

Donald observed me for a moment, lit a cigarette, and took a deep drag.

"So, what? Do you expect me to believe you've been out doing some exercise at three in the morning? You've been gone for hours," he said, cocking an eyebrow.

I plopped my clothes on my desk, and climbed into bed in my pajama pants and T-shirt. I pulled the blanket up close and turned toward the wall.

When it became apparent he wasn't going back to bed, I turned around to face him and said, "Are you going to leave the light on?"

"I woke up when you shut the door," Donald replied, ignoring my question.

He kicked his blankets off, sat up in his bed, and leaned against the wall.

His expression was one of a cat catching the canary.

"I had to get out. Sometimes I can't get any shut-eye. It helps to get some air," I said, avoiding his glare and shutting my eyes as if I could go to sleep with the bright light of the lamp shining in my eyes.

"You must need a lot of air because you were gone for quite a while, sir," Donald said.

I could smell the smoke of the cigarette wafting in the air. It made me hack with a raspy cough.

"Do you have to do that in here?" I said, opening my eyes again, and staring at him.

"Sorry!" Donald said, holding up one hand in surrender and stubbing out the cigarette into a random glass ashtray from Yosemite Park in the shape of a bear.

I closed my eyes and turned back around in my bed, burying my face in the pillow.

"I'm going to sleep now," I groaned.

"You're no fun," Donald accused. "Are you not going to tell me about that handsome Jap guy I saw you go into the net factory with? That is after you got Sanders to leave you alone."

I immediately jerked up and turned around to face him again. I could feel the anger rising in my throat.

"What the hell? Are you following me?" I demanded.

Donald scratched his nose and shrugged.

"Well, you did wake me up, and I didn't think I'd be able to fall back to sleep so quickly. So, yeah, I got up a couple of minutes after you left and snuck into the hallway. I looked out the window and saw Sanders standing awfully *close* to you," he said, with a sly smile.

I shook my head. This guy was unbelievable. Why didn't he just stay out of my business?

"I don't know what you're talking about," I said feebly. "You're reading into things."

Donald clicked his tongue and said, "I don't think so, Jack Henry. I wasn't born yesterday. Sanders had the same *talk* with me a couple of nights ago when he came across me coming back from the mess hall by myself. Only thing is I took him up on it. Of course, now I regret it."

In shock, I swallowed hard. I couldn't believe the words that had just came out of his mouth. Could he be saying what I thought he was saying?

"What…do you mean?" I asked slowly.

Donald sighed loudly. "You know what I mean. You know *exactly* what I mean. I'm not proud of it, but it happened in his office. I just…I don't know…felt so confused and lost about my decision to come here to begin with. *It* made me forget. Come on, Jack. Let's not play games. We both know which side our bread is buttered on, so we might as well be open with each other about it. I'm not going to say anything to anyone about anything."

"And I'm supposed to trust you? The guy who's following me around?" I countered. Then I added with a crack in my voice, "I still don't know what you're talking about."

Donald rolled his eyes.

"I know…I know I shouldn't be following you around like I'm one of the Hardy Boys," he said. "But I was bored. Goddamn, it's boring out here in the middle of nowhere with sometimes only relentless dust and wind to keep me company half the time. These weeks have felt like an eternity. I hoped at least *you* were up to something interesting. So, yeah. It's true. I looked out the window and watched Sanders talk to you. When you took off, he went back inside. After that, I snuck outside and got lucky, picked up your trail, and didn't come across any guards or anyone along the way. I stayed a good ways back and followed you to the net factory. That's when I saw you with the *very* nice looking Japanese guy sneaking, I assume, into the net factory. I can't imagine anyone making netting at three in the morning. Who the hell around here would be that dedicated?"

"I don't know what you think you saw…" I started to say even though I knew my defense was growing weaker by the second. There simply wasn't a good way to explain it away as me not being up to something I shouldn't.

"How did you meet him here?" Donald asked. "Your *friend.* Especially with the two sides hardly mixing."

"Look," I said, trying to sound nonchalant. "We know each other from LA before he got sent here to the camp. We were friends. So, we were just..."

"Oh, I know what you were doing," Donald interrupted. "Good for you. He's a handsome devil."

"I...uh..." I stammered.

"You can trust me," Donald said. "Sure, I can be a bit of a gossip, but not about this. I know what's on the line. After all, I told you about me and Sanders. So, we're even. All I can say is be careful what you do."

I gave up trying to deny the truth because as he said, I knew about what he did with Sanders. So I would have to trust we were equals on the scandal protection level. And I had to admit, it would be nice to have someone to discuss some of this with. I hadn't had that before...*ever.*

"I will be careful," I said. "And you and Sanders?"

Donald shook his head and folded his arms.

"That's not going to happen again. Well, at least I don't think so. Hell, I can't lie. Who knows?" He grew quiet for a moment. "You got something special with this guy?"

"I think so, but what can we do about it really?" I said sadly.

"But at least you have that something *special.* I never have. Treasure that. I've only had...brief encounters with people I met on the street or the well-dressed men I'd meet at Café Gala and later spend a night with."

"Café Gala?" I said curiously.

"You've never heard of it?" Donald said, his eyes growing wide.

"Nope."

"I've got some wild stories from that time. There's a lot of places back in LA you can meet men and not just the parks. We could have fun going out and checking things out," he told me. "Be friends. It'd be a lot more fun than doing those things alone."

His voice had a twinge of loneliness in the tone. I knew how he felt during my own nights living in the shadows of downtown Los Angeles.

"You could bring your friend from here, too," he said, before stopping and really thinking about what he said. "I suppose that is if things ever get back to normal. That is "normal" not being here."

"You think things can ever be *normal* after this war or after this place especially for the people on the other side of camp?"

"I don't know, Jack Henry. I don't know. We better get some sleep. I don't know why you insist on keeping me up," he said, with a laugh.

Donald reached over and switched off his lamp.

I pulled the covers up close and willed myself to get a least a couple of hours of sleep after what had to be one of the most exciting yet strange nights of my life. Just knowing that Hiro was so close, even if worlds existed between us for all intents and purposes, gave me a sense of peace I hadn't experienced in a very long time.

Just about all I could think about the next day, Friday, was getting the opportunity to see Hiro again. Since I was giving a test that day, I spent most of the day sitting behind my desk for the first time since I began teaching at Manzanar. The students, for the most part, took their studies seriously, so the classes remained quiet as they focused on their exams. I had begun to realize that for many of them school provided some semblance of normalcy in their otherwise less than regular teenage lives. At least in class, they could focus on the lessons and maybe, just maybe forget they were in what passed for a prison even though they'd done nothing in their young lives to deserve such a fate.

I should have spent the quiet time planning for the next week. Instead, all I could think about was meeting up with Hiro in the community garden that he was helping put together. I wondered what would be the best excuse I could come up with if a staff member really pushed me on why I wanted to be there when it was the weekend and I could be anywhere else, even if just out drinking at a watering hole in one of the nearby tiny towns.

That night, I went with the rest of the white teachers to a small diner in nearby Lone Pine where I indulged in a hamburger and fries. Getting a break from the mess hall food was a treat, but it was hard to enjoy myself when the Japanese-American teachers were back at camp having the latest questionable canned food creation. The situation added to my general uneasiness I had regarding working at Manzanar and the freedoms I had that most there didn't.

I eased around Donald some and the mood in the room we shared relaxed. I realized he had as much to lose as I did if our secrets got out, and I had to admit that it was kind of nice to have a friend to talk about my "shadow life" with.

"Are you arranging to see your *friend* this weekend?" he asked when we made it back to our rooms after dinner.

"I'm supposed to meet up with him tomorrow at a garden he's helping build," I answered, collapsing on my bed.

Donald sat at his desk, lit a cigarette, and raised an eyebrow.

"You better have a good story and reason for why you're over there. You know the two sides don't really mix outside of work unless it's baseball."

Baseball had turned into quite the camp passion for both sides, staff and internees. I heard the games at the makeshift ballpark were always well-attended by everyone.

"I know," I said. "I've thought of saying I wanted to see it because I was thinking of starting a gardening project for the high school."

Donald shrugged and said, "Could work. Just make sure and have your story straight."

I nodded and pulled the scratchy blanket toward me. The barracks had a constant draft it seemed, but I knew it couldn't compare to what I heard the Japanese had to go through with wind whipping through the cracks in the floors and walls of theirs. As a group, they were always moving from their barracks to the mess hall to the latrines, but in reality, they were never really going anywhere.

The next day after breakfast it was warm to the point you could've sworn summer had made a hasty return. The sun beat down on the rocky terrain with an unrelenting force and made it hard to see from the glare. The endless dust drifted in the air, coating everything, including myself, in a thin layer of dry powder.

As I walked between the barracks, children ran and chased each other around the buildings. The screams and shrieks were often ear piercing, and no parents were in sight. Women carried large loads of laundry to be washed. Each latrine had a long line with many people holding their toiletries and towels in their hands. Some people looked restless as they tapped their feet, or their eyes darted around and looked impatiently at the slow-moving line. Others looked worn down and defeated as they stared ahead at nothing in particular.

I got more than my share of skeptical looks as I walked through the rows of barracks and amongst all the internees. Obviously I was no guard, so I'm sure many of them wondered what business I must have there. They probably assumed that whatever it was it probably wasn't anything good.

Eventually, I made it to the garden area in the block Hiro had directed me to go to and found myself the first to arrive. I stopped on a dime as I viewed the scene. Here, in the middle of this stark landscape, another beautiful garden was being created. To see a thing of beauty behind barbed wire was truly a sight to behold. An intricate gazebo had been fashioned from what otherwise could be described as a bunch of random twigs. More wood had been used to build a small bridge that crossed over a small concrete pond. Rocks had been carefully arranged to create borders and paths throughout the garden. A few trees and flowers such as the silver lupine had also been planted.

I paused at the sight and found myself suddenly overwhelmed with emotion to find a pocket of such beauty surrounded by such struggle and many times desperation. The garden gave me the sense of being at some peaceful place far away from Manzanar as I'm sure it did for the residents. The garden represented hope in an otherwise sometimes hopeless place.

"It's coming along nicely, right?" I heard Hiro's voice say behind me.

I turned and saw him, with his trademark smile, carrying gardening tools: a shovel, a pick, and a bucket.

"How long have you been watching me from over there?" I asked.

"Just for a few minutes," he said, with a sly smile.

"I can't believe *this* is here," I said, still in amazement and looking over the garden again.

"There are others all around the camp. I'll show you around one day," he said, walking toward me and handing me a shovel. "I hope you're ready to get to work."

I took the shovel and laughed. "I didn't know there'd be actual work involved."

"I already know you're not afraid of working up a sweat," he said softly and with a wink.

"Who's that?" a booming, deep voice called from behind us.

When I looked over I saw two other young Japanese men. Both were probably around Hiro's age with one being on the shorter side and a little portly while the other one was very tall, with a slender build, and hints of Caucasian features in his face.

"A new friend?" the tall one asked.

The booming voice had been his.

The shorter guy just stared at me in amazement as if I were a unicorn and couldn't possibly be standing before him.

"This is my friend from LA, Jack. He's working at the high school and is one of Lily's teachers, too." Hiro began. He pointed at the tall guy first. "This is Nathan."

"Hey," I said trying to sound upbeat and friendly, but even at a distance I knew what he saw.

Jailer. Captor.

"Hey yourself," he said in such a deep skeptical voice I wondered if he could be a baritone singer.

"And this…" Hiro said pointing to the shorter guy, "is Dan. They both live in the barracks next to me."

Both Dan and Nathan continued to stare me down, and I knew exactly what they were thinking.

"What is he doing here?"

"So, you knew each other from Los Angeles?" Nathan said, sounding a bit skeptical.

"Yeah," Hiro said, apparently he hadn't thought his story through. "I…uh…used to do some business at his family's store downtown. Now, he's here, too. He's thinking of starting a garden near the high school with some of the students, so I thought I'd invite him along to see what we're doing over here."

Dan nodded and looked a little more relaxed, but Nathan appeared to still be on guard.

"Hope you're ready to work then," Nathan said, eyeing my shovel.

"Yeah, and here to learn," I said, trying to sound positive, but I was quickly beginning to wonder if this was a good idea. There just didn't seem to be a way for me to spend time with Hiro outside of a secret location without raising eyebrows. "You guys have done some great work here."

"Guess you could say we've found ourselves with some time on our hands," Dan said, finally speaking.

I nodded and swallowed hard. The sun began to come out in a force I hadn't ever experienced before, and beads of sweat careened down my cheeks.

"You can start digging over there," Nathan said, pointing to where a pile of rocks had been neatly stacked. "We're going to extend the pond in that direction."

"Sounds good," I said, shooting Hiro a look meant to gauge if this was really okay.

"I'll help you get started," Hiro said, leading me over to the digging spot.

We spent the next hour or so tilling the soil, and I found myself appreciating just how difficult it was to turn a plot of mostly lifeless, cement-hard land into something of beauty.

Nathan and Dan gradually relaxed a bit around me once they saw me roll up my sleeves and really dig into the work.

"You're not doing so bad, Teach," Nathan said, surveying my work.

"It was mostly Hiro," I said.

Nathan shrugged, but I knew I'd won a tiny bit of approval from him.

When Dan and Nathan went off to gather some more wood from an area just outside of camp, it gave Hiro and me a few minutes to talk.

"Are you hanging in there with the heat?" Hiro asked, grinning and wiping the sweat off his forehead.

Besides the sweat, both of us were covered in dust particles.

My bad leg ached from deep within, but I wouldn't have complained for anything, just to spend this time with him. And compared to the Japanese, I had nothing to complain about.

"I'm doing okay," I said, wiping my forehead with the sleeve on my shirt.

"You said you wanted to spend time together," Hiro teased. "You didn't say anything about not wanting to do manual labor."

"I don't mind. I'd just be sitting in the barracks, probably playing cards and watching the clock slowly tick the minutes away."

"But at least you're in Beverly Hills over there," Hiro said, and I could pick up a hint of tension in his voice.

The internees had begun to refer to the much better built staff barracks as Beverly Hills.

"How's your family?" I asked, as I kept shoveling away despite the worsening pain in my leg.

Hiro stopped digging and leaned against his shovel.

"I'm worried about my mother," he said, his gaze avoiding mine.

"Why? What's wrong?" I asked, immediately feeling stupid for asking the question.

A lot was probably wrong.

"She's not eating. The food's been making her sick. That and she worries about my father constantly," he said.

"You still haven't gotten any word on him, huh?"

"No," he answered. "I feel so powerless. I'd do anything to help bring him back, to help my family, and to somehow make things better for us in here. I'm the man in the family now, and I feel like I'm letting everyone down."

"Don't say that," I said, stopping shoveling.

I wanted to reach out, take him in my arms, tell him I knew how impossible things must feel for him right now, but I couldn't do it here…or anywhere in public.

"I have to figure something out," he said. "I *have* to. I miss just being a young guy in his twenties, going to school, and helping out at my family's restaurant. Before, I thought my life was complicated. Now I know just how easy things have been."

At that moment, Lily showed up carrying a pitcher of water and some cups. She froze for a second when she saw me, but then continued to walk toward us.

"Just in time," Hiro said, leaning his shovel against the gazebo. "Mr. Henry came to help us with the garden."

"I see," she said, pouring two cups of water and handing one to each of us.

"Thank you, Lily," I said. "You're a lifesaver."

She gave me a thin smile and a skeptical glance.

I wondered what was really going through her mind after finding me here of all places with her brother. Just how much had she put together about our relationship?

"How's Mom?" Hiro asked.

A look of distress swept over Lily's face, and she shook her head.

"Not good. Still in bed. When are you coming home?"

She cut her eyes back at me.

"When are you coming back home and leaving this guy?" I could imagine her saying.

"We're almost done for the day. Talk to Mrs. Tanaka next door. See if she still has some plain rice left over that we can cook in the kettle for Mom. She can keep that down at least."

"Okay," Lily said. "Where's Nathan?"

I saw her face light up a bit when she said his name, and it was the tell-tale sign of a crush. I could relate since Hiro made me feel the same way.

"Getting more wood. Why?" Hiro said.

"Just asking!" Lily said, defensively.

"Okay, okay!" Hiro said, holding his hands up.

"Just come home when you can. I need help with Mom," Lily said, before turning and walking away.

"Yeah, she still doesn't like me," I said, once Lily was out of earshot.

A middle-aged man with thick Coke-bottle glasses came up to the garden, saw me, and gave me a disgusted look before turning and walking away.

"And I don't think she's the only one," I said.

"People are just scared right now," Hiro said. "And as for Lily, I just think she's confused. She doesn't know what to make of you...of us exactly."

"Has she mentioned anything about me to your mother?"

"No, no," Hiro said, shaking his head. "We're both working hard to keep our mother from getting any more upset or despondent than she already is now. Without my father, it's like she's floating with no place to land."

"I'm sorry," I said.

"I'm just only now beginning to understand a small bit of what she must feel. When I didn't think I'd see you again..."

"I know. I felt the same way."

We both heard Nathan and Dan's voices as the two made their way back.

"Meet me again tonight at the net factory at one," he said, in a hushed tone.

"Is it safe to meet there again?" I asked, concerned.

"For you, I'm willing to risk it," he said.

"Me, too," I agreed.

I would have met Hiro on the moon if he'd asked.

That night a little before one, in the cold desert night, I made my way to the net factory and the same location where we met previously. I passed a guard I'd seen before in the mess hall and recognized from the staff baseball team. He was a young skinny guy, with patches of acne still on his face, no more than twenty, and an air of friendliness to him. He was leaning against one of the buildings in Block 2.

I didn't know whether to turn around at that point and make my way to the factory using a different path, or to keep heading in the same direction as if I had a perfectly legitimate reason to be out at this time of night.

Just when I started to turn around, I stepped on and broke a twig in two causing a loud snap. The soldier startled and stood straight up and at attention holding his rifle next to him.

"Sir," he said, as I continued walking in his direction.

I couldn't afford to turn around and stir up suspicion.

"Nice night, huh?" I said, and as I got closer I saw that this young solider looked visibly upset, and once I stepped into the light his eyes were red. He looked as if he may have been out here crying.

"Yes, sir," he said, even though I was probably just a few years older than him.

I started to ask if he was okay, but I realized even if something was wrong the chance he'd talk about it with me at that moment was quite slim. From the way he averted my gaze, I figured he was just eager for me to keep walking.

"Have a good night," I said.

"You, too, sir," he answered, still standing at attention.

I could only guess what had him upset, but I already knew Manzanar could conjure up so many different types of emotions for someone held behind its fences.

I continued on to the net factory and made my way to the entrance where I'd met Hiro before. I checked my watch and saw it was one on the dot, but he wasn't anywhere in sight.

I blew hot air on my hands to warm them up and stuffed them into my pockets. Even though Hiro lived probably just a few blocks from here, I knew it had to be a journey fraught with all sorts of dangers, much more so for him than for me. If he were to get caught doing anything considered out of line, the consequences could be major.

After another fifteen minutes, I started to really worry.

"Hi. Sorry," he said, as he rushed up toward me. "We need to get inside."

He opened the door with a key that I still didn't know how he ac-quired, and we stepped inside. He immediately shut the door behind us, and I could barely make him out in the bit of moonlight that came through a window.

"Is everything okay?" I asked.

Hiro pulled me toward him and embraced me. I could smell his scent, clean and masculine. His body felt like heaven, warm and inviting.

"I wasn't sure if I would make it," he said, still holding me tight. "Two guards stopped me on my way here. I gave them a story about not being able to sleep and wanting to sit in the garden. I thought they were going to send me back, but they got distracted when they heard a domestic squabble in a nearby barracks."

He pulled back, and I saw the fear and worry in his eyes.

"You made it though. It's going to be okay" I said, pressing my lips against his, and we hungrily kissed each other as if we gave each other the very breath we needed to survive.

When I pulled back I could still see the tension in his expression.

"What's wrong?" I said, clasping his hands. "Besides the obvious day to day here. You can tell me."

He sighed loudly and guided me over to the threadbare sofa in the corner of the office.

"Mother is getting worse," he said at last. "Each day she seems to slip a little more away from us. Lily is getting angrier by the day. No one around here will give us any information about where my father is. The only…"

He stopped and seemed to be considering carefully what he said.

"What is it?" I asked.

He shook his head and said, "How far would you go to help your family if they needed it?"

The seriousness in his voice scared me. There was something he wasn't telling me. I could sense it.

"I know how much you care about your family," I said.

"And you. I've grown to care about you, too. You know that, right?" he said, a desperation in his voice.

"Of course. I feel the same about you," I said, putting an arm around his shoulder.

"Sometimes when I can't sleep I think about that night we stood in front of the ocean," his voice said, drifting off into the memory. "The sound of the waves crashing drowned out everything behind us. The vastness of the ocean made everything feel full of possibilities even with the challenges we faced. I wish we could go back to that mo-ment…before all of *this*."

"One day we'll feel that again. I promise," I said, kissing his cheek.

He gave me a smile, but it was one that suggested he was just hu-moring my naïve comment.

"I hope so," he said finally, pulling me in for another deep kiss.

And, at least for a short period of time, we were able to lose our-selves in the moment and leave our seemingly impossible situation, the war, and Manzanar behind.

Later, I must have fallen asleep with Hiro holding me from behind as we lay on the sofa together. We could barely squeeze both of us onto the tiny space.

"Jack?" Hiro said in a half whisper.

"What? What time is it?" I said.

"We need to get back to our barracks," he said, letting me go and pulling himself up from the couch and reaching for his shirt.

I sat up and yawned.

"I wish we didn't have to go back. I don't want to leave you," I said desperately.

Hiro finished buttoning his shirt and knelt down beside the sofa.

"I'm so happy I got the chance to meet you, Jack," he said, before giving me one last kiss on the lips.

He then quickly got up and went to the door.

"Be careful going back," Hiro said, rushing out the door.

But I should be saying that to him, I thought.

"Hiro!" I called out, but he'd already left, and I felt a sudden pang of deep loss.

I had barely opened the door to my room before I heard Donald jumping off his bed and running toward me. He looked frantic and worried.

"Sanders has been by three times tonight looking for you. I had to tell him I thought you went to Lone Pine," he said, his tone rushed.

"Sanders?" I asked. "Why?"

"He got a call from your father back home," Donald answered.

My stomach twisted in knots. A call from my father in the middle of the night could not be good news.

"What is it? What happened? Is it my brother?"

"No," he answered, reaching out and putting a hand on my arm. "It's your mother."

"What? Why? What happened?" I said, feeling the beat of my heart going into overdrive.

"She's in the hospital. That's all I know. But your father said you needed to come home immediately," Donald answered, handing me a piece of paper with an address. "They're supposed to be at this hospital."

I quickly began to pack a small bag. It didn't matter if it was the middle of the night. My father was *not* an over-reactor. If he meant for me to come home now, I should listen.

Chapter Twelve

Sleep-deprived and bleary-eyed, I hopped out of my truck as soon as I arrived at the hospital parking lot. The morning sun was just beginning to shine brightly. I made my way up the sidewalk to the main entrance and immediately saw my father standing outside. He held a paper coffee cup in one hand and a cigarette in the other. I hadn't seen him smoke in a long time, ever since he started to complain about the price of a pack. He quit cold-turkey after announcing a pack just cost too damn much now.

When I was just a few feet away from him, he still hadn't noticed me, and I could tell even in the early morning light how haggard and stressed he looked.

"Father," I said.

We weren't exactly a touchy-feely type of family, and when most family members might hug during such a crisis, my father just nodded at me.

"Son," he said, taking a long drag off his cigarette.

I wondered if he'd purchased a pack or just bummed one off someone.

At closer look, I could see his eyes were bloodshot and deep, dark lines under his eyes practically dominated his face. I'd only been gone a short time, but he looked like he had aged a few years.

"How is she?" I asked, scared I might hear the worst.

He shifted his weight from one foot to the other and loudly exhaled a deep breath like he'd been holding it for way too long.

"The docs said it was a mild heart attack," he said.

A lump appeared in my throat.

"Heart attack?" I said, not sure I heard right.

Wasn't she too young for such a thing? And I thought they usually happened to men.

"How?" I asked. "Why? Is she going to be okay? Can I see her?"

Father held up a hand, and I knew I was rattling off too many questions at once when he looked so tired that he might collapse at any moment.

"She's going to be okay. The doc said so. She was sleeping finally when I came out here for a smoke," he said, in what I knew was his most assuring voice, the one he used to use when we were little and had cut or bruised ourselves. "He said it was probably stress related."

"Stress?" I said. "How bad has it been?"

"We haven't heard from Edward in weeks, and she's just petrified someone from the military is going to show up with bad news. The store hasn't been doing well. It feels like even the rich are holding on to their money during the war. Jane's been acting out in school, probably because of everything going on. She worries about you."

As soon as he said the last sentence, he immediately looked like he regretted it.

"We know you're doing okay. It's just the first time you've been so far from home."

Immediately, I felt pangs of conscience consume me. I left to go teach at Manzanar to get away from my life and to delay having to make any decisions in Los Angeles. I hadn't thought how my absence might add to my mother's stress level when she had so much else going on, too.

"I'd like to see her," I said.

Father dropped his cigarette on the ground and put it out with the sole of his shoe.

"Come on," he said. "I'll take you."

We entered through the double doors of the hospital front entrance. A middle-aged plump receptionist smiled at us as we walked inside.

"Did you need some help?" she asked, with a look that contained a mix of sympathy and patience.

"Thanks," Father said. "I know where we're going."

The receptionist nodded and looked back down at the book she was reading.

We began to make our way through an endless cavern of hallways, one after the next. I don't know how my father could remember where to go. Everything looked pretty much the same with each corner we turned, and the smell of bleach and antiseptic wafted through the air and almost burned my lungs.

As we walked by various rooms, doctors and nurses darted inside and out of them, and I could hear various patients' moans and pleas for help. All of this made me grow more and more anxious. Neither of my parents had ever so much as made a quick trip to an emergency room, much less actually get admitted to the hospital.

"Where is Jane?" I asked, knowing how especially frightened my little sister must have been at the moment.

"She's with your Aunt Carol," Father said. "She drove up in the middle of the night to stay with Jane. Try and spend some time with your sister while you're here, okay? I think it'd make her feel real happy."

"Of course," I said.

"When do you have to go back?" Father said, motioning to a room with an open door to let me know it was Mother's.

"When I told the principal, he told me to take whatever time I need. They're having such a hard time finding teachers they can't be too strict," I said.

"You can tell me more about it all later. For now, when you talk to your mother, remember *no stress*," he emphasized.

I almost told him that, of course, I knew that, but I reminded myself that he was exhausted and likely very shaken up. So I just nodded and braced myself.

"What medicine do they have her on?" I asked before we walked into the room.

"Just rest and some blood thinner. He said she was very lucky," Father said, his voice growing softer as we walked into the room.

When I walked in, I almost gasped in shock. She, too, appeared to have aged years in a matter of weeks. Her skin looked pale and as thin as onion paper. Her hair looked as if it had more gray than the last time I saw her. How could that be in such a short period of time? I couldn't wrap my head around it.

A sheet and blanket covered her almost completely except for her neck and head. Her eyes were closed, and she looked so odd sleeping like this as she never slept on her back but on her side.

"How long has she been asleep?" I whispered to my father.

But before he could answer, her eyes fluttered open and widened when she saw me.

"I am dying, aren't I?" she said in a raspy voice. "You called Jack to come home."

My father, much gentler than he normally was with her or anyone else, reached under the covers and took her hand into his.

"You're going to be just fine. But I knew Jack would want to be here. See. He's perfectly fine. Fit as a fiddle just like when he left," Father said, stroking her hand.

Mother pulled her other hand out from under the covers, waved me over to that side of the bed, and patted the edge. I walked over and perched myself on the fringe.

"How are you?" I said.

"Just very tired. But I hate being here. You know I hate hospitals. That's why I even had Jane at home," she said, her voice fading in and out.

"Go back to sleep," Father urged. "We're not going anywhere. You need your rest."

Not having the strength to answer vocally, she just nodded and closed her eyes.

Father put her hand under the blanket and motioned that we should go back outside.

"The doctor says the more sleep she gets the better," Father said once we were back in the hallway.

"Why don't you go home and get some rest? I'll stay here," I offered, but Father was already shaking his head no.

"No, no…" he said, his voice trailing off.

"I will call you if anything at all changes. Go home. Take a shower. Lie down for a bit. The more energy you have the better for her, too," I insisted.

He looked at me as if it were the first time he'd really *seen* me in a long time.

"When did you boys get all grown up? Edward at war. You off teaching hours away from home," he said. "It all went by so quick."

He startled me by reaching out and putting his hand on my shoulder.

"I know you hear your ma and me say all the time how fast time goes as you get older. You probably think we're just a couple of old fuddy-duddies, but it's true, son. Just remember that. Moments like this remind us just how real it is. Time just gets faster and faster until…well, you don't know where it went."

I nodded. I had never seen him look so emotional, even on the verge of crying. Not even at funerals had he looked so emotive. Yet standing in that hallway, under the buzz of the fluorescent lights, he looked positively lost. I thought about how he and my mother had rarely been apart since they had gotten married. I thought about Hiro and how much I wished I could have that type of life with him. If we were lucky enough to be able to continue being together, it would have to continue to be in the shadows, and we'd have to be highly selective of letting anyone at all know the nature of our relationship. But between the war, the camp, and our cultural differences, I felt lucky to have anything at all with him, and as sad and worried as my father was, I couldn't help but feel a little jealous of what he could publically have with my mother.

"Everything will be okay. You'll see. Go rest a bit. I'll be right by her bed in case she needs me. Promise," I said.

Father's shoulders slumped and his eyes grew heavy.

"Maybe just for a couple of hours and a shower," he said, slowly being talked into it.

"She'll be fine," I said.

"Okay," he said, taking a deep breath.

"Are you okay to drive? Should we ask to use the phone and call someone?"

He shook his head, "Nah, nah. I'll be okay. You just keep a close eye on her."

"I will, and I'll call home if anything happens."

He nodded and said, "Thank you."

"You don't need to thank me. Now go," I said.

Finally, he turned and started making his way back down the labyrinth of hallways.

I made my way back into Mother's room, and an older nurse with a kind, slightly wrinkled face and crisp white uniform followed me.

"Hopefully, she'll sleep for a bit. She needs it," the nurse said in a hushed tone as she looked my mother over.

"Is this common?" I asked. "You always hear of this happening to men and usually older ones."

The nurse looked at me sympathetically and said, "It's not common, but it most definitely can happen. She was lucky though. She stabilized quickly. What's most important is that we keep her calm and relaxed."

I nodded, and the nurse gave me one last smile and left.

I took the seat next to the bed, and I could sense my eyes growing heavy. I'd been up for over twenty-four hours by that point. I didn't know when it happened, but I must have nodded off. The next thing I knew someone was gently shaking me awake.

I popped my eyes open, and I had to blink a few times to make sure I saw correctly. Sally was kneeling on one knee and shaking my forearm.

"Hi," she said quietly. "I'm sorry to wake you. I just wanted to see if there was anything I could do."

She wore a matching red box coat and half hat that perfectly complemented her raven pin-curled hair. She gave me a warm smile and all of the anger that had been there since the last time we saw each other had disappeared.

"I hurried over just as soon as I heard. Your parents' neighbor called mine after she saw your father getting home this morning," she said.

"Thanks for coming," I said, and I meant it.

Seeing Sally with her friendly, good-natured personality automatically helped put me a little at ease. It had been one of the things I'd always liked about her the most. She almost always had a way of making me feel like things would work out somehow.

Mother, still asleep, began to stir in bed.

"Let's go out in the hall," I said.

I got up and had to stretch my bum leg, which was killing me, before following Sally out into the hallway. I glanced at my watch and saw it was past noon. The corridors of the hospital were in full swing now with even more doctors, nurses, and orderlies dashing here and there.

Leaning against the wall, I stretched out my leg as best I could.

"Hurting you?" Sally said, motioning toward it.

"Yeah. Still starts hurting if I don't move it after a bit," I said.

"How is she?" Sally asked, her voice full of concern.

My mother and Sally had gotten along from the get-go. They both loved to bake, talk about the latest fashions, even though my mother rarely bought anything, and enjoyed gardening. She'd started to look at Sally as another daughter and friend.

"Docs say she was lucky. We just need to keep her calm. All of this stress with everything happening. I don't know. Maybe if I hadn't gone off to teach," I said, regretting it as soon as I said it.

Sally looked down for a moment and acted as if she were checking her shoe, but I knew she didn't want to face me. After all, my heading to Manzanar was the straw that broke the camel's back for us.

"I'm sure she'll be fine," Sally said, looking back up at me.

I knew her well enough to know she was trying to keep her tone even and cool. I could see some of the pain and the hurt still in her eyes.

"Thanks for coming down here. It means a lot," I said, hesitating before adding, "So, how have you been?"

I knew it was an awkward question, but I cared about her still.

"Fine," she said. "You? How is the teaching going?"

"The students are good, but it truly is in the middle of nowhere," I said. "And you?"

"A little challenging at first," she said. "Can you believe I got accused of being too strict by the principal?"

I chuckled. "You? As easy-going as you are? I don't believe it!"

"Well, I guess I came on a little strong at first wanting to establish authority," she said, with a little laugh. "But then I had to remember that they are second graders."

She looked like she was going to say something else, but then she paused as if thinking better of it.

"What is it?" I asked. "You can say it. Whatever it is."

"It's just…" Sally said, fiddling with the handle of her purse. "Now's not the time. I just wanted to make sure you and your family were okay. I should let you rest."

I held out a hand and stopped her.

"Really, Sally. It's okay. Say what you would like. I know things didn't end too well between us, but I'd like to think we can still consider each other friends."

I didn't know how she'd react to "friends" and if she still harbored feelings for something more, but she visibly relaxed when I said it.

"It's just that you'll probably hear eventually, and I don't know. Somehow, I feel like it's still better if you hear it from me."

"I'm listening," I said, standing up straight.

"I've started seeing someone new. He's another teacher at the school and the football coach. He's a nice guy. I think it might *lead* somewhere. Or, to be honest, I'm hoping it does," she said shyly.

Even though I knew I had no right to feel anything but happiness for her, I couldn't help but feel a slight bit of sadness. Sally moving on with someone she could maybe actually have a future with, was another sign of something that would probably be unattainable for me at least in the conventional sense.

"I'm happy for you," I said finally. "You deserve to have a good guy and so much more, Sally. You were right to force things with us and cut things off. I wish…I wish I could explain it to you, but I'm not sure I could have ever been what you needed, what you deserved, I…" I started stammering.

"It's okay, Jack," she said. "I've come to terms with it, and I really do believe that things usually happen for the best even if they do hurt us at some point."

"Yeah," I said, agreeing. "I wish you nothing but the best."

"Well, I should be going," she said. "Please let me and my family know if we can do anything at all. I mean it. You know how fond I am of your mother."

I reached out and took her hand.

"I'm really happy to see you're doing so well. Take care," I said, giving her hand a squeeze.

There was so much I wished I could tell her at that moment to explain why I had done some of the things I had in our relationship, and that none of it had anything at all to do with her.

I must've had a look on my face that read as wanting to say more because she looked at me quizzically and said, "Are you all right, Jack?"

"Yeah. Just worried about Mother," I said.

"I can imagine," Sally replied. "I'll call your house later to see how she is."

"Thanks again."

She gave me a sympathetic smile and turned to walk away.

I stood and watched her make her way down the hallway. I felt a new sense of peace where Sally was concerned now. She would be okay. I hadn't permanently broken her as part of me feared deep down.

That night, Father went back to the hospital to stay with Mother who was expected to be released the next day.

At home, I looked after Jane once Aunt Carol had to head back to San Diego.

I had been gone such a short time, but Jane already appeared to have grown up a bit. As she sat at the kitchen table picking at the peanut butter and jelly sandwich I made her, I could see the worry and concern on her young face.

"Not hungry?" I asked, sipping on a cup of coffee, not having much of an appetite myself.

"What if it happens again?" Jane asked, looking up at me, tears in the corners of her eyes.

"What do you mean?" I asked.

"What if Mama gets sick again? Or what if it's worse next time?" she said, her voice cracking a little.

"She's going to be just fine," I said. "She just needs some rest. Try not to worry."

I knew not worrying was easier said than done, and it must have been especially hard for Jane. So much had changed for her in the past few months with Edward and me both leaving and now Mother having a heart attack.

She drank a little of her milk and then said, "I miss Edward. I miss *you*."

"I know, Monkey," I said, using the nickname I gave her as a toddler when she constantly tried to climb all over me while I tried to study. "I miss you, too. I promise I'll write you more, okay? And next time I'll bring you something back."

She nodded, but she didn't look very placated.

"What if Edward doesn't come back from the war?" she said.

"What do you mean? Of course he will. You know how big and strong Edward is. He'll be back and be just fine," I said, hoping she couldn't sense my own fears coming through in my voice.

"Jeanie Smith, in my grade, her brother, he didn't come back. Soldiers came to her mama's house to tell her. Jeanie didn't come back to school for a few days after that. I felt sad for her."

I swallowed hard, and said, "I hate to hear that."

How could I possibly explain to a little girl why mankind does things such as war when I couldn't understand it myself?

"But Edward is going to be okay," I replied.

"How do you know?" Jane countered in a hardened tone I had never heard from her before.

"Because I have to believe it," I said honestly. "And you do, too. Okay?"

She hesitated, but then she nodded.

"Why don't you go take your bath, and then I'll read to you some," I suggested.

"Alice in Wonderland?" she asked, sounding a little bit more like the young girl I knew.

"Anything you want," I said.

"Okay," she agreed, pushing the plate with her barely touched sandwich away from her.

She climbed down off her chair and headed to her bedroom without another word.

I hoped and prayed that she wouldn't have to experience what her classmate and so many other children would have to endure during the course of this war.

When Mother returned from the hospital, Father and I had to constantly run after her to make sure she didn't overexert herself. She had always had a tendency to sort of downplay anything wrong with her health. So when she tried to start cleaning and cooking as soon as she got home, Father snapped at her like I had never heard him before.

"What are you trying to do? End up back in the hospital? Give *me* a heart attack?" he barked from what I knew was lack of sleep the past few days. "You're going to *bed*."

"But I'm fine," Mother tried to insist, as Father practically dragged her back to the bedroom with Jane, still shook up from Mother's heart attack, on his heels.

"Please rest, Mama," she pleaded.

"All this fuss!" Mother tried to argue but the fight in her voice slowly drained away and fatigue set in again.

Once Father got her settled back into bed with Jane lying next to her and reading a book, he came back into the kitchen and began to heat up a day-old half pot of coffee in the percolator.

"You need to get some sleep, too," I suggested.

"I need to check on the store," Father said, slowly moving through the kitchen, half asleep.

"I can check on it for you," I said. "I'll stay as long as you need me to."

"I appreciate it, son. But I know you need to get back to work," he said, putting a teaspoon of sugar into a chipped mug with a Hawaiian scene painted on it, a gift from an uncle who took a cruise.

"I can call the principal and ask for more time off. He's a reasonably nice guy."

Father, who could be just as stubborn as Mother, shook his head.

"No, you need to get back to work. We'll be fine. I'll call you if I need you. I spoke to your Aunt Carol this morning, and she's going to come back tomorrow for a few days to keep an eye on your mother and Jane. But I appreciate you getting here so fast."

He motioned for me to sit down at the table.

"Coffee?" he offered.

"No, thanks. I think I've already had enough for a week in the past twenty-four hours," I said, sitting down.

He nodded.

"Tell me how you are. How is that…camp?" he asked.

I hesitated to answer and shifted uncomfortably in my seat. I knew how anti-Japanese the war had made my father. Could I possibly convey how what I'd seen impacted me in a way that would generate sympathy from him?

"It's strange," I finally said, fiddling with a paper napkin on the table and avoiding eye contact.

"How so?"

"It...well...it's not how they describe it in the papers, you know like some sort of nice community there for the protection of the Japanese-Americans. It's much closer to a prison and often feels like one with the barbed wire and the armed guards."

I studied his face, but I didn't pick up on any sort of emotional reaction from what I said.

"Well, that's just the way it needs to be," he said flatly. "We can't be too careful."

I wanted to disagree, to talk back and tell him how unjust it was, but I didn't want to get him riled up at that point. I also realized that sometimes you just had to accept that some people's minds might not ever change no matter what evidence was given to them to the contrary. To do so would force them to have to rethink not just that particular situation but how they viewed so many other things in the world. So many people lived in black and white with gray being downright scary for them. I understood because I might have been the same way if I had never met Hiro in Pershing Square. Why did it take us getting to know someone branded as *other* to view them with the humanity they deserved? Why was it so hard sometimes for people to be empathetic?

"How is the work?" he asked.

"Good. The students work hard for the most part. I try to...I guess engage them in class and maybe they can forget about where they are at least for a little bit. I want them to feel like they're just regular high school students, but there's only so much I can do I suppose."

He took another long sip of coffee, and I could tell the caffeine was taking effect as his eyes became a little more alert.

"You're a good man, Jack," he said.

Those five words hit my heart hard. My father had never said anything like that to me before. I had always assumed that on some level he blamed me for John's death and that my limp served as a reminder of the son who should have been there if not for me. He might have had a son who was more athletic, more rough and tumble like Edward, more well…a man by 1940s standards. Instead, he got me, a son who helped teach the enemy, let a good girl go, and seemed to be drifting without a clear path. Yet here he was telling me I was a good man.

"Thank you," I said, feeling my throat close up and tears stinging at the corners of my eyes. "That means a lot, Father."

Usually a man of few words when it came to emotions, he simply nodded, gave me a smile, and reached for the copy of yesterday's paper. Maybe he didn't understand why I did what I did in my life, but he was able to see past that to who I was as a whole.

The next day, I prepared to head back to Manzanar. Jane, wearing a long face, sat on the edge of my bed as she watched me pack up my final items.

"When will you be back?" she asked.

"Don't worry, Monkey," I said, reaching out and tousling her hair. "I'll be back one weekend soon. I promise. I'll bring you back a surprise like I said I would. I'm a working fella now so I can afford it."

She brightened up a bit as any child would at the thought of a present. The war had made my parents' finances much tighter and who knew how much the hospital bills would be. I made a vow to help out as much as I could.

Mother walked into the bedroom wearing her yellow housecoat. Her silver-streaked hair had simply been brushed back behind her ears. She still looked a little pale, but some of her sturdiness had started to make its way back in her demeanor.

"All packed up?" she asked.

"Yeah, I think that's it," I said zipping up the suitcase. "Are you sure I shouldn't stick around longer to help out?"

"You need to get back to your life. We'll be fine, won't we, Janie?" she said, gently pushing back some of my sister's hair with her hand.

Jane gave an unconvincing, "Yes."

"I heard Sally came by the hospital," Mother said.

I could pick up on the twinge of hope in her voice.

"She did," I said. "It was good seeing her."

"Maybe..." Mother started to say.

I cut her off and said, "She's dating someone new, the football coach where she teaches. I'm very happy for her."

Mother's shoulders slumped a bit and she sighed loudly.

"Well, she is a good catch. You can't expect her to stay available for long."

"I'm happy for her," I repeated, hoping to dispel any possible hopes of a reconciliation.

"Jack's going to bring me back a present next time he comes home!" Jane exclaimed.

"Is that right?" Mother said, smiling before turning back to me. "I finally got a letter from Edward today."

"How is he?" I said, my stomach knotting up as it always did when I thought of my brother and what he may be facing on the battlefield.

"He seems to be in good spirits," Mother said. She shook her head. "This war can't end fast enough."

"You promise to call me if you need anything?" I said.

"Yes, yes. Promise. Now all of you need to stop treating me like an invalid."

I walked over and gave her a peck on the cheek. The show of emotion looked to catch her off guard.

"Please promise me you'll take care of yourself," I pleaded.

"I will," she answered softly before play-slapping me on the arm.

As I made my way outside with Mother and Jane behind me, I found Father sitting outside on a stool and drinking yet another cup of coffee. I don't know how he managed to ever sleep with the amount of it he drank.

"Next time you come home we'll change the oil in that truck. You want to keep on top of the maintenance," he said, in the best way he knew how to show concern and affection.

"Yes, sir," I said. "I'll try and make it back in the next few weeks. There's not like there's much to do there on the weekend to begin with."

I secretly hoped that somehow I would get to spend some time with Hiro on those long days when school wasn't in session.

I knelt down and gave Jane a hug. She held me so tightly I wasn't sure she'd let me go, but finally she pulled away, looked at me, and said, "Remember my present."

I laughed and said, "Promise."

"Take care, son," Mother said.

"I will."

Father gave me a nod, and I made my way to the truck. I turned around and glanced at the three of them one last time.

There were so many unspoken words between all of us. So much was always left unsaid. Being with Hiro had awoken in me what it was like to truly share what you were feeling with someone else. A sadness came over me, and I wished I could be the same way with my family instead of everyone being so stoic, so afraid to really speak what was in our hearts.

Would that ever change?

Chapter Thirteen

I made it back to Manzanar just as school was letting out for the day. I saw the students pour out of the classroom area carrying their notebooks. We were already short on teachers, so I couldn't imagine whom the principal could have gotten to cover me for the time I was out. To keep my students on track, I knew we'd need to catch up from the missing past couple of days.

A wave of emotions came over me as I parked and looked at the barbed wire, guard-towered compound in which I worked and the person I had begun to care so much about...it was hard for me to say the word "loved"...was detained, to put it nicely. It would be hard to go back inside, but I knew the students needed me, and just the thought of getting to see Hiro for brief moments was enough to make me deal with the unsettledness of the place.

I got out of the truck, grabbed my bag, and headed for the barracks to unpack. Suddenly, I heard a female voice call out, "Mr. Henry!"

I turned and saw Lily on the other side of a fence.

"Hi!" I called back and walked over, surprised at her wanting to speak to me. "How has class gone the past couple of days?"

"I need to talk to you," she said, ignoring my question.

"About class?" I asked, noticing the edge in her voice.

"No," she said, shaking her head. "About Hiro."

From the look on her face and the tone of her voice, I got a sinking feeling in the pit of my stomach.

"Let me drop this off. I'll meet you outside the school," I said.

She nodded, and I rushed inside to drop off my bag.

Donald had just made it back to the room from work and had plopped down and stretched out on his bed which he tended to do right after the workday ended.

"Hey!" he said, sitting up. "How's your mother?"

"Doing better. Thanks," I said, dropping my bag on the bed. "I'll be right back. I need to see someone."

"Your special friend?" he asked with a wide grin.

"Something like that," I replied, before walking out.

As I walked toward the school, I saw Lily sitting on one of the steps leading to the classrooms. She had her schoolbooks on the ground next to her. She looked preoccupied studying a hangnail on her right hand as I observed her from a distance. Everything about her tense, antsy body language conveyed anxiety.

The closer I got to her, the more I began to dread what she had to say.

"Lily," I said, once I was just a few feet away.

Just now realizing I was there, her head jerked up, and she looked at me with a defeated expression.

"What's wrong?" I asked.

She dug into her schoolbag and pulled out an envelope with my name on it.

"I brought it with me in case you came back today. But then you weren't there again, but I saw you pull up into the parking lot," she said, sighing.

She held the envelope out toward me.

I took it from her, and I recognized Hiro's handwriting on the front of it. All that was written on it was "Jack."

"He's gone," Lily said, in a sad matter-of-fact, weary voice.

"What?" I said, shocked, my pulse quickening.

No. How could this be?

"He left last night. He made me promise to give that to you. I haven't read it. I swear."

She averted her gaze, and I wasn't sure whether to believe her or not.

"Why did he leave, Lily? *How* did he leave?" I asked, knowing Hiro simply couldn't have just decided to walk out of the wired enclosure.

"Lily! Are you coming?" a girl, maybe a year or two younger, called out a couple of buildings away.

"I have to leave," Lily said, grabbing her school materials and getting up. "I need to check on my mom, too. I'm the *one* that has to watch over her now."

She shielded her eyes from the glaring sun and looked in the direction of the girl who had called out.

"I'm coming!" she called back.

She started to walk away, but I grabbed her hand. She acted as if my touch sent a shock of electricity through her body and stumbled back a couple of steps.

"Lily, please! Tell me what happened. This doesn't make sense. Is Hiro in trouble?" I begged for more information.

She glanced back at the girl still waiting for her and turned back to me.

"He said he had to do something to help the family, to help maybe bring our father home, and to prove his patriotism," she answered. "He couldn't tell us exactly. And then, all of a sudden, he was escorted out and left."

I saw tears at the corners of her eyes, and she, embarrassed, turned away again.

"I have to go. Maybe your letter will tell you more. Maybe it will tell you more than he told *us*. I promised not to read it," she said with a harsh and bitter tone in her voice. "I guess I'll see you in class."

And with that she took off and headed into the direction of her friend.

I looked back down at the letter and at Hiro's neat cursive writing.

How could I have been gone just a few days right after we connected and now he was gone again? What could have happened to him? A wave of fear for him overwhelmed me. I had heard of people being sent to Japan even if they were US citizens and had never stepped foot on Japanese soil if they were deemed troublemakers. Had Hiro done something for the government to send him away? Did someone find out about us? Was that what was happening? But then no one had said anything to me about it.

There was an unusual number of staff and detainees milling about near the high school and some of the kids were in groups talking and horsing around. They were obviously in no hurry to get anywhere, but where would they go anyway but back to the tar barracks?

I knew I had to be alone and someplace quiet when I opened the letter, so I made my way to the Presbyterian church. When I walked inside, the cooler air greeted me and a mournful looking picture of Jesus looked down upon me from the altar. Luckily, no one else appeared to be around. I sat in a second row pew, took a deep breath, and opened the letter.

Dear Jack,

I'm hoping that Lily delivers this letter to you. Please excuse any hostility she may show towards you. There's so much she's confused and worried about these days, not just wondering how you fit into the equation of my life. She's worried we'll never see our father again. She's petrified that our mother sometimes appears to think that she's still in Los Angeles with her words and acts as if she's living in a completely different world from us. Yesterday, she told Lily to go next door to our neighbor's in Los Angeles and see if she could borrow a cup of sugar. It feels like our mother is slipping away from us inside this place and going to a world that only her eyes see. Lily also doesn't understand why I'm having to leave, and I can't explain it to her at this point...or to you.

I thought I would never see you again after those brief but wonderful moments we got to spend together in Los Angeles. I had never come across a man like you. Somehow with your kind eyes, tender touch, and caring heart you managed to bring about feelings in me I had only heard others talk about but had never experienced myself. When you ended up here in Manzanar and our paths crossed, I couldn't help but hope that maybe this was fate. Maybe despite all the odds against us getting to know more about each other, we were meant to somehow be together. That's why saying goodbye for now is so achingly hard.

I've been presented with an opportunity to help the United States during this time. I wish I could tell you more, but I am not really supposed to reveal details. Leaving you, Lily, and my mother hurts like hell. But it's been suggested that I may be able to help my family and ultimately my missing father by taking this next step. This is why I must leave.

Please know that you'll remain in my heart, and when this nightmare for all of us comes to an end, I hope that we get the chance to see each other again one day just so I may see that sweet, caring smile of yours again. Even though my heart is broken, I would rather it have its cracks than to have never known you.

Hiro

Stinging tears streamed down my cheeks as I finished the letter.

Right when I thought I'd probably never see him again, he had, just as surprisingly as the first time, appeared in my life. And just as quick as it was the first time, he was gone.

When I finally made it back to the barracks, I found Donald sitting at his desk grading papers.

"I've been worried about you," he said, his voice full of concern.

"I'm okay," I said, sitting on the bed.

Donald turned his chair around to face me.

"Then why do you look like you just lost your best friend?" he asked. "What happened?"

I glimpsed down at the envelope in my hand, and I surprised myself by handing it to Donald. My hurt so overwhelmed me at that moment that I very much needed a friend and someone who might just understand what I was going through.

"Do you want me to read it?" Donald asked, double-checking.

I nodded, and then buried my face in my hands for a moment. I could hear Donald opening the envelope and unfolding the letter within. There was a minute or so of quietness as I tried to steady my breath and ward off the tears that threatened to pour out of me at any moment.

"Oh, my God," Donald said.

I looked back up at him, and he, too, looked on the verge of tears.

"I'm so, so sorry, Jack. This is so sad," he said, in a comforting voice I'd never heard from him before. "You two really cared about each other."

"Yeah," I said. "I know we didn't have much time together, but what I felt for him was unlike anything I've ever experienced. First I'm scared to death I might lose my mother and now this."

Donald surprised me by getting up, sitting next to me on the bed, and giving me a hug.

"I wish I could say something that would make this better," he said.

"It is what it is," I said, taking a deep breath.

"At least…" Donald said, his voice trailing off for a moment. "You had this with someone. That's something to always treasure. And, who knows? You managed to find each other again here. Who's to say it won't happen again?"

I nodded, but could I really be blessed enough for him to enter my life a third time?

That night around ten, when most staff and internees had retired to the bunks, I told Donald I needed to get out of the barracks for a bit, and I walked to the garden that I had helped Hiro and his friends with the few days prior. The tiny pond had been expanded with the holes we had dug and the rocks had been positioned to lead to a new bench under a lone tree big enough for shade. I sat down and took all of it in. At that moment, under the twinkles of the night stars and the sounds of insects humming their songs, everything felt at peace.

I wondered where Hiro was at that moment. What was he doing that he thought would help perhaps save his family? I pondered over how I could have been so lucky to find him only to have him taken away twice almost as quickly. Then I found myself feeling fortunate that I had gotten to help a tiny bit in the building of this space that managed to be serene even behind the wire. Maybe the garden would provide others with some moments of tranquility that would ease their hearts, at least temporarily, on being sent to this place simply because of who they were and what they couldn't change.

Under the moonlight, I saw a black-tailed jackrabbit hop in front of me a few yards away. The hare paused for a moment to stare at me, too. The animal looked in the direction of the staff barracks and then turned back to me for a moment before hopping away as if to say, "It's time to go back now."

Chapter Fourteen

The next few weeks found me just going through the motions of what I needed to get done during the day. I planned my lessons, gave my lectures and exams in class, and attended all of my faculty meetings. However, I knew I had lost some of the pep that I'd displayed that first week in class, and the sometimes bored or wandering looks of my students confirmed the fact.

Donald tried to lift my spirits by arranging some outings for hiking and dinners outside the camp with some of the other staff and asking me if I wanted to talk. But I just didn't want to do much of anything. I felt like a vise took hold of my heart.

Lily appeared listless in class, and my worry for her grew. I could only imagine what she was going through with both her father and brother missing now. Hiro's comments on his mother's mental state was another concern.

One day after class I asked Lily to stay behind for a few minutes with the excuse that I wanted to talk about her essay.

Once all of the other students had left, I motioned for her to sit down.

"Are you okay?" I asked her.

"What do you care?" she retorted, not bothering to hide her animosity at all.

The day after reading the letter I told shared with Lily that it hadn't provided any additional information on where Hiro went, but I wasn't sure she trusted what I told her.

I wondered if she blamed me for Hiro's leaving or if I just provided an outlet for her frustration.

"I'm worried about you," I said.

"You just want to know about my brother," she said, staring down at her notebook and tearing off tiny bits of paper.

"I care about your brother," I said, before adding, "A lot."

She raised her eyebrows at that comment.

"And because I care about him, I care about you. I know how much he loves you," I said.

"I don't know anything about where he is or what he's doing. All I know is that he left me here to deal with our mother by myself. Every day she's getting worse."

"Have you talked to one of the doctors at the hospital?" I asked.

She stared at me like I had gone mad and said, "I can't tell anyone that's she's not making sense when she speaks or that she seems to think we're back in our home in LA at times waiting for my father to come home from work at the restaurant. If I tell them, what if they take her away, too?"

Panic set in her voice.

"But if she needs help…"

"No!" Lily yelled. "This is none of your business! I should have never given you that letter, either! You didn't deserve it!"

She jumped out of her seat, grabbed her books and ran out of the room.

"Lily!" I called after her, but I already heard the door leading out of the school slam shut.

I so badly wished I could have done something, anything to make her feel better. I knew Hiro would have liked that, but I had no idea of what it could be.

That day happened to be a Friday, and I had promised my mother that I would visit that weekend. I had packed my bags the night before but I almost forgot the card game and penny candy I'd bought for Jane from the drug store in Lone Pine. I would have never heard the end of it if I had returned without my promised present. I stuffed the presents in my bag and looked over at Donald who was reading an old issue of a movie magazine.

"You're going to miss the big party Dottie's throwing in her room tomorrow," Donald said, just a bit sarcastically. We were all getting a little restless spending time with the same people over and over as if we were stuck on a ship far out in the ocean. "She's baking cookies! She talked the kitchen staff into letting her use the space."

"Hate to miss it," I said dryly. "Why don't you visit your family one weekend?"

He chuckled, but it wasn't a happy laugh.

"I think they're just fine without a visit from me," he said.

Over the course of the now couple of months we had shared living space, Donald had spoken very little about his family. Although, he'd excitedly tell me stories about secret bars where men like us could meet in Los Angeles. He still promised to take me to one as soon as we were both back in town.

"Why don't you come down to LA one weekend with me?" I offered. "You can meet the family and then we can visit one of those notorious haunts you've been talking about."

He put his magazine down and perked up a bit, "Really?"

"Yeah, why not?" I said.

"Maybe next time then," he said, sounding a little cheerier.

In those first few days we'd known each other, I had done my best to keep Donald at a distance, and I never would have dreamed we'd end up becoming friends. His demeanor scared me a bit, and I worried it would somehow reveal my own truth. But after losing Hiro again, I realized how much my newfound friendship was to me. In a way, Donald already knew me better than anyone else ever had.

As soon as I pulled the truck up into my parents' driveway, Jane came skipping out of the house to greet me.

"What are you still doing up?" I asked as soon as I stepped out of the truck since it was past nine o'clock.

"There's no school tomorrow, silly!' she said, wrapping her arms around me and giving me a big hug. "Did you bring my present?"

"Yes! Yes!" I said, laughing. "Give me a moment to get inside and unpack. Then I'll give it to you."

"Howdy!" I looked across the yard and saw my father stepping out of the house. "We were wondering when you'd get here."

I headed towards the house carrying my suitcase.

"Where's Mother?" I asked.

She had always been the first one to greet anyone.

I saw a twitch in my father's eye at the question.

I glanced down at Jane and could see the worry on her young face. I looked back up at my father.

"Come on in. We've got some fried chicken your Aunt Carol dropped off," he said.

Aunt Carol. Not my mother.

What had happened now?

"She's sleeping. Let her rest," Father said, when I stopped in front of their bedroom door after dropping off my bag in my room and giving Jane her gift.

"She's asleep?" I asked, surprised.

He raked a hand through his hair, shaggier than the last time I saw him.

"Where's your sister?" he asked me.

"She's in her room," I answered.

"Let's go eat," he said, heading down the hall to the kitchen.

I followed behind him.

On the table sat a platter of my aunt's fried chicken, sliced bread, and a bowl of green beans.

"Iced tea?" Father offered, as I sat down.

"No thanks," I answered. "I'll get some water in a minute."

He nodded, and poured himself a glass from a pitcher on the table.

"Hungry?" he asked.

I was, but much more than that, I needed to know what was happening.

"Why is Mother in bed? She's never asleep at this hour. Tell me what's happening," I said, in a hushed tone so Jane wouldn't hear.

Father sat down, grabbed a drumstick off the platter, and set it on a plate.

"We had another scare," Father said finally. "We had to go back to the hospital."

"What? Why didn't you call me?"

"She was fine. The doctor sent us home soon after. I didn't want to worry you."

"Father, you should have told me. What did the doctor say?"

"He says she needs to rest and not work for a while. He gave her something to rest which is why she's sleeping now," he said, taking a bite of chicken and chewing methodically.

"How long will she need?" I asked.

"I don't know. It could be a while. The important thing is that we keep her as stress-free as possible, but I know she's worried about Edward, maybe to the point of making her sick."

"How are you going to handle everything? Taking care of the store and Jane?" I asked.

"We'll figure it out. We always do," Father answered, trying to sound confident, but I could hear the cracks, the doubts in his voice.

Out of the corner of my eye, I could see Jane, clutching her favorite stuffed bear from when she was younger, and standing in the hallway listening in on our conversation. She looked lost and worried, and I could see all the stress that was weighing down her young mind.

That's when I knew what I had to do. As brave of a face as Father was trying to put on, I could easily see the worry in his eyes. I would have to leave Manzanar, put my teaching career on hold, and come home to help out my family. Even though I had left to put some distance between me and them to try to figure things out, my love for them was bringing me back to the place that not that long ago I had run away from.

Chapter Fifteen- April 2004

"Wait!' Tate exclaimed, as we made our way down 395-South, close to Death Valley and nearing the Manzanar site. "That was it? Did you go back to Manzanar at all?"

I set my now empty thermos of coffee on the floorboard and turned to my great-nephew.

"Just for a day. I had to tell my principal I needed to return to help out my family and pack up the few things I had there. It was sad because I had grown to care for my students and their education. Going to school was one of the few "normal" things they had to do in their teenage lives. And part of me wished I could keep an eye on Lily to help in some way. Although I'm not sure how I could have done so, but I wished I could have tried. But your great-grandparents needed my help. There's no way my father could have taken care of Jane, my mother, and the store by himself. I didn't go back to teaching until I moved to San Francisco and your great-grandparents sold the jewelry store and retired in Arizona."

Tate nodded solemnly and then asked, "What about Hiro? Did you hear from him again?"

"No. Never. I don't know where he was sent or what happened to him or if he survived the war," I said, looking down at the crisscross of deep blue veins on my hands.

"That's so....sad," Tate said, after a few moments.

"That's life sometimes, kid," I replied.

"Did you try to find him?" Tate asked.

"It's not like today. You kids can just look someone up on your computers. Back then, it was much easier to lose track of people and never know what became of them. I did hear from Donald about a year after I returned to Los Angeles. He's the reason I made it up to San Francisco!"

"How the hell did that work out?" Tate asked, passing a worn-out Cadillac that sputtered down the highway.

"He ended up moving there after finishing a year at Manzanar. Turns out that San Francisco was where the military was processing and releasing all the men they determined to be "sexual deviants" aka gay. That's how San Francisco ended up becoming sort of the gay mother-land, all thanks to the US military."

"Seriously? I didn't know that either," Tate said, his eyes widening.

"I'm a wealth of information, my child," I said, with a wink. "You don't get to eighty-five without knowing some stuff. Anyway, I had given Donald my mailing address when I last saw him, and he wrote me a letter right around the time my parents were getting ready to sell our store. The letter said that San Francisco had a lot of what he called "our friends" now. I knew what the coded language meant. He offered me to stay with him if I ever wanted to move up. So we ended up becoming roommates for about a year and remained friends until he died…well, about ten years ago. Funny to think how I tried to avoid him at first, and he ended up being my longest friend."

You don't get to be my age and not lose a lot of loved ones, friends, and family. Even though the hurt never goes away, you learn to accept it begrudgingly, I thought.

"After everything you described, why did you really want to come here today?" Tate asked, his voice very serious.

I saw a sign for Independence, California, and I knew we were very close now. After so many years, so many decades, it was hard to believe I was returning.

"I've thought of Manzanar often even though I was only there a few months and some of the internees were there for years," I told Tate. "But I often wondered how my students there fared. Were they able to overcome the hardships our government had foisted upon them? And I thought of Hiro and his desperation to help his family. Did he do what he set out to do? Has he thought of me over the years? Did he even survive the war?

"When I read in the newspaper about the opening of the Interpretive Center museum at the old Manzanar site, I knew I had to visit and even if the chances were slim, I still needed to go. This place and my time there had always haunted me. It was the place that stole what little innocence I had left at that age. It showed me first-hand what normally good-hearted people can do when they let fear overwhelm them. Of course, my brother Edward, who fought many battles across Europe before returning home to us, had it even worse. He never spoke of his time during the war, but would always get a far-off look in his eyes if someone brought the topic up. You knew he was remembering harrowing sights and sounds that could never be erased in his mind."

"I remember meeting Uncle Edward just a few times before he died," Tate said. "I think the last time was at my grandmother's sixtieth birthday party. He always struck me as a quiet man."

"He was always reserved, humble. We didn't always agree or even get along, but I always respected him for the hard worker and provider he was for his family," I said, also remembering how grateful we'd been when he returned home from the war alive and physically well. Not all of Edward's friends had been so lucky.

"Do you think of Hiro a lot?" Tate asked, obviously moved by my long tale during our car ride.

"I do. You never forget your first intense crush…or love," I said.

Tate grew quiet for a moment, and then he asked in a soft voice, "What if Connor was my first love and I let him go too easily?"

"Then, if you think so, you shouldn't keep letting time pass by. You might need to slow down a bit to let love properly develop. You know, maybe really give Connor or one of these boys you meet a true second glance and see what can happen."

Tate shook his head, stared ahead at the road, and said, "Guys in San Francisco only want one thing."

I could hear a bit of hurt in his voice, and I knew there were probably stories of heartbreak he hadn't shared.

"As long as you believe that, those are the only guys you'll meet. Take it from me. I've been there and done that, as they say."

All of a sudden, I saw the reconstruction of one of the guard towers and a parking lot full of cars. I recognized what I read to be the old high school auditorium that was built after I left. It now served as the new Interpretive Center.

My heart quickened.

"We're here," I uttered.

"Yeah, I see that. It popped up out of nowhere," Tate said, slowing down to pull into the parking lot.

I could feel my stomach twisting.

What if I found out something I didn't want to know during this visit? It was this fear that had probably kept me from searching for more information earlier. But now in the twilight of my life, I knew I couldn't wait any longer, and fear was a weak excuse for possibly discovering the truth.

After driving around for a bit, we finally found a parking space. The grounds were packed with cars with license plates not only from California but neighboring states as well.

"Are you ready?" Tate asked.

Am I? Can I face so many memories or people I have seen wronged for no reason beyond their ancestry?

I nodded and said, "Yep. Ready."

"I'll help you out," Tate said, hopping out of the car and running around to open my door.

After such a long ride, my bad leg didn't want to move, and I started to try to pick it up and move it with my hands.

"Wait, Uncle Jack. Let me help you," he said tenderly.

And he reached into the car and helped me get my leg moving.

I noticed a change in him after hearing my story. His day had changed from just driving me to some far-off museum to driving us to a place that impacted so many innocent lives. I think he also saw in me the young man I used to be and was reminded on how far our community had come since I was his age. I could see the emotion on his face and a new level of respect. It wasn't that Tate was ever disrespectful to me. In fact, he'd been an amazing great-nephew, but in his eyes, I could see he'd been changed by my story. I knew I had planted the seeds for many new thoughts and reflections on the past.

Once we were out of the car, he took my arm and said, "Lean on me. We'll get there."

"Thank you, young sir," I said, and he smiled.

We made our way through the parking lot and crowds and toward the Interpretive Center. It warmed my heart to see so many people of all ages and backgrounds there for this occasion. Every time I saw a Japanese-American my age I wondered if they had been in one of my classes or had they lived there during my brief stay. I saw young people, teens and children, there with their families, and it gave me hope that they might be the start of a new generation that would never allow this to happen to any other group of people. Awareness is usually half the fight, I've learned.

I thought of Donald and how amazed he would have been at this moment to see so many people returning to pay respect to the past and what these people endured. He stayed at Manzanar much longer and had been there during what was called the Manzanar Riots in December 1942 when internees protested the arrest of a Manzanar kitchen union leader for the beating of another internee. Two internees were killed by the guards during the riots, and many more were injured during a protest. Years later, he told me he almost left after the riots, but he had become so fond of his students that he returned when the schools were permitted to reopen months later.

Tate opened the door of the Interpretive Center for me. When we walked in I saw park rangers answering questions from the guests and a small bookstore.

"Welcome," a young Asian woman with a bright smile greeted us as we walked inside. She wore a name tag that said, "Volunteer - Anne."

"Thank you," I said.

She handed us a pamphlet that featured the exhibits and a map of the camp as it had been during the 1940s.

"We're screening a film in one of the theaters in the next ten minutes," she told us. "Please be sure to ask us if you have any questions. This evening we'll be hosting a Manzanar After Dark program. Former internees will be there to share their story."

"In person?" I asked.

"Yes. It will be a very moving evening," she told us.

"Thanks," Tate said, helping lead me through the thick crowd that had gathered in the gift and bookstore area.

"Did you want to see the film?" Tate asked.

I turned to the right and saw a huge reproduction of a sign that read, "Japs Keep Moving! This Is A White Man's Neighborhood!"

"In a moment," I told Tate.

I immediately found myself gravitating toward the exhibits. I could see a reproduction of one of the barracks, samples of ID tags that were actually attached to people before they got on the trains, and a wall with thousands of names on it of those interned at Manzanar.

"You okay, Uncle Jack? Do you need some water?" Tate asked.

"I'm fine," I muttered, making my way to the wall of names.

I wondered if *his* could be there.

Tate was right behind me as I maneuvered myself around some small children to the wall of names.

"I have to see," I told Tate.

He nodded and I knew he understood.

I began to scan the names until I came across the two that stood out to me personally.

Hiro Narita.

Lily Narita.

I reached out and ran my fingers over the engraved letters, and before I knew it I began to cry.

"Uncle Jack!" Tate said, putting a protective arm around me. "Are you okay?"

I hadn't been prepared for this moment and what seeing those names would mean to me. All that suffering and injustice that I saw, and all I did, for the most part, was watch, as many others had. What if we, the non-Japanese-Americans, had stood up for our fellow citizens? Could this blight on our history have been avoided? Why did it take retrospect to get us to really look at our supposed morals and sense of humanity?

Out of the corner of my eye I could see some of the other people sneaking glances at me, the old man sobbing. I'm sure some might have wondered why I cried so. After all, I didn't have the face of someone who probably looked like they should be this upset. Within the confines of the camp, I was part of the privileged ones. But what I saw others going through during my brief time there had haunted me all these years later. I had watched it, but I knew I would never be able to fully understand how the experience had truly impacted Hiro, Lily, their family, and all the rest of the internees.

I sucked in a breath and tried to regain my composure.

"I'm sorry," I managed to say, more to the names on the wall than to Tate.

"Don't be sorry," Tate said, and I could see the concern in his eyes. He looked lost, as if he didn't exactly know how to handle me at the moment. "Do you want to sit down?"

"No, no," I said. "Let's keep looking around."

I removed my glasses and wiped my eyes with the sleeve of my shirt.

Tate nodded and took my arm, and began to lead me to a re-creation of the inside of one of the barracks. I saw the metal cot with the rough straw mattress and the small desk cobbled together from what looked like leftover wood pieces. I never saw the inside of one of the barracks of the internees, and now for the first time, I saw the true bare starkness people had to live with. It wasn't much better than camping. I remembered the relentless wind and dust and realized how hellish it must he been living in these barracks with all the cracks and crevices in the wood.

"I never knew it was this bad inside where they lived. Not even Hiro told me," I said.

"It's hard to believe," was all that Tate could manage to say.

I could tell that the combination of my stories and now seeing the recreations had really shook him up.

"This happened in America," he said, but it was perhaps more of a question than a statement.

"Yes. Fear will drive people to do all sorts of illogical things," I replied.

I looked down at the map of the park and saw that the locations of the old gardens had been marked, and I was able to locate the one I had briefly helped Hiro and his friends with that day.

"I know where I want to go next," I told Tate.

We went back outside and used the map to guide us to the remains of the garden I had played a small part in building. Many of the rock formations and indentions of where the ponds had been remained.

"What was this place?" Tate asked.

"A place of hope," I answered simply, before adding, "I want to go tonight and hear the stories of those that lived it."

Later that evening, in the VFW hall, a few miles away, we joined a crowd of others to hear first-hand stories of those who had called Manzanar home, not by choice but by political decree.

I looked a couple of rows up, and saw a very regal looking Asian woman around my age stand up. Something about her struck me immediately. There was a familiarity about her that I couldn't quite put my finger on. Her still mostly dark hair had been swept up with an elaborate studded hair pin. She wore a bright flowered printed dress, and even from a few yards away I could see her makeup was flawless and included ruby-red lips.

Tate must have noticed because he put a hand on my arm and said, "What is it, Uncle Jack?"

"I…uh…" I stammered.

I couldn't take my eyes off her. She popped out to me in this sea of people.

Then, she turned to the right. I had to squint, but I saw it, the beauty mark on her right cheek.

Lily. Could it really be?

I blinked to make sure I was seeing right. Of course she had aged just as I had. And even though she seemed so young back then she must've only been six or seven years younger than me.

She started to make her way to the back where a table had been set up with coffee and water.

I turned to Tate and whispered, "I'll be right back."

He cocked his eyebrow, and I could tell he was worried if he should let me go off on my own.

"I'll be fine," I insisted. "Promise."

He hesitated but eventually nodded.

I got up from my seat and made my way to the aisle and headed to the back of the room. The woman, who I thought might be Lily, was adding sugar to a Styrofoam cup of coffee.

Suddenly, I could feel my nerves. What would I say to her if she was Lily? Would I after all this time find out what happened to Hiro? So many times over the years, I had wondered if I would somehow ever find out his fate.

The woman turned around to head back to her seat when I approached her.

"Excuse me," I said.

She stopped and looked at me with a curious stare.

"Yes?" she said, eyeing me curiously.

"Are you Lily Narita?" I asked.

She smiled slightly and answered, "Yes. Well, I was. It's been Lily Sato for a very long time now."

My heart leapt at her answer, and in her eyes, I could tell she was trying to place me after many decades.

"And you are?" she asked.

"My name is Jack Hen…"

"Jack Henry!" she interrupted. "You were my teacher and my brother's friend, weren't you?"

"Yes," I said, a lump in my throat. "I know I've changed a lot…obviously."

She chuckled and said, "As we all have. But I see it now. I see it in your eyes. You always had such kind eyes."

"Thank you," I replied, and I could feel the tears stinging at the edges of my eyes again. "I wasn't sure, but I thought it may be you."

Out of the corner of my eye, I could see Tate looking back and watching us to make sure I looked okay.

"I'm afraid I wasn't the best student back then," she said, with a kind laugh.

"You were going through some incredibly hard times. I'm sure I could have been a much better teacher," I said.

Her eyes continued to search mine.

"You want to know about my brother, don't you?" she said. "You want to know about Hiro."

Just hearing her say his name after all these years overwhelmed me so that a few tears escaped and rolled down my cheeks.

"Oh," she said, struck by the sudden show of my emotions. She reached out and took my hand. "Why don't we step outside for a few minutes?"

"Of course," I replied.

"Let me just go tell my husband, Nathan," she said.

"I'll wait here," I said.

She worked her way back to the crowd, and I waved at a worried Tate to let him know all was okay.

When Lily came back, she directed me to the exit.

"Let's get some air, shall we?" she said, in a very sweet tone.

"Yes," was all I could manage to say.

When we walked outside, the air had cooled considerably and the night sky was illuminated by countless stars that I could never see with the city lights of San Francisco.

She gestured to a bench, and we sat next to each other.

"Well, after all this time," she said. "It all feels so long ago, but being back here it also makes it feel just like yesterday. I remember so much of it clearly each time I come back here. Just the feel of the sharp winds takes me back."

"I can imagine," I said.

"The first time my husband wasn't so sure we should come back here," she said, taking a sip of her coffee. "He was here, too. He was a few years older than me. He worked in one of the kitchens at the time. You might think we would talk about our time at Manzanar with each other, but...." She shook her head. "There were so many bad memories here for both of us. He was the best thing to come out of all that for me, my silver lining if you will. After we got married, we ended up owning a restaurant for years just as my parents had."

"Where?" I asked.

"In San Francisco," she answered.

"San Francisco?" I said in awe. "I've been living there since the fifties!"

"What a small world it is!" she said. "Our restaurant was right on Post Street and near Fillmore. We sold it and retired about twenty years ago."

I marveled at how close we had been living to each other.

"I taught in San Francisco for years before retiring," I said.

"So, you stayed a teacher?"

"Yes," I said, pausing for a moment before working up the courage to ask, "What about Hiro?"

She smiled at his name.

"He was such a good man," she said.

Was?

"He passed away just last year," she said.

My heart sank and my shoulders lowered. At our ages, this was always a distinct possibility, but seeing Lily here had filled me with a surge of hope that I might see him again.

"I...I'm sorry," I managed to say.

"I'm sorry, too," she said. "I know you were probably hoping not to hear that."

I nodded.

"After the war, he ended up living on the East Coast in New York. He ended up teaching Japanese at a college there. He had a partner, Hiraku. They met when both were in the MIS."

"The MIS?" I asked.

"I'm sorry," she quickly added. "I forgot you probably don't know where he disappeared to while we were here."

"Please tell me," I pleaded. "For so long now, I've wondered what happened to your brother. He meant a great deal to me. He was my first..."

"Love," she finished. "I guessed as much. Back then, well, as you know very well, things weren't so open, and our Japanese community was so conservative, and still is in many ways. I was very confused by my brother's life back then. I know I took some of that out on you. I'm sorry for that."

"Please, don't apologize. You were just a teenaged girl, and it was a different time."

"Well, I did eventually accept my brother for who he was much later in life. I wish I had much earlier though. But it took me some time to fully accept him. In the end, I was actually very close to his partner, Hiraku. He passed a few years before Hiro," she said, her eyes lighting up. "Ah, yes. The MIS. The Military Intelligence Service. It was a special military unit of linguists during the war. Almost all were *Nisei*, second generation Japanese, who worked as translators for the US military."

"Hiro studied linguistics," I said, more stories of the past slowly coming together for me.

"Exactly, and he was recruited straight from Manzanar. Since it was a secret branch of the military at the time, he wasn't able to give us much information. They sent him to training at Camp Ritchie in Pennsylvania. It was all hush-hush then. But they ended up being one of the most decorated units in American military history. I remember the morning he left."

The morning after our last night together, I remembered.

"He told me he was doing something to possibly help our father make his way back to us. By proving his patriotism to the United States, he hoped to reunite our family. At the time, I was extremely angry with him for leaving me alone with our mother, who wasn't doing very well herself. But later, as an adult, I understood what he did and the sacrifice he made. Unfortunately, our father had a stroke and died and never returned to us. The US held him at the Tule Lake camp supposedly because they thought he had spy connections through my uncle who still lived in Japan and was a part of the Japanese army. Our father was never charged or convicted of a crime during his time there, and he died there."

Lily was now the one wiping away tears.

So much pain, so much heartache for these people, I thought. Yet, so many of them had still managed to work hard and pull their lives back together.

"Hiro's hope to serve and help our father return home never materialized. Although, he remained quite proud of his military service. It also brought Hiraku in his life, too."

My heart brimmed with sadness now that I knew that I would never get the chance to tell Hiro how much he meant to me. It had been him that first got me to open my heart to another person. But how lucky I felt at finding and getting to speak with Lily.

The door opened, and a young man wearing wire-rimmed glasses poked his head out.

"Lily Sato? You're next," he said.

"Thank you. I'll be right there," she told him.

The young man smiled and went back inside.

"I'm supposed to speak," she said.

"Oh, sorry," I said. "I didn't mean to keep you."

"No problem at all. In fact…" She paused, opened her purse and dug around for something.

She handed me a card, and I saw it had her name and phone number on it.

"I think I may have something for you," Lily said

"For me?" I said, a little taken aback.

"Yes," she answered. "Call me next week if you have time. I'd love to have you over for tea, and then I can show you what I'm talking about."

I ran my fingers over the raised letters and numbers on the card. I still couldn't believe I had found Hiro, sort of, after all of these years.

"I'll do that," I said.

She stood up and held out her hand which I shook.

"It was nice seeing you, Jack. I look forward to getting the chance to speak more."

"Thank you, Lily," I said, squeezing her hand. "You have no idea what this means to me."

She smiled and said, "We'll talk soon."

As she walked back inside, Tate walked out.

"I'm sorry. I just had to check on you," he said, sounding like a worried mother.

"Have a seat," I said, patting the other side of the bench. "You'll never guess who that was."

"Who?" Tate asked, his curiosity piqued.

"Lily, Hiro's sister," I answered.

His eyes widened, "Seriously? Oh, my God! Where is he?"

"Well," my voice quietened. "He's already passed."

Tate's face fell and he sucked in a breath.

"Uncle Jack," he said. "I'm so sorry."

"Thanks, but I knew it could be a possibility at our ages," I said, taking a deep breath and looking up at that vast open Manzanar night sky. "But I still had hope."

"Were you able to find out why he left and what happened though?" Tate asked hopefully.

"Yes, and I'll give you the details later. The important thing is that it sounds like he was happy at the end and had someone that loved him, just like I had my Howard."

Tate let out a sigh of relief and said, "I'm glad to hear it."

"Me, too," I answered, feeling slightly overwhelmed with so many emotions. "But I want to go hear Lily speak now while I have the chance. Let's go back inside."

"Are you sure you're okay?" Tate said, hesitantly.

"With you here to support me, yes," I said.

Tate's face brightened, and we both stood up to head back.

I heard Tate's cell phone make that vibration sound. He took it out and read one of those text messages. I knew instantly from the widening of his eyes who had sent the message.

"It's from *him*. It's Connor," I said.

"Yeah," Tate said, stuffing the phone back into his pocket.

"You're not going to respond?" I asked.

"Maybe later. I want to go back in with you. That's what's important now."

"Sure?"

"Positive," Tate said, clearing his throat.

"If you say so," I replied, even though I could tell from the look on his face that part of him wanted to reply.

What was it with young people? Why did they think they had forever to reveal their true emotions? If I looked back on my life, I can remember so many times life would have been much easier if I had just said what I felt and did what I truly wanted. Time, as always, was the greatest teacher, but why did she often show up late for class?

When we walked back inside, we grabbed the closest available seats in the back. Lily was at the front and holding a microphone. Next to her stood a woman maybe thirty-five years her junior. Obviously, she had to be Lily's daughter. They both had the same high cheek bones and height, and even from this distance, I could see she had the same sparkling dark eyes as her mother. She looked so much like I remembered Lily from when she was in high school. The resemblance was uncanny.

"My very first night in the camp," Lily began.

She paused, and I could tell she was getting emotional due to the memories that must have been flooding her mind. She took in a deep breath and continued.

"I woke up in the middle of the night after a fitful bit of sleep under the scratchy wool blanket on a lumpy Army cot. Besides my mother and brother, we shared an area with a married couple with three children. We hadn't met this other family before moving into the barracks, and the stress of leaving our home and now sleeping next to strangers with zero privacy I think made it even harder."

She stopped and gazed upward for a second. Her daughter, who looked to be holding back her own tears, put an arm around her mother's waist which seemed to give Lily the strength to continue.

"There was just so much that happened so fast. None of us had time to really process it, and in front of strangers, I think we had an even more difficult situation since we couldn't discuss things within the family privately. My father had been arrested and accused of being a spy weeks before, even though he'd never be formally charged."

In the short amount of time Hiro and I both lived at Manzanar, he'd told me very little of what his family went through. I knew there was probably much, much more than I'd ever imagined.

"I got up to use the bathroom in the middle of the night," Lily continued. "Everyone else in our barracks had finally fallen asleep, and the only sound was the strong winds whipping around our new home and through its walls and through its floors. I could feel dust settling on my face. And I couldn't understand what we had done to make people hate us, hate me, this much that they would do this to my family. My parents had always instilled strong values in us and pride in ourselves and our country, but our country had locked us up even when we supposedly did all that was expected of us. If that was possible, my young mind wondered, then what else in my life would prove to be untrue?"

Lily opened her mouth again to speak, but then she sat the microphone down and allowed her daughter to lead her back to a chair.

Few things are quite as painful as the shattering of youthful innocence, I thought.

Chapter Sixteen- May 2004

I meant to call Lily soon after we returned to San Francisco, but somewhere along the way I picked up a horrible flu. At my age, the flu can do a lot more than just leave you feeling icky for a few days. It can be life-threatening. I was stuck in bed for a week with Rita coming by every day to check on me. She warmed up endless cans of chicken soup and made sure I kept my fever down as much as possible. Some days I could barely lift my head.

Tate got concerned after calling a couple of times, and I didn't answer. He let himself in with the key I kept hidden under an aloe vera plant by the front door.

"Uncle Jack!" he exclaimed, when he entered my bedroom. "Jesus! Are you okay?"

"I'm sure I've looked better, and I know I've felt better," I managed to say.

I reached for the TV remote and switched off a rerun of *The Golden Girls*.

"Why didn't you call me?" Tate demanded, as he surveyed the line of empty Gatorade bottles and empty boxes of saltine crackers. "How long have you been sick?"

"Since the day we got back from our trip," I croaked. "Don't get too close. You might catch it."

"I'll be fine," Tate said, picking up the thermometer from the bedside table next to a picture of Howard and me not long after we met.

He practically rammed the thermometer into my mouth.

"Did you tell Grandma you were sick?" he asked, referring to my sister.

I started to open my mouth to answer.

"Don't speak!" he demanded. "Wait for the thermometer to beep!"

Despite being perturbed by my great-nephew's bossiness, it did warm my heart that he cared so much. We had always had a good relationship with Tate standing in as the grandson I never had, but the trip to Manzanar had definitely made us closer. I think he was able to for the first time to see me, *the young me*, who had many of the same hopes and dreams about life and love that he had.

To be honest, telling Tate my story had been good for my soul, too. The trip to Manzanar had brought back many more feelings, old wounds, and questions that I had carried with me over the years. I had finally begun to feel some sense of closure.

The thermometer beeped, and Tate pulled it out of my mouth.

He exhaled loudly when he saw the reading.

"What's the damage?" I asked.

"It's ninety-nine," he answered.

"See there!" I perked up and exclaimed. "I'm almost normal. But, hell, I've always been *almost* normal."

"Seriously, Uncle Jack," Tate said, sitting on the bed next to me. "You should have called me and told me you were sick. Have you even been to the doctor?"

"Don't need one. As you can see, I'm on the mend anyway," I said, pulling myself up into a sitting position on the bed. "I've had Dorothy, Blanche, Rose, and Sophia to keep me company."

Tate shook his head and groaned.

"Next time you're sick, I want you to call me. I can stay here and look after you," he said.

"You have to go to work to that big marketing job you have," I said, waving him off. "I'll be fine."

I neglected to tell him of when everything went black the day before, and I came to lying on the floor next to the bed. I had no idea how long I had been out or what exactly happened.

"And what about Connor? Did you call him back yet?" I asked, deliberately changing the topic on him.

"No, not yet," Tate admitted.

I slapped him on his arm and said, "Why not, for crying out loud? What are you waiting for? Did my *long* talk on our drive not teach you anything? Don't waste time especially in matters of the heart."

"I'm just scared of getting hurt again," Tate said, looking away.

I saw him staring at the picture of Howard and me on the wall. In it, we're both holding up impossibly large margarita glasses on a cruise ship bound for Mexico.

"I wish I had what you and Howard had," he said.

"We didn't find each other until our fifties," I reminded him. "If you think you've got even a small shot of having something that special with Connor you need to call…no, wait. You need to meet him in person. All of you young people spend far too much time on the phone. I miss the days of pay phones. People said what they needed to say, and then they got the hell off the phone and met in person if needed."

Tate laughed and asked, "What's a pay phone?"

I play-slapped him again and said, "You know what I'm talking about. You're young but not *that* young."

I then patted him gently on the arm.

"Time's ticking. Take it from an old man," I said.

He smiled noncommittedly and said, "When are you going to go see Lily and find out what she has for you?"

I had told Tate my whole conversation with Lily on the way back to San Francisco, and he'd almost as curious as me to find out what she had for me.

"As soon as I get out of this bed," I said, already starting to feel better than I had in days.

"Let me know. I can drive you," he offered.

"It's okay. Rita can take me the next time she's here. I'll probably go on a weekday."

I would actually probably take a cab, but I figured it was best to leave out that detail at this point. I don't think anyone trusted me to get from here to there on my own anymore regardless of where *there* was.

"Well, let me know if you need me to. I can go with you on the bus or in a taxi," Tate said.

I nodded, smiled, and said, "I will let you know."

"Is there anything I can get you? I can run to the market down the block."

"Well, now that my appetite has come back a bit, I am sort of craving that Chunky Monkey ice cream," I admitted.

"Be right back. I'll go to the corner store," Tate said, jumping up. "Don't go anywhere!"

"Where the hell would I go?" I retorted.

"With you, who knows? Be back in a jiffy!"

As he left the room, I called after him and said, "Maybe you can call Connor on your way there on that phone you always have with you!"

"We'll see!" Tate called back in a tone that told me he wouldn't be doing that.

I flipped back on the TV to find out *The Golden Girls* had been replaced by *Designing Women*. Julia was giving some misogynistic man a talking to in a restaurant. They just don't make TV like they did in the 1980s, I thought.

And even though I had felt like hell the past few days, suddenly, I was overcome with a sense of peace I hadn't experienced in years. I glanced over at that picture of me, Howard, and the margaritas, and I felt overjoyed to know that Hiro, too, had found someone to love.

A week, a cab ride, and a lot of ice cream later, I stood on Lily Narita Sato's front step and knocked on the door. The previous day I called, and she had been pleased to hear from me. She said she had grown worried she might not hear from me after so much time had passed, and there were still things she needed to say.

"Jack!" she said, with a warm smile, when she opened the door. "It's so good to see you!"

"You, too, Lily," I said, handing over a bouquet of daisies I'd bought at the florist on my block. "For you."

"How thoughtful!" she said, opening the door wider. "Come in."

I walked into the foyer of her Edwardian-style home in Japantown. The house was spotless with many family portraits hanging on the wall. I did a quick survey of the pictures.

"Are these your children?" I asked.

"Yes, and grandchildren," she answered. "We had two daughters, and they gave us three beautiful grandsons."

She pointed at a formal portrait of the three generations together.

"You're very lucky," I said.

"Thank you," she said, before adding, "Oh, and here's one of Hiro from about ten years ago."

She pointed out a picture of a man who was decidedly older than I remembered him with his white hair and signs of age creasing around his eyes. However, it was definitely Hiro with the same twinkle in his eyes and charming smile that had disarmed the walls I had built around my heart. He stood next to the Lincoln Memorial in DC.

"That was from a trip he took with his partner," she said, before adding with a hint of sadness in her voice, "It was the last big one they took together."

"He was still very handsome," I said. "The years agreed with him."

"It's true," Lily said, with a smile. "We always kidded him that he hardly ever aged."

"The same's true for you," I told her.

"You're too kind," she said, holding up the flowers. "I'll go put these in water. Would you like some tea?"

"That would be wonderful," I answered.

"Please," she said, directing me to the living room. "Have a seat, and I'll be right back."

I made my way to the living room and sat on an overstuffed brown leather sofa.

"Make yourself comfortable!" Lily called from the kitchen.

"Thank you!" I called back.

The room had a comfy, cozy vibe as only a home that had been lived in for decades would have. Shelf after shelf of leather bound books lined the walls and more family pictures were placed on tables and shelves around the room. The glass coffee table had issues of Better Homes and Gardens and Readers' Digest on top of it. It was the type of room I felt like I could spend hours in curled up on the sofa and reading a good novel.

Lily returned carrying a tray with a teapot, two cups, sugar, cream, and a plate of lemon cookies.

"Can I help you?" I asked, starting to get up.

"No, no. Please sit. I'm fine," she said, sitting the tray on the coffee table.

"Thank you. I could use a pick-me-up this afternoon," I said. "I just got over a flu last week. It took a lot out of me."

"I'm so sorry to hear that," Lily said, pouring both of us a cup of tea.

The smell of sweet jasmine from the tea wafted through the air.

"It takes a little longer to bounce back these days," I said, taking the cup and saucer when she handed it to me.

"Tell me about it," she replied with a chuckle, before adding, "It's such a small world with you living so close by."

"And the driver passed what was your family's restaurant on the way here. I visited it several times over the years."

"We had a good run," Lily said, sipping her tea. "My husband and I enjoyed the business. We're both people persons, so the business worked well for both of us. What's ironic is that when I worked in my parents' restaurant as a little girl I swore I'd never work in a kitchen as an adult, but there you go."

"It's true that we turn into our parents to an extent," I agreed.

I thought of my father's habit of rising before dawn and having two cups of coffee by sunup that I had adapted. I also tended to be bad with first names but great at crossword puzzles like my mother.

"Hiro came here many times to visit. I wish that the two of you would have had the chance to meet and catch up," Lily said. "I know that would have meant a lot to him."

"And to me," I said, my voice drifting off again.

Even though I was well into my eighties, the heart never forgot.

"He was a wonderful brother," Lily said. "Although, it took years for me to forgive him and to understand why he left my mother and me at the camp. We argued over it for some time, and I'm afraid to say it kept us at a distance for many years. Of course, we weren't the only family where the stress of the camp did its damage. And it took me a while to accept him for who he was. We had a mutual friend that owned a flower shop that my restaurant used in the 1970s and 80s and Hiro knew him from our old neighborhood in Los Angeles. When he died of AIDS, well before all of these new medications, we came together over our mutual grief and frustration at the lack of what the government was doing to help."

I shook my head and said, "Those were the days that I went to more funerals than birthday parties. Sometimes I feel like it's a miracle I'm still here. I lost so many."

Lily nodded knowingly and said, "I started volunteering with a local food bank that helped patients who couldn't shop for themselves anymore. It opened up my eyes quite a bit. Not only did my brother have to deal with the prejudice of being Japanese-American during the war, he had to persevere when he came out of the closet. Ours was often a very conservative culture. Both of our parents were gone by the time he told me, but it actually ended up making us closer."

I nodded and thought of my sister, Jane, in the early 1980s. My coming out to her also made our bond deeper. She told me she'd figured it out long before and regretted that I had felt the need to distance myself from her to keep my secret. I never told my brother, Edward, which was something I tended to regret as I felt it kept a remoteness between us. He never truly knew me and vice-versa. Now, looking back, I had no idea how our relationship might have developed if there had been no wall between us.

"I'm glad the two of you were able to come back together," I told her.

"Me, too," she said with a sigh. "It would have been awful if that had never happened."

She cleared her throat.

"So you're probably wondering about what I told you I had for you," she said, with a twinkle in her eyes.

"I am quite curious," I admitted.

"You might remember that Hiro also loved to paint, but he didn't really embrace his artistic side until he retired. By then, you could barely get the paint brush out of his hand. He went through canvases faster than I could certainly give them as gifts. A lot of his paintings had to do with Manzanar or surviving in New York during the AIDS crisis. I think it was his way of processing all of those emotions."

Her voice had grown hoarse, so she took another sip of tea.

I wondered where on Earth this could possibly be headed.

"After he passed, I distributed many of the paintings that were left to his nieces, nephews, cousins, and friends, but I kept a few that touched me in a special way. There was one in particular that something just told me I needed to keep."

She got up, walked behind the sofa, and picked up a canvas to show me.

In surprise, I sucked in a breath when I saw what had been painted.

"It's me," I muttered.

"Yes, standing in one of the gardens of Manzanar. I believe it was one that you helped him with one day."

I couldn't find my voice at the moment, so I just nodded. There in the picture stood an expert likeness of a much younger me smiling and leaning on a shovel. The realness of the painting took me right back to that moment just as any photograph would.

"When did he paint it?" I managed to say, my heart pounding.

I set my tea cup on the coffee table, and Lily walked over and handed the twenty by twenty-four canvas to me.

"Just a couple of years before he passed away," she said.

She pointed to the bottom right hand corner and I saw his name painted.

"And if you turn the canvas around you can see what he named it," Lily said.

I carefully flipped the canvas over and saw written in ink on one of the corners, "*Love. August 2000.*"

"He named the painting 'Love'," I said, a little breathless.

"Yes," Lily said with a wide smile. "I believe you were his first love, too. He never forgot you to the point that even after all of those years he could paint you with such a striking resemblance just from memory."

"I don't know what to say," I said, feeling my eyes well up with tears.

"I want you to have it," Lily said.

"Are you sure?"

"I'm positive," Lily said, placing her hand on my arm. "Like I said, I believe there was a reason something told me to keep the painting in the first place."

"Thank you, Lily," I said, choking back the tears. "This means so much to me. It's like…"

"He was still able to talk to you and send you a message," she said, finishing my sentence.

"Yeah," I replied. "Exactly."

I held out the picture again to look at it while an overwhelming sense of peace came over me.

That night when I returned home, I leaned Hiro's painting against the wall on top of the mahogany dresser in my bedroom. I could barely take my eyes off it. Even if we didn't get to speak in person, this still felt like a miracle of some kind. I sat on the edge of my bed and just stared at it. I still couldn't get over how striking the realism of the portrait was.

"You've been staring at that picture for quite a while," Rita said, removing the blood pressure cuff from my arm and writing something down in the small notebook she carried.

"An old friend painted it," I said. "I just received it as a gift."

Rita turned and surveyed the painting. Her eyes pivoted from the painting and back to me.

"Is that you in it?" she asked cocking an eyebrow.

"It is," I answered. "A much younger me."

She walked over to the painting for a closer look and said, "Well, I'll be. I can see the resemblance."

"Even after all these years?" I asked with a chuckle.

"Of course," she said. "And I would know those soulful eyes anywhere."

She turned and smiled brightly at me. "You want me to heat up some dinner for you before I go?" she asked.

"Nah. I'll just have a yogurt," I said, waving her off.

"You need more calories than that, Mr. Henry. I've told you about…"

"I know. I need to keep up my calories," I said, still looking at the painting.

I got up from the bed and walked closer to the painting, and for the first time, I noticed a small bird flying heavenward in the upper right hand corner.

"At least have a banana with that yogurt," Rita scolded, as she put her blood pressure machine back into her bag.

"Okay, okay," I said.

What kind of bird was it? An eagle?

"I'll be calling to check on you," Rita said. "We have to make sure that flu doesn't come back."

"Okay. Thank you," I said, a bit dismissively.

All I wanted to do was to study this painting more to see if I could find any other possible messages from Hiro.

"Okay. I'll let myself out," Rita said.

"Okay," I mumbled.

"Are you sure you'll be okay?"

I nodded.

"So, you said an old friend painted it, huh?" Rita asked, her curiosity piqued even more as she took a closer look at the painting.

"Yes," I answered, "a very special friend from a long time ago."

Later that night after studying the painting from every angle, I took a pain killer for my bad leg. It had been acting up again with a vengeance lately. I put on some pajamas, and crawled into the bed. I pulled the afghan Jane knitted me on top of the blanket. My bones had been growing especially cold in these San Francisco evenings.

I took a sip from the glass of water I always kept next to my bed, and glanced at the clock. It was 10:13. Tate said he would come over tomorrow and take me out to my favorite diner for a chicken fried steak I loved there. Rita would be upset about the fried part, but at least it had the calories she was always concerned with me consuming.

I scooted down and laid my head on the pillow, and as usual these days, I drifted right off.

I woke up with a start, and bleary-eyed I looked over at the bedside clock. It read 3:23 AM.

"Jack," a familiar voice said on the other side of the room.

"What?" I said confused and half-asleep.

Who the hell was that?

I turned and saw a figure walking toward me, and eventually, from the light shining through the window, I saw it was my deceased partner, Howard.

"Howard!" I exclaimed, sitting up and suddenly very awake.

He looked around the age he had been when I first met him in his early fifties. He wasn't the feeble and tired man whose hospital bed I sat next to as he died. Howard looked fit, even athletic, and had the same thick mane of white hair I remembered.

"Hello, Jack," he said to me, with a warm smile.

"I don't understand," I said, feeling frightened and confused all of a sudden.

This had to be one of those nightmares where you *dream* you wake up, but in reality you were still asleep.

"It's okay. There's no need to be scared," he said, holding out his hand. "It's time."

"Time for what?" I asked.

With trepidation at first, I slowly reached out and touched his hand. I could feel him! A warmth generated from deep inside me, and I got out of the bed. I felt overwhelmingly compelled to walk toward him. At that moment, I realized that all the aches and pains of my old age had disappeared. Even my bad leg felt strong and sturdy again.

"It's time to go now," Howard said. "You need to come with me."

"Go where?"

"Jack," I heard a young boy's voice say.

I looked to the right, behind Howard, and I saw a boy walking toward me.

"John!" I exclaimed when I recognized him, feeling a wave of emotions flood me at the sight of the younger brother who died when it so easily could have been me instead.

John, wearing his favorite pair of overalls, ran and threw his arms around my waist.

Howard let go of my hand, and I knelt down to look my little brother in the eye.

"John, is it really you?" I asked, sobbing.

John wiped the tears from both of my cheeks and said, "Don't cry, Jack! It's okay."

"But I…it was because of me…" I stammered.

"No, Jack. It wasn't because of you," he said, in a soothing wise tone. "There were reasons I had to leave, but it wasn't your fault. It just needed to be."

"Don't you blame me?" I cried.

John smiled and said, "There is no one to blame, but it's time to go now. You need to come with the three of us."

"The three of you?"

"Hello, Jack," another voice I remembered from many years before called out.

I looked up and there he stood before me after all of these years.

Hiro.

He looked just as I remembered him the last time I saw him: young, strong, and as handsome as ever.

"You're here, too!" I said in shock.

"Yes. We're all here for you and to take you to the next stop," Hiro said. "There's no reason to be scared."

"The next stop?" I asked, perplexed. "What is that?"

"The place on the other side. It's always been right there, but most people don't realize it," Hiro said.

"I still don't understand," I said, looking from Hiro to Howard to John.

The three of them stepped aside and the brightest, warmest light I've ever experienced appeared. As I stared into it, I could see two more people far away in the distance.

John took my hand, and I looked down at him.

"It's Mama and Pops," John said, using the names only he had used for our parents. "They're waiting on you, too."

The light filled me with a calm and sense of serenity I couldn't remember ever feeling before, and all of my resistance to anything melted away.

"It really is time, isn't it?" I said, accepting what was now at hand.

Howard, Hiro, and John all smiled at me.

"Let's go," I said, wanting nothing more at that moment that to follow them wherever they'd like me to go.

Howard took my other hand, and Hiro gestured toward the light.

"Welcome home, Jack," Hiro said warmly.

Epilogue- May 2004, Tate

"Uncle Jack!" I called out, as I walked into his apartment. I knocked and knocked for a good ten minutes, but when he didn't answer I felt a knot in my stomach. Somehow, I immediately knew that all was not right.

The air in the apartment felt stuffy and still. A sense of emptiness drifted through the air.

"Uncle Jack!" I called out again.

On the coffee table was a copy of a tome of Shakespeare's sonnets. I glanced at it and saw it had been left open on Sonnet 98 and the first line had been highlighted.

From you have I been absent in the spring…

Uncle Jack's reading glasses sat next to the book.

The door to the bedroom had been left open. I knew in my heart what I would find on the other side, and I couldn't seem to get my feet to move in that direction. The finality of what I thought I might see filled my heart with an undeniable heaviness.

Eventually, I worked up the courage to head inside the bedroom, and as soon as I walked in, I found Uncle Jack still and under the covers. Even from a good ten feet way I could see he wasn't *really* there anymore.

I reached into my pocket, took out my cell phone, and dialed my grandmother's number.

After the EMTs arrived and took Uncle Jack away, my Grandmother Jane and I sat on his bed for a moment in silence. She'd rushed over when I called her and embraced me the moment she saw me.

"Poor, baby," she said, "I'm so sorry you had to be the one to find him."

As usual, she was dressed in one of her long denim skirts and peasant blouses. Her wavy shoulder-length salt-and-pepper hair framed her face, and she wore her trademark extra-large gold loop earrings. She'd always been what she described as a late in life hippie. In contrast, her daughter, my mother, had always been Miss Trendy and Polished.

"I called your mother," Grandmother said finally.

"Is she coming up from Laguna?" I asked.

"Tomorrow. There's nothing that she can do here today," Grandmother said.

Grandmother had always had a flair for the dramatic. A hangnail could be the reason for a meltdown, but now, here with her brother passing, she appeared almost eerily calm while I kept trying to fight back tears.

"Are you okay?" I asked her.

She ran a hand through her wild hair and answered, "I'll be fine. When you get to be my age death becomes something more suspected than a surprise. Jack was a good man."

At the last sentence, I heard her voice begin to break, but she pulled herself together.

"He had a nice long life and plenty of people that loved him including you," she said, wrapping her arm around me and pulling me to her.

"I just knew the moment I walked in," I said, still trying to process everything. "We just took that trip together a couple of weeks ago."

"Hang on to that memory and know how much it meant to him," Grandmother said. "He loved it when you'd visit him."

"I should have done more," I said. "Visited more often. Helped him out."

"You did a lot. He loved you so much. You were one of the lights in his life."

"This is going to sound strange," I said. "But I feel like I really got to know him for the first time during our trip to Manzanar. I could picture him as a young man during the stories he told me along the way. I can't help but wonder now what other untold memories he could have told me. I came over today partly to tell him I finally called Connor."

"You did?" Grandmother said, perking up just a tad.

She had always loved Connor. The two had immediately bonded over a family dinner during which they discussed various styles of yoga.

"Yeah. I told him I wanted us to talk about things if he was willing. Maybe we can somehow figure out a way to make it work."

"When there's a will, there's a way," she said. "I'm glad you two are giving it another try."

"Just hearing how difficult it had been for Uncle Jack to be with the person he loved, I realized how maybe I was taking a lot for granted. I wanted to thank him, but now…"

I guess neither one of us could hold it in any longer we both began to shed tears. We hugged each other as both of us let our grief finally cascade over us.

After a couple of minutes, we both pulled back and wiped the remaining tears out of our eyes.

That's when I noticed the painting on top of his dresser.

"Look at that!" I said, noticing the piece of art for the first time since I'd been so distracted. "That painting is new."

"What?" Grandmother asked, and I pointed to it.

I got up and walked across the room, and Grandmother followed me.

"It's a young Jack," she said in amazement. "Where did this come from?"

I saw the name "Hiro" signed at the bottom, and suddenly, it clicked. This had to be what Lily had for Uncle Jack. I tilted the painting forward to look at the back and saw the title and date on the back.

Love. August 2000.

"From a place deep in someone's heart," I answered, gently putting the canvas back in place, and feeling tears flood my eyes again.

I intertwined my hand with hers, and for a moment, we just stared at this uncannily realistic portrait of my Uncle Jack, young, full of life...

And hope.

About the Author

Michael Holloway Perronne is a writer living in Los Angeles. He has a BA from the University of Southern Mississippi and a MFA from the Creative Writing Workshop at the University of New Orleans. His debut novel, A Time Before Me, won Foreward Magazine's Bronze Award in Gay & Lesbian Literature. "Gardens of Hope" is his seventh book. For more information on Michael, please visit his website at www.michaelhperronne.com.

www.ingramcontent.com/pod-product-compliance
Lightning Source LLC
Chambersburg PA
CBHW070333260626
47160CB00003B/1029

9 780977 050642